DOREEN

DOREEN

Ilana Manaster

RP|TEENS
PHILADELPHIA • LONDON

Books published by Running Press are available at special discounts for bulk purchases in the United States by corporations, institutions, and other organizations. For more information, please contact the Special Markets Department at the Perseus Books Group, 2300 Chestnut Street, Suite 200, Philadelphia, PA 19103, or call (800) 810-4145, ext. 5000, or e-mail special.markets@perseusbooks.com.

ISBN 978-0-7624-5962-9

Library of Congress Control Number: 2016934245

E-book ISBN 978-0-7624-5963-6

10   9   8   7   6   5   4   3   2   1
Digit on the right indicates the number of this printing

Front cover image: Fashion Portrait © Thinkstock/heckmannoleg

Designed by T. L. Bonaddio
Edited by Lisa Cheng
Typography: Baskerville, Times New Roman, Port Vintage, and Sabon

Published by Running Press Teens
An Imprint of Running Press Book Publishers
A Member of the Perseus Books Group
2300 Chestnut Street
Philadelphia, PA 19103-4371

Visit us on the web!
www.runningpress.com/rpkids

To my family

The one that I made and the one that made me.

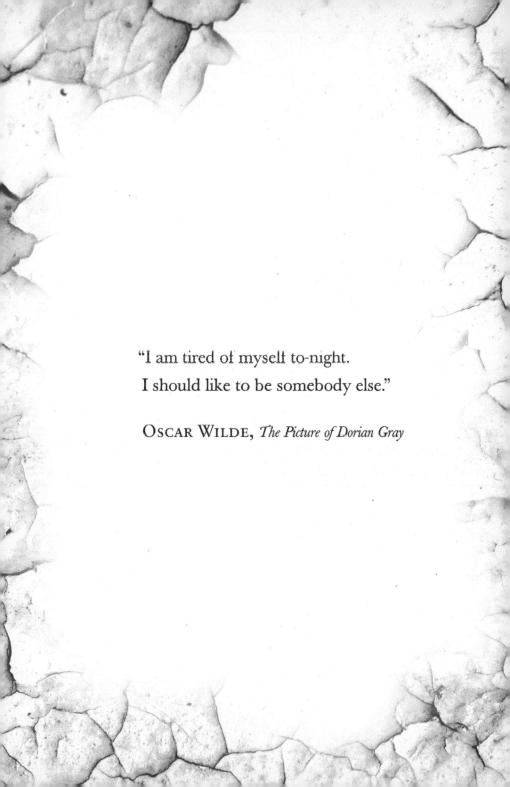

"I am tired of myself to-night.
I should like to be somebody else."

OSCAR WILDE, *The Picture of Dorian Gray*

1

The charms of late summer seemed a very humdrum topic for an imagination as wild as Heidi Whelan's, but she nonetheless found herself, on the first day of her last year at Chandler Academy, laid across a leather love seat in the sitting room of her suite, eating pistachios and feeling rather satisfied by the green and blue and pink of things as she peered out onto the as-yet unpopulated quad.

"Isn't campus great when nobody's here?" she called to her roommate Biz Gibbons-Brown. Biz was not visible from Heidi's perch on the couch but could be heard shuffling around in their bedroom. "Before the arrival of all those loathsome people."

"Speak for yourself," said Biz, entering the common room wearing the kind of thing that Biz always wore, that is to say, an outfit made of beautiful individual elements—an exquisite white blouse, a perfect navy linen skirt—but thrown together without thought for their overall effect. In this case the blouse was worn open over a T-shirt from last year's pumpkin festival, the skirt was hopelessly wrinkled, and she'd finished the outfit with her beat-up yellow Converse All Stars. "I don't think they're all so very *loathsome.*"

"Oh please," said Heidi. She swung her thick blonde mane behind her as she sat up on the sofa. "You know better than anyone how empty, shallow, mean-spirited—"

"It's a new year, Heidi. Can't we indulge in a little optimism? At least until classes start? Now, where are my glasses?"

"Over by your desk. New shirt?" Heidi asked with forced nonchalance. It had a subtle white-on-white stripe and looked very expensive, even from across the room. Biz slid on her wire frames and looked down at her top as if seeing it for the first time.

"Oh, this? Yeah. You like it?"

If it were Heidi's, the blouse would be among her most prized possessions, but Biz wore it like flannel pajamas. No matter, Heidi thought, relaxing back into the love seat. She had full access to the treasures in Biz's closet. Heidi gazed out at the quad, imagining herself crossing it in that gorgeous top and congratulated herself once again for the good judgment she demonstrated by finding and befriending Elizabeth Gibbons-Brown two years earlier.

"It's lovely. Who makes it?"

"No idea. Mumzy picked it up in Paris, I think. She forced it on me for some party out in the Hamptons."

"Of course she did."

Biz didn't really call her mother "Mumzy." Or she did call her that but only as a way to express her contempt. Gloria Gibbons-Brown was a flitting kind of woman, thin in a way that was only attractive on the young and tall (she was neither). What wasn't brittle on her was bought— dresses made of thick silks, jewels the size of geological events, and a face that had been lifted, folded over, and smoothed by the best surgeons on the planet. She ate nothing and drank much, so evenings at her table often included long, winding stories about salespeople or flight attendants or waiters. Her own role in these anecdotes was always the same: demander of justice, voice of the truth, a superhero for the unbusy and overindulged.

Biz, of course, despised her.

For good reason. Heidi could see Mumzy for what she was: a shallow, unfeeling, insensitive person who seemed to have had children out of a sense of obligation to her bloodline. But Heidi knew, also, that she could learn a lot from Gloria. After all, the woman was the quintessential old-money society maven, comfortable in her position at the top of the food chain, offended by anything common or unrefined. Which is why she'd swept in and replaced every piece of furniture in their dorm room. Instead of standard-issue, Biz and Heidi had mid-century modern chairs, a leather chesterfield sofa, a gorgeous antique rug, a brass-footed onyx coffee table. Curtains had been installed for privacy, and shelves built for books. Heidi had never lived in such sumptuous quarters, and now she could not imagine living any other way.

Only Biz's desk had avoided Mumzy's touch. On that front, Biz was firm. The desk was all hers—evidenced by the stacks of books, the papers, but more than anything, the photographs. The wall behind her desk was loaded with pinned-up photos—her own, as well as the work of others that she found inspiring. She had wires hanging across the ceiling clipped with more photos she changed out in a constant cycle. Images overwhelmed the small space: full-color, black-and-white, landscape, portrait, animals, people, interior spaces, exteriors, abstracts.

Heidi could not look at the collage for long without feeling dizzy. She agreed with Mumzy that the tumult took away from the clean lines of the rest of the room, but secretly she also admired Biz's dedication and talent. It must be nice to produce something tangible with one's gifts.

"This one's new, right? Is it from this summer?" Heidi walked over to a photo clipped to one of the wires. Biz's mother sat at a dressing table. She was turned toward the camera with a sponge in her hand, her mouth open as if she was talking, her expression annoyed. She looked exhausted, like someone who would rather stay home, but the evening gown was in the background, hung on the back of the closet, and the makeup would go on the face. Somehow, she would have to pull it together and find the right pose. It was like a behind-the-scenes photo, but the stage was this woman's entire life.

"What? Oh. Yeah. Not bad, right? Anyway, do you have anything you need to do today? I mean, could you scram for a little while? I need some quiet."

Biz seemed nervous, shuffling little things around her desk as if trying to tidy up, an activity she did rarely and only when pressed. And now this mysterious request for privacy? Clearly the girl was withholding information.

"Why don't you cut the crap, Biz, and tell me what's going on. Are you having an affair?"

"Don't be ridiculous."

"You little she-wolf! And I bet I know who it is, too. That teacher! What's his name, from your photography class. Mr.–"

"Mr. Cameron?"

"No doubt! With the late nights poring over nudie shots."

"You're insane."

Heidi giggled. Of course, she had been a willing participant in a number of seedy little scenes herself, but the idea of Biz's promiscuity seemed so uncharacteristic, so utterly unacademic that Heidi found herself positively thrilled.

"Elizabeth Gibbons-Brown in love. I, for one, never imagined that the day would come!"

"I'm not in love, Heidi. Can you just drop it?"

"In lust, then. Even better! Even less likely! Oh, Biz, to think that you might make space in that determined little brain of yours for thoughts of the dirty variety, it's just so, I mean, I'm floored. I'm flabbergasted. Of course, I knew that Mr. Carson—"

"Cameron."

"Oh. Pardonnez-moi! I didn't mean any disrespect. That Mr. *Cameron* was after more than an extra set of hands. Or maybe that was exactly what he was after."

"Heidi!"

"It's just so delicious! Am I glowing? You certainly are."

"That's enough! Now look, she's going to be here soon."

"*She!?*" The pitch of Heidi's voice approached a squeal. She felt the impulse to applaud.

Biz collapsed into the tobacco-brown Italian leather club chair. "Listen, it's not what you think. Her name is Doreen. She's my cousin."

"Your *cousin?!*"

"Don't be gross, okay? For once? Look, do you remember me telling you about Mumzy's brother, Roland?"

Heidi froze.

"Uh, Heidi?"

"Oh, sorry. You were saying? You have an uncle? How interesting!" She pulled at the end of her ponytail and looked out the window. Surely anyone could see the blush in her face! Heidi told herself to calm down, breathe.

"Yes. My mother's brother, Roland Gibbons—he used to be married and have a daughter. Well, I guess he still has a daughter, but I haven't seen her since I was a little kid. Her name's Doreen, and when her mom was married to Uncle Roland she was the only cousin my age. So we were always together. Doreen and Elizabeth. I remember we planted a garden out behind the compound in Amagansett. We spent hours and hours digging holes with our little fingers and weeding. I don't think we got a single sprout to grow that whole summer, though." Biz laughed. "Of course, Uncle Roland had to go and ruin everything."

"Oh!" said Heidi, too loud, too eager. *Pull it together, you sow!* "Oh, ha ha. Yes, I remember him now. His wife is foreign, right? Didn't you say he married a European lady? Is that this cousin's mother?" She wound a strand of hair around a finger. Tight.

"What? Why are you talking like that? I can barely understand you. Anyway, that's his second wife, Constantina. They got divorced, too, but their kids are little. Doreen's our age, like I said, and she's transferring to Chandler. She'll be a junior. After the divorce she and her mother moved to the Midwest somewhere. Illinois? I can't remember. I haven't seen her since that summer when we were kids."

Heidi stood up. She couldn't believe what she'd just

been told. "Your uncle Roland has a daughter our age, and she is coming to Chandler Academy."

"Yes. To our room, actually. Any minute now."

Heidi whirred to life. "Oh, I wish I'd known, I would have prepared something. Biz, you should have told me. We will have to make this work somehow." She raced around the common room, fluffing up pillows and tossing pistachio shells into the trash. She picked up shoes from under the sofa and threw them into their bedroom.

"Wait. Heidi, stop! Just cool your jets for a second, will you please? There's something else. Sit down."

"What? What is it? Come on, out with it. She'll be here any minute, you said."

"Sit down!"

"Fine! I'm sitting. What is it?"

Biz sighed again. "She was bullied."

"And why would that be remarkable? She went to public school, right? I know you've never been to one of those, but I can tell you from experience that 'bullying' is how most American schoolchildren say howdy-do."

"No. It was bad. Worse than just your regular run-of-the-mill bullying. Okay? Like, her and her mom, they were afraid for her safety. That's why she's coming here. She has the opportunity to have a different kind of experience at Chandler and I want her to feel welcomed." Biz shot Heidi a reproachful look.

"Wait," Heidi protested. "Do you mean to imply that I would be somehow *ungracious*?"

"Ugh! Would it be so terrible for you to find somewhere to go, just for an hour or two? Give us an opportunity to get reacquainted? Is there any chance I could get you to do that?"

"Certainly not!"

"Don't you have anything better to do, Heidi? Must you be involved in every mini-drama on campus? Can't you just . . . just do something else with your time? Jesus!"

"Excuse me?" Heidi leaned back in the couch and pursed her lips. For a moment she did not say anything.

"Hey, I didn't mean—"

Heidi held up her hand. Her voice was steady and soft. "I wonder if you have any idea at all what I would do to someone who spoke that way to me, say, in the cafeteria. I wonder if you understand the storm of humiliation I could make rain down on a person's head with a few text messages and a wave of my hand."

"Let's not overreact, okay? I was only trying to—"

Heidi snapped open a pistachio. Her cheeks burned. "Do you understand how easy it would be for me to take away the things you love here? The library, your classes, even photography. You think that's all guaranteed to you? Why? Because of tuition? Because of your fancy name? Ha!"

"Heidi," said Biz, "hey, I was only joking, okay? Seriously." Biz seemed more embarrassed than frightened by Heidi's threats. And as she calmed down, Heidi felt embarrassed, too. She'd overreacted. But Biz had insulted her. She had implied that Heidi was some sort of parasite who lived off other people's lives, and not what she was, which was an artist. Maybe she didn't shove a camera in everybody's face, but Heidi did engage in a kind of art practice—the art of manipulation, of gaining and maintaining power.

"Never mind. Let's forget it, okay?" Biz could have laughed at her theatrics, but she'd left Heidi with her dignity, a class act as always. "I'll tell you what I'm going to do. I am going to sit right here and greet your cousin with the warmth and goodwill expected of a Chandler woman. How does that sound?" She flung her hair over the arm of the sofa.

Biz laughed. "Okay, okay. You win. You do realize that girls like you have probably abused Doreen her whole life."

"Not possible, my dear. There are no other girls like me."

"You know what, Heidi? I think you're right about that."

"You betcha," Heidi said with a wink.

A knock sounded.

2

Heidi could not quite identify what it was about Doreen Gray that produced such a visceral reaction on her part. Certainly she looked terrible. Her skin was simultaneously oily and dried out, with shiny pimples on her forehead and chin and red dry patches on her cheeks and neck. Her hair was a forest of black frizz with curls that seemed to be variously tight and loose, depending on the section of her head from which they originated. Her body was neither trim nor plump but lumpy, and she carried her flesh in a worn-out, army-green jersey dress as if carting home meat from the market.

However, though there was no doubt in Heidi's mind that these physical facts, among others, contributed to the girl's horrendous presentation, they did not account for the whole effect. As Biz and Doreen chatted politely, Heidi sat unusually mum on the couch and studied the girl. Because beneath the bad hair, skin, clothes, etc., there was a kind of beauty to her. Her cheekbones were high and wide, and when she finally looked up from the carpet Heidi saw that her eyes were a remarkable bluish-purple.

They were something else, the peepers on Doreen Gray. Doreen appeared able to take in more light with them, to draw the world into her. Heidi found herself wishing that she, too, would be taken in by those purple eyes, even though they were housed in that mess of a face. But she couldn't capture them, couldn't keep their focus. The eyes darted around the room fretfully, returning over and over again to the ground.

Biz sat at full attention, obviously trying to make her cousin comfortable. "I don't know that I'd even have recognized you, it's been so long. Are you all settled in your dorm?"

"Am I settled? Oh yes, thank you," said Doreen from deep in the armchair where she'd burrowed herself.

"Which dorm is it?" Biz inquired.

"Which dorm? Oh. It's called, um, it's West Hall? Is that bad?"

"No. West Hall isn't bad at all, is it Heidi? We know a ton of people who have lived there. My brother, for example. Addison. Do you remember Addison? He lived there—what? His junior year, wasn't it, Heidi?"

"Yes."

Biz waited for Heidi to elaborate. She did not. Biz gave her roommate a stern look: *Are you just going to sit there?* Heidi shrugged. Watching Biz try to make small talk was hilarious.

"So, uh, Heidi and Addison used to date," Biz continued with some desperation. She picked up her camera and held it, apparently for comfort, as she did not seem interested in capturing the moment for posterity. Unusual. "That's how we became friends, actually. He brought her home for Easter our sophomore year. She was quite the hit of the party, Mumzy just loved her! Then she shattered my brother's heart into a million pieces." Biz forced a laugh. "That wasn't very nice of you, Heidi. Really. Not nice at all," she said with her mouth while her eyes said: *Mayday! Mayday! Help me out for crying out loud!*

Heidi languidly deposited some nutshells into a Japanese bowl on the coffee table. "I dumped him in the third-floor study lounge at West Hall, actually. He sobbed like an infant."

"I'm sure," said Doreen. "I mean, I'm sure he was very sad. I mean, you're so—"

Doreen looked up at Heidi. In a flash, Heidi saw her whole self reflected back in the deep color of Doreen's remarkable eyes, until they found their way back to the carpet.

"Yes, well," Biz continued, smiling broadly, "any-who." *Anywho?!!* "It's a fine dorm. Whatever Heidi might think of Addison, he was always very popular."

"Oh, well," said Doreen, miserably.

"And I suppose you got your schedule? You should let me see it. I'll tell you all about the teachers you have and if you want I'll even show you where—"

"Don't you want to be popular?" Heidi asked with a level stare at Doreen.

". . . where your classes are, if you want. But the first thing you'll need to do is—"

"Biz, hush. I asked your cousin a question. Tell us, darling, won't you? Do you want to be popular? Here, at Chandler."

"Heidi!"

Doreen's expression, as she looked from Heidi to Biz, was an incredible mixture of eagerness and horror. A plan was beginning to unfold in Heidi's mind as she watched a flush climb up the girl's throat from her chest. "Do I want to be popular?" Doreen repeated dumbly.

"You don't need to restate the question, dear, only answer it."

"Don't listen to her, Doreen," said Biz. "Popularity is not as important to most people as it is to Heidi."

"But it is to our Dorie, isn't it? Which is why I proffered the question. Biz said that her brother had lived in West and that he'd been very popular, to which you replied 'oh well,' as if popularity, while something desirable to you, is not something you see yourself acquiring. And while I'll admit respectfully that it is difficult to imagine popularity in your current state, I am a true American in the sense that I believe that one can achieve anything when one is smarter than everybody else."

"Heidi! My cousin did not come all the way here from Wisconsin for the right to be insulted."

"Indiana," said Doreen, her eyes fixed on Heidi.

"Huh?"

"I came from Indiana," said Doreen. "And I don't feel the least bit insulted." The girl's spine had straightened. Hope came into her violet eyes. "The truth is—I feel kind of strange talking about it, but since you asked—I guess I would want that. I'd like to be popular. Who wouldn't? I've never, I mean, in my old school—"

"Yes, Biz tells me you were very badly bullied," said Heidi gravely.

"I'm sorry," said Biz. "I shouldn't have told her. It wasn't my place—"

"That's okay," said Doreen. She reached out and touched Biz's knee. "Hey, that's in the past, right?"

"That's right!" Biz said, aglow with her cousin's attention. "Exactly."

"What was it? Name-calling? Frogs in your locker? That sort of thing?"

"Heidi! Didn't we just say it was in the past?"

Doreen shrugged. "No, it's okay. Sure, yeah, name-calling. No frogs, but somebody did put a pair of bloody underwear in my locker once. Which everyone in the whole school saw flying out onto the floor."

"Oh, Dorie," said Biz.

"That was fine. I could take that. And the pushing. And the tripping. And the time someone put something in my drink so that I threw up during my biology midterm. I learned how to be careful. Eat in the library. Keep my head down. But then I got a message on Facebook. A *boy*." Doreen paused and gathered her strength. "Judah was his name. He was new, or he was going to be new, moving from another town and he wanted to make friends. We got to chatting." Her eyes welled.

"Who was Judah? Who was he *really?*" asked Heidi. She knew the old social media fake-out. She'd employed it herself, not directly, but through a minion or two, as a tactic for social maneuvering. But she was never cruel for cruelty's sake. Nobody ever got seriously hurt. That made a difference, surely. But something unpleasant gnawed at her from the inside. Remorse? Guilt? No matter. She soothed herself with the satisfying pop of a splitting pistachio shell.

"A girl from school. Her boyfriend, I don't know. A bunch of people. They started posting some of the stuff

I'd written to Judah. But it was totally out of context, you know? So humiliating. My mom wanted me to transfer to a different public school, but I knew that was worthless. They would follow me anywhere. I deleted my Facebook account, I would get through it. But my mom . . ." Doreen swiped at her eyes. Her efforts to downplay how it had all affected her made the story even more heartbreaking. Heidi felt terrible for having asked about it. She should have minded her own business. She sucked the rough salty remains of the nut from the empty shell.

"Children," said Biz. "They can be so awful. And for what? What's the point? I don't get it."

"I'm so sorry," said Heidi. And she really was.

"My mom saw some stuff someone had written on one of my books. Nothing out of the ordinary. 'Kill yourself, bitch.' That sort of thing. 'Nobody likes you, you should die.' And that was it for her. She called my dad and made some serious threats if he didn't get me in here. So that's my story! The life and times of Doreen Gray."

"Well, you're here now," said Biz. "Nobody has to know a thing about your old school. And listen, if you want to be popular, we can definitely help you. I have legacy here, a kind of built-in social status. And Heidi has the proper—"

"Cynicism," said Heidi.

"I was going to say ruthlessness. To manage your, what would you say? Your rebirth."

"Really? Thank you." Doreen's eyes lit up, hopeful. "Thank you so much!"

"You're welcome," said Biz. She blushed. "If it's what you want, then I want to help you."

"Yes! Okay, marvelous. Operation rebirth. Let's begin." Heidi paced around the room, her fingers in a dome under her chin, as if giving dictation. "Now, Doreen, as Biz will attest, I have made quite a little study on the subject and I can say with some confidence that being popular in prep school carries with it a number of requirements. For example, one must be thin. This is of utmost importance. And though a closet full of beautiful clothes is obviously ideal, one need only possess a single major piece from a recognizable designer—a bag for example. Louis Vuitton is the classic but not the only option, set off by simple, well-fitting black apparel. One's complexion must be perfect, and one's ponytail thick and long. If this last proves unobtainable, short and sporty might be passable, but such a coif carries with it the responsibility of joining a team, of which only soccer and field hockey are acceptable, of course. To be truly popular one must not only be on a team, but must either be the best one or the captain or both, and so, if achieving excellence in this regard does not seem likely, I recommend maintaining a long, lustrous head of hair."

Heidi regarded the length of Doreen's piteous appearance. "Had you begun as a freshman rather than a junior, I would have suggested dating a senior as a quick and painless way to make immediate inroads, especially if you break his heart without sleeping with him. As it is, however, to uphold unreasonable prudishness at your age would make you seem as if you were undesirable in your former school. I think it would be wiser to take an appropriate boyfriend right away and sleep with him late enough to avoid seeming desperate, but early enough to suggest a passionate appetite for sex. Giving a high school senior the best sex of his life is simpler than one might expect—assuming he never dated me," Heidi added with a twinkle.

"But this is hopeless!" cried Doreen. "I don't see how—I mean, I'm not any of those things, Heidi. Oh, this is impossible, just impossible. I knew that changing schools wasn't going to make any difference." She covered her face with her hands.

"It's okay, Doreen." Biz hunched by her cousin, rubbing her back. "None of that stuff really matters. Seriously. And most of the popular kids here are really boring so . . . I never really cared about any of that stuff, personally. I'm actually kind of relieved—"

Doreen emitted a single agonized sob.

"Nonsense!" Heidi declared. "True, we have our work cut out for us, I won't argue that, but I believe we can launch you into Chandler, my dear, as a success. It simply requires a little art direction. Hair. Makeup. Lighting. Props. And we shall begin with your GryphPage profile." With that, Heidi disappeared into the bedroom.

"What's a GryphPage?" Doreen asked Biz with a sniffle.

"It's pretty stupid. See, our mascot is the gryphon. Do you know it? It's a mythological creature from ancient

Greece." Biz rummaged through a desk drawer. "It's got the body of a lion and the head and wings of an eagle. Here." She handed Doreen a Chandler Academy notebook. The creature was there in the middle, standing on its back lion paws with its wings outstretched.

"Like a dragon," said Doreen.

"Sort of. Interestingly, gryphons are said to mate for life. Even after one dies the other continues alone–they think that aspect of the myth was perpetuated by the church in order to support its view on marriage." Biz would have been happy to continue on to more mythological details, but she could see Doreen looking around the room. "Anyway, GryphPages is a localized social network, strictly for students at Chandler."

"Did you take all these pictures?" asked Doreen. She was scanning the photos on the wall. "Oh! That's Heidi. And Addison! I remember him now." She stepped closer to a photo of Biz's brother in silhouette, driving golf balls off a cliff near their Connecticut estate.

Biz smiled. "Everyone here calls him Ad-rock."

"Really? How stupid."

"Thank you!" said Biz. "Right? Anyway, I didn't take all of them. Some of them are just inspiration."

"So you're an artist."

"I don't know if I'd say–"

"Oh my god! This one of Aunt Gloria is amazing! The colors are so vibrant. Wow. Wow! I'm impressed. You are a great photographer, Biz."

"I'm, you know, well, that's nice of you to say."

"I didn't say it to be nice." Doreen squeezed her cousin's arm.

Heidi reentered the common room under an armload of clothes and deposited them with a grunt onto the sofa. "Everybody has a profile."

"Not everyone," said Biz. "I, for example, do not have a profile and I can assure you that I don't believe myself to be at all lacking—"

"Right. Let me rephrase," said Heidi. "Anyone who has any social aspirations whatsoever at Chandler has a Gryph-Page profile. Come over here, will you, sweetie? Let's see what we can do."

Doreen left Biz's photo collage and stood awkwardly in the middle of the room, her body resigned to Heidi's machinations. Heidi chose a black wrap dress from the pile and held it up over Doreen, studying the effect with a frown on her face. It was one of a few Mumzy purchased at Liberty of London in a panic, after Biz had arrived for a ten-day trip carrying only a backpack. "Too dull," Heidi pronounced and snatched the dress from Doreen, replacing it with a yellow silk.

"This is nice," Doreen offered. "I like the color."

"No, no," said Heidi. "It's entirely too, I don't know, Nantucket bridesmaid." She flung the yellow on top of the black wrap on the reject pile and stood with her hands on her hips, her perfect forehead creased in concentration. Biz sat at her desk chair and opened her laptop. Clothing bored her.

"Isn't there anything with a little sex?" Heidi complained as she picked through the pile on the sofa.

"Listen," said Biz. She entered Doreen's name on the GryphPage home screen and gave her account a password, cousin1. "If you don't like the pickings, why don't you go into your own closet?"

"Aha!" said Heidi. "Of course, the Dolce." She produced a tiny scrap of shiny, baby-blue fabric from the pile and held it overhead like a captured flag. "I wore this to winter formal last year. Doreen, the boys were driven near to lunacy!"

"But—" Doreen protested as Heidi pressed the frock into her arms. "Isn't it a little, I don't know, small?"

"Try it on, won't you, dear? We'll be honest. Let's just see what we're dealing with, hmm?" Heidi ushered Doreen into the bedroom.

"I don't know . . ." Doreen studied the minidress like she did not know what she was meant to do with it.

"It's the kind of dress that looks better on. Trust me. You pull it on over your head." Heidi closed the bedroom door.

Meanwhile, Biz had filled in Doreen's GryphPage profile with information about her cousin that she remembered from their shared youth at the beach house. Under "Interests" she'd written, "Gardening, mosaic-making, sailing, and board games." Now she was straining to remember something about Doreen's musical tastes. Biz smiled to herself as she recalled playing the pieces she knew on the heirloom baby grand the family kept in the great room while Doreen hopped and twirled and flittered around like a fairy. Whenever the music stopped, Doreen would spiritedly demand more. "Mozart," Biz wrote in the music column. "Bach, Chopin, Beethoven."

"What do you think you're doing?" Heidi asked. She bent over Biz and read what she'd typed over her shoulder.

"Huh? I'm helping."

"Board games? Do you really think that is an appropriate interest for a high school junior? And classical music? She wants to be popular, Biz, not middle-aged."

"You like classical music."

"Of course I do, but I'm not going to advertise it on the Internet. Here, move."

"This is my desk! I'm not going to—"

"MOVE!" Heidi commanded. Reluctantly, Biz complied.

"You're so bossy," said Biz with a defeated sigh, but Heidi didn't look up from the screen. "Lie carefully!"

At last the bedroom door opened. "You guys?" said Doreen in a small voice. "Heidi? Can I take this off now?"

"Oh, dear," said Heidi. "Oh no, that's not going to work at all." The dress hugged Doreen's flesh in a uniquely unflattering way, emphasizing the lumpiness of her hips and tummy while flattening her chest. Heidi wondered if this project was beyond even her considerable powers.

"I told you," Doreen sulked.

"Don't feel bad, Doreen. That dress looks indecent on everyone. Even Heidi."

"Hey! Yes, Doreen, you were right. Please take it off. We'll think of something." As Doreen disappeared to change,

Heidi paced around the common room. "Sexy isn't going to do it. We're going to have to go for drama." She spotted the *Vogue* magazine she'd purchased for the bus back to campus. "Hold on a second. I saw something in here."

Heidi flipped through the pages. "Ah, yes! Here it is. This is perfect. Doreen?" she called through the door. "Honey, can I come in?"

"I really wish you wouldn't."

"She's upset," said Biz. "This is exactly what I was trying to avoid."

Heidi waved Biz off. "That's okay," she told Doreen through the door in her sweetest voice. "But do me a favor? Go into Biz's closet there, the one on the right. Toward the back you'll find a red strapless dress. Do you see it?"

"I really don't want to do this anymore, Heidi."

"This is the last one, okay? I promise. It's red and strapless and the label says Carolina Herrera." She grinned at Biz. This was going to work, she was sure of it.

Biz plucked the open magazine from Heidi's hand and regarded the picture. "Is this a joke?" she deadpanned.

"Shh! No negativity," Heidi whispered. "Find the place where you keep your can-do attitude, Miss Gibbons-Brown. You're going to need it."

"Or what?"

"You know better than to cross me, Elizabeth. Or don't you want your cousin to like you?" Heidi snatched the magazine back from Biz.

"Is that another threat? They're really coming fast and loose today."

"Just get your tripod, okay? And dispense with the histrionics." Heidi rolled her eyes. It was tiresome, doing everything oneself. Finally the door opened again. Biz and Heidi stood up to behold their project.

"Well? What do you think?" Doreen asked.

"Perfection!" Heidi managed. "Yes, that'll do just fine." She spun Doreen around. The dress did not fit altogether perfectly—it tucked right under the fat part of Doreen's armpit, and an inch or two of zipper remained open at the top because her back was too wide for the fabric. But it was a lovely dress. She did not look beautiful, but Heidi was sure she could work with it. "Next up? Makeup."

3

The moon shining through the window gave Doreen's skin a soft effervescence, as if she was a ghost or an angel. She'd scrubbed her face of the makeup Heidi had slathered upon it for the photo shoot, pulled the hair that Heidi had so painstakingly curled back into a messy bun, and reclothed herself in the green knit dress. So it was Doreen Gray as her natural, pimply, frizzy-haired self upon whom Heidi gazed so admiringly.

Perhaps it was the excitement of the day's activities, or the comfort of a friendly welcome—or it may simply have been the night, coming through the window thick and velvety in the late summer, but Heidi saw majesty in Doreen. "You looked great, Doreen. I think you're going to like the picture."

"Really?" Doreen's smile was full of gratitude.

Biz sat at her computer, hard at work. She uploaded the photos from that afternoon's session onto her computer and clicked through, looking for the picture that best mimicked the one from *Vogue* that she'd torn out of the magazine and pinned onto the wall. One photo in particular caught her attention.

It was a medium shot, with Doreen gazing directly at the camera, commanding the viewer take her in, to feast on her beauty. It was a good picture—great even—and since she'd taken it herself, Biz was proud of the results. She checked it against the magazine picture and thought Doreen looked so much more vivacious than the dull model. Of course, Biz admitted to herself, you could see the imperfections of

Doreen's skin and the awkwardness of her body, but with her soul so available, what would that matter? Anyway, she could easily clean up the blemishes.

Biz pulled the photo into her design program. Just a couple little touch-ups here and there so that Doreen would be proud of herself. Biz wanted her to feel confident—to see the beauty that was so apparent to her but more hidden from shallower types like Heidi or Mumzy. She zoomed in on Doreen's face and began to smooth and gloss her skin.

"I think," Doreen said to Heidi, "that Biz thinks you will be a bad influence on me."

"Of course I will," said Heidi. "If I am any influence at all, I will be a bad one, because that is the only kind of influence there is!"

"What do you mean? You don't believe in positive influence?"

"Only when you are the influencer, then there are oodles of benefits. You see, Doreen, most people find the freedom of life to be too stressful. Choices oppress these people. To relieve them of their burden, you just make their choices for them. Of course, it's a delicate process. Though they want to be freed from freedom, they still have an ego. As an influencer, it's up to you to ensure that even as you deliver them from their free will, they can uphold the make-believe that they are proceeding on their own chosen path.

"But in the meantime, you have to be vigilant in the matters of your own desires. Differentiate yourself from the sheep by loving freedom, by refusing to forsake it for any reason. You must, in other words, make yourself a fortress, barring yourself from outside influence so that you maintain the power over your own life and the lives of others."

Doreen's face took on a peculiar look, as if she'd uncovered some long-buried truth and the discovery made her euphoric with recognition.

"There is something special about you, Doreen," Heidi continued, keeping a careful eye on the effect of her words on Doreen's face. "I saw it as soon as you walked in here. I think it would really be something if you gave yourself the liberty to satisfy yourself. Let life work in your favor; let all that you want be delivered to you. I'll help you."

"Will you, Heidi?" Doreen asked breathlessly, her eyes darting back and forth across Heidi's face. "I would like that so much! Will you really?"

"Heidi, what are you saying?" said Biz, her face lit blue from the glow of the computer screen. "Whatever it is, don't listen, Doreen."

"Biz, don't lecture," said Heidi, with a conspiratorial roll of her eyes at Doreen. The girl smiled—at her cousin's expense! Oh, this was too easy. "And aren't you done yet? The anticipation is torturous."

"Almost, almost." Having finished with Doreen's face, Biz moved onto her body. A little smoothing, she said to herself, nobody is perfect. Anyway, she was only giving Doreen's picture the same attention the model had received in *Vogue*. She trained her digital airbrush over Doreen's arms and torso.

"There. That's perfect. Now I'll just upload it to your GryphPage so you can see it *in situ.*"

"No!" Doreen blurted, springing to her feet. "I mean, can I see it first? Before it goes, like, public?"

"Oh. Sure. Of course. Here, let me print it." Under her desk, Biz's professional-grade printer whirred to life, a gift from her father. "I think you're going to like how it came out."

"Don't be nervous." Heidi patted Doreen on her knee. "You looked amazing in that dress."

"I'm not nervous," Doreen insisted as she cracked every single knuckle in succession.

"Yeah, right."

"Here we go." Biz removed the page from the printer and gave it a satisfied nod. She laid the photo on the coffee table in front of Doreen and Heidi.

In the picture, a stunning girl sat on a chair in the middle of a field, wearing a red strapless dress that fit her perfectly, as if she was sewn into it. The girl's skin was flawlessly smooth and white, and her violet eyes met the camera directly, with an audacity befitting her incredible beauty. Her thin arms rested comfortably at her side while ringlets of black hair cascaded dramatically down her back. In the porcelain white of the face, Doreen identified some recognizable features. That must have been her nose, after all, and though the lips were so perfectly shaped in their light-pink stain, it was her mouth in the photo, the same mouth that gaped openly at the picture she beheld, naked and dried out from nervous chewing.

"Why, Bizzy Bear, you've quite outdone yourself! Our little Doreen looks so—"

"Unrecognizable! Oh, what have you done? No. No!" The picture shook in Doreen's hand. "You're making fun of me. I should have known!" Doreen buried her head in her hands.

"Huh? Making fun of you? What would make you think that?" Biz looked mortified. "I thought you would like it. I just touched it up a tiny bit."

"Ha!"

"I'm sorry, I didn't mean to—I thought, I don't know. I was trying to give you what you wanted."

"To look like an idiot? How can I possibly claim that this is a picture of me? It looks nothing like me! If people see it . . . It's cruel what you've done. Both of you! Oh, I should have known."

"Doreen, calm down. Nobody is making fun of you," said Heidi, but the girl continued to sob. "You don't like the picture? Fine! Biz, delete the file from your computer. Give me the photo." Heidi held a hand out to Doreen. "Really, you needn't make such a fuss. Poor Biz was simply trying to help you." Heidi was disappointed with the scene Doreen was making. She hadn't thought the girl would be so gushy and unreasonable. "Give me the photograph, Doreen."

"Why?" Doreen asked. She pressed the picture to her chest. "What are you going to do with it?"

"I was going to destroy it. Isn't that what you want?" Heidi stood up and paced around the room, her hands in fists. "I cannot tolerate this inconstancy. Resolve yourself. If you don't like the photograph, I will rip it to shreds. Otherwise get a hold of yourself so that we may discuss the issue like adults. Your cousin was trying to be kind to you. She does not deserve to be spoken to with such ugliness!"

"You're right. I'm sorry. Please don't be mad at me. I'm sorry, Bizzy. I just—don't you understand?" Doreen looked down at the photograph with a new tenderness. "Oh, I wish this was me in the picture." She wiped tears from her eyes. Crying had brought out the splotchy redness of her complexion, making her look even more unlike the photo. "I would give anything to be this girl!"

"But it is you!" said Biz softly. "All I did was clean it up a little. That's what they do in the magazines."

"I really appreciate what you did, Biz. But when I see this picture, it shows me everything that I'm not. I'm not beautiful or glamorous. I could never be this girl, as much as I would want to be her. Look!" Biz and Doreen looked down at the picture together. "See how easy her life must be! How everybody must love her! That isn't me. That isn't how—" Doreen's eyes welled up again. Biz gently ran a hand along her head.

"Shh," she said. "It's okay."

"And I don't want you to rip it to shreds, Heidi. Because it's so—it's beautiful. It's the most perfect picture I've ever seen. I love it, in a way. Only . . . I'm jealous of it. Have you ever heard of anything so ridiculous? To be jealous of a picture." She shook her head, smiling. "I really am a piece of work."

"You've had a long day," said Biz. "You must be exhausted." Doreen leaned her head against her cousin's shoulder and Biz stroked her cheek. Heidi could not remember Biz displaying so much affection for a human before.

"That's right, Biz. We've all had a long day of it." Heidi sensed that she was losing Doreen to Biz, but she was not ready to give up yet. So the photo shoot had been a bit of a disaster, so what? She could still recover her position. After all, popularity was not something one gave up on so easily. "Listen, Doreen, why don't you drop by here tomorrow at around eleven? We'll get you dressed and then we can appear together at lunch. Maybe the GryphPage profile was the wrong starting point."

"Listen, Heidi, I think we've had enough of all that. Popularity is a waste of time. I'll show you around campus tomorrow, Doreen. Wait till you see the technology at our disposal here."

"As your friend?" Doreen asked Heidi, unclasping Biz's hand.

"I'm sorry?"

"Will you introduce me to people at lunch—as your friend? Would you really do that?"

"Of course!" said Heidi. She tucked an errant batch of wiry hair behind Doreen's ear and put an arm around her shoulders. "I will introduce you as my friend as well as a representative of the midwestern branch of the Gibbons-Brown family."

"Oh, please," said Biz. "Do you hear yourself? How absurd."

"Okay. Okay. I'll see you tomorrow at eleven." Doreen gathered up her things to go.

"But, Doreen, I thought, is that really—"

"I really am tired, so I think I'll head home. Good-bye for now. Thank you, Heidi. Thank you so much for everything. I'm sorry for my outburst. Good-bye, Biz! I'll see you tomorrow!" With the photograph still in her hand, Doreen let herself out of their room.

"Well!" Heidi said when she heard the door close. She sank onto the sofa beside Biz. "What a fascinating evening!"

4

"Are you asleep?" Biz asked.

"No," said Heidi. "And apparently neither are you."

Biz sat up in her bed and flicked on the lamp on the nightstand. "Can I ask you something then?" Without her glasses, Biz looked like a mole person.

"What? Oh, sure. Shoot. What is it?"

"Why are you so interested in Doreen? She's not exactly made of the same stuff as the girls you normally associate with." Biz clasped her legs over the covers and nuzzled her chin between her knees.

"I can't help but point out that she's your cousin. Which means she's made of precisely the same stuff of someone I normally associate with—you."

"Yeah, but, I mean . . ."

"What is it?" Heidi could see that Biz was having a hard time getting out whatever it was that she needed to say.

"That's about my brother, right? Isn't that why you became friends with me? I thought it was some sort of revenge thing against Ad-rock."

"No. Maybe a little, at first. Anyway, I knew you before I knew him."

"At the campus tour? You were hardly interested in being my friend."

"You don't know that. Plus, Ad-rock and I are ancient history. If I only wanted to be friends with you to get back at him, I would have cut off ties after he graduated."

"I guess."

"Biz, I have to associate with those other girls, the Chandler types. Otherwise I wouldn't . . . it's hard to explain, I just have to. But I don't hang out with you because I have to, I do it because I want to."

"Why? We have nothing in common."

Heidi could not understand why Biz was bringing all this up now. "Let me ask you this, why do you hang out with me?"

Biz looked over at Heidi. "I don't know. I guess because you're here." Heidi laughed. "What? What's so funny?"

"Nothing, nothing. Look, Biz, you're smart and I'm smart. Intelligence makes a person interesting. You are incapable of being manipulated, you are malice-free, and most importantly, you are not boring. Which, I may add, gives you a giant lead over your dimwitted brother, who is about as fascinating as oatmeal. Okay?"

"Yeah. Okay. You're not boring, either," Biz said. She yawned and lay back on her pillow.

"Stop it. I'm gonna cry."

"And Doreen? What about her?"

Heidi looked up at the white ceiling. "Doreen is a blank canvas. What could be less boring than that? Anyway, there's something about her I can't quite put my finger on."

"I know what you mean," said Biz. "She's always had it. A kind of quality, like she understands what you're thinking and feeling. She's really sensitive, I think. It probably accounts for the bullying."

"Huh," said Heidi. "I'm sure you're right."

"Of course I am. Anyway . . ." Soon enough, Biz was snoring.

———◦◦———

Heidi still couldn't sleep. In the common room, she wrapped herself in a cashmere throw and looked out onto the empty quad. She thought about her own first day at Chandler Academy. Heidi had not been so different from Doreen then. She was prettier, better groomed, but she was a transfer student, too. And even though she grew up a few miles from the private elementary schools where the Manhattan contingent of Chandler had learned their ABCs, it may as well have been another planet. She remembered distinctly the feeling of being lost, like she'd gotten off the bus a stop too early.

But unlike Doreen, she had prepared for the moment. *He'd* groomed her for it. He taught her how to talk, how to walk, how to present herself as a person who belonged. And after everything she'd risked to get into the school, she made sure to appear perfectly at home from day one. She thought of herself at the campus tour on her first day, how nervous she was in her painstakingly chosen outfit, a slight smile on her face that she hoped made her appear dignified and at ease. She stood tall. She moved with grace.

All of this was lost on Biz. Charged with leading Heidi on a fifteen-minute tour of the campus, Biz had been too full of information and enthusiasm about the wonderful academic resources at Chandler to keep it under forty-five.

But Heidi had more pressing items on her agenda than rare book collections and jazz ensembles. So when the tour was finally over and Biz asked at last if she had any questions, Heidi found herself asking if she happened to know Addison Gibbons. They stood at the edge of campus, near the field house. It was an innocuous question, Heidi thought, and she did a decent job of asking it without betraying the stakes involved.

Biz, who had been introduced only as Elizabeth when they met at student services, stopped her forward progress and flipped to face Heidi. "Gibbons-Brown, you mean?" she asked.

"Uh, yes, of course. I'm, uh, our mothers know each other and I was told to look him up." Heidi's was the smile of a cartoon doe.

"Who is your mother?" the girl demanded. She squinted at Heidi through her filthy wire frames like her lie was written on her face.

"Oh! Uh, it's just . . ."

"Because Addison is my brother," said Biz. "So his mother is also, goes without saying—"

"Your mother! Of course. I didn't, I mean, you probably haven't heard . . . They know each other very . . . well, she probably wouldn't even remember. A charity function. In the Hamptons over the summer, I guess they got to talking." In fact, there had been a party. A beautiful party in a mansion. Gloria had gone on and on about Addison. Not to Heidi's mother—who had never stepped foot in the

Hamptons and only gave money to the Catholic Church—but to Heidi herself. *Oh, how I wish Addison were here so I could introduce you! He would adore you, wouldn't he, Roland? Oh, you're cute as a button. It would be nice for him to bring home a girl with a little intelligence. Roland, why didn't you insist that I bring him here to meet her? Well, you'll meet. Of course you'll meet.*

"Talking?" Biz sniffed. "She certainly has been known to do *that.*" Her lips spread into a contemptuous grin. "And she mentioned Addison, but not me? Elizabeth? Because you and I are the same age."

"Oh. Maybe she mentioned you. I'm sure she did, so, great to, I mean, it works out that, and everything," Heidi said. She should have waited to establish herself on campus before digging around for his nephew. But she couldn't stop herself. She'd gotten away scot-free and still it wasn't enough.

"Nice to meet you, too," said Biz. "And Addison is right over there." She pointed to a field where boys were kicking around a soccer ball. "He'll be the one not wearing a shirt. He rarely does."

"Oh. Okay."

"Here, I'll introduce you. Addison! There's a pretty girl here that Mom wants you to meet!" Biz screamed across the quad. The kid looked up from his game and smiled before slow-jogging over in nothing but a pair of faded sweats and sneakers.

"Thanks, Elizabeth," Heidi whispered.

"Biz," she said. And she walked away.

As it turned out, Ad-rock was as dumb as the mineral deposits in his moniker, and so full of himself that a few delighted squeezes of his bicep were enough to win his heart. *Make them feel like you're giving them what they want, like they are the ones coming out ahead.* That's what she'd been taught, and it worked like a charm. She fed Addison a never-ending stream of compliments and assurances that his insecurities were unfounded. He, in turn, brought her into the fold of the leading cliques on campus. Once she felt sufficiently entrenched, and when it became too exhausting to maintain the appearance of interest in the inane things that occupied Addison's feeble mind—workouts, video games, golf, eating large quantities of meat—she dumped him. Hard. Which broke his silly little heart and took her from unknown transfer student to fascinating object of desire, practically overnight.

Win-win. Looking back now, it remained one of her most effective social strategies. But she had to admit that choosing Addison was stupid. With so many worthy older boys on campus, getting involved with Roland's nephew put her in danger of exposing their arrangement. She could have lost everything. So why did she do it? And why, when it ended, did she immediately befriend the niece?

But Heidi only needed to look at Biz's cluttered gallery of a desk to find the answer. What she'd told her before was true: Biz was interesting. She remained one of the only souls on the Chandler campus who did not bore Heidi to tears. So she happened to be Roland's niece, what of it? In their two years of roommatehood, Roland had hardly ever come up in conversation. Biz didn't like her uncle, rarely spoke of him.

And wouldn't the same be true of Doreen? She obviously had little to do with her father. After all, Roland rejected Doreen, too, hadn't he? And the poor thing, she seemed so friendless and alone. Heidi had every confidence she could help her. And if she could, wouldn't it be cruel, immoral even, not to do everything in her power to turn it around for the poor sucker? What better way for Heidi to spend her last year at Chandler than to use the power she'd accrued to help someone less fortunate than she was? There were many other ways for Heidi to relieve herself of boredom, but maybe she could take the high road this time, use her gifts to create something great, the way Biz did with her photography.

Heidi sighed. She flicked on her desk lamp and fished a slinky gold watch from the top drawer. She spun the diamond-encrusted face toward her. The watch had been a gift, delivered to her care at the concierge desk of the Montauk Inn where she'd been employed the summer she met Roland Gibbons. It was a replacement for a less elegant timepiece she had left behind in Roland's room the previous evening, before they went to the party that would change her life forever. Roland could not tolerate ugly things. And so he'd tossed the other watch and sent this beautiful trinket, a gift and also an upgrade, the next step in his Heidi improvement plan. She hadn't minded. At the time, she thought the watch was the most beautiful thing she had ever seen—certainly the most beautiful thing she had ever owned.

Three a.m. Heidi dropped the watch back in the drawer and slammed it shut. Her dad would be getting up soon to make his shift. She imagined him waking up next to her mother in the old wooden bed under the cross. Roland had everything and acted like he got a bad draw, but Heidi's father was content with the nothing he had. He liked to sit at the bar in O'Keefe's with a seltzer—he'd given up drinking around the time that Heidi was born, but sitting around a bar is what guys like Heidi's father did with his friends, so that's what he did. He sat with his seltzer and told funny stories about his life and the life of his family, stories that were true, or true-ish, or could be claimed as true by someone like Brian Whelan, a guy with the gift of blarney.

He was always so proud of her. Every time she brought home a report card, he carried it with him to work. "The beauty she gets from her mother, I had nothing to do with that. But smart! Smart like her old man," he would say.

"I'm proud of you, honey," he said when she told him about working at the Montauk Inn for the summer. Wide-palmed, he clapped her on the back. "She's gonna go out to the Hamptons and schmooze with the hoity-toits this summer," he'd told the guys at O'Keefe's when she came by to get him for dinner. "Pretty soon you're gonna be too big for us, here." But that's what he wanted, wasn't it? He couldn't have wanted her to stay in Yonkers forever.

"You gotta be the first one there," he said when he presented her with the watch from Macy's. It had a white face and a black leather band. "Every time. Don't let nobody get there before you do. Get there early and get a lay of the land, like. Know what you're up against." She said she would do it, whatever he said, whatever it took. Her father had lived through enough disappointments. She vowed not to be one of them.

In the darkness of the sleeping campus, Heidi grieved for her father's lost watch, tossed into the wastebasket for the hotel maid by a spoiled playboy. She would give anything to have it again. Sometimes she felt the shame inside her might swallow her up.

But she was going to change that. She was going to be good. To help Doreen, that was the right thing to do. She could even tell her father about it. *I used my gifts to help a sad, lonely girl make a better life, a fresh start. Aren't you proud, Dad? Isn't it just what you would have wanted?*

"Mornin', Pops," she whispered, allowing herself to relax into her natural accent.

"'Nighty-night, Heidi-bear," she imagined him saying back. She was tired, too tired to think. Her thoughts were getting all jumbled. She stretched out on the sofa and faded off.

5

As soon as Doreen opened her eyes, she felt possessed by a weird feeling. Probably from spending her first night in a new place, she thought. She lay back on her pillow and replayed the events of the previous evening—how happy she'd felt, reveling in the attentions of Heidi, a girl prettier than even the most popular girls at her old school. But then the memory of the doctored picture brought her right back down to reality and she felt rotten again.

Biz was just trying to be nice, she reminded herself, though she felt a sharp pang at how much Biz needed to change her image in order to make her presentable. Still, Doreen was anxious to look at the picture again. The fantasy of it delighted her. She pulled it from the drawer in her nightstand where she'd placed it the night before. "I'll look one more time," she said to herself. "And then I will rip it up into a hundred pieces." She knew better than to waste her time on what could never be. But she would indulge one final glimpse. She turned on the reading lamp beside her bed to get a better look.

The picture looked nothing like she remembered it. She brought it closer to her face. Instead of the beautiful stranger, she saw that the subject of the photograph was the real Doreen, sitting self-consciously in a chair in the woods, in an unflattering dress and too much makeup, her smile strained with effort. Doreen blinked at the image. Had she imagined the pure-skinned angel? Could her eyes be playing some sort of trick on her? She launched herself out of bed and opened the blinds. But the light, now everywhere, only confirmed that the girl in the picture was no ideal of grace and beauty but Doreen as she knew herself to be—utterly, painfully flawed.

Doreen cried out. How could she have mistaken her own pathetic body for the goddess in her imagination? Oh, how she hated her looks, her face, her skin. She stepped in front of the mirror to relish in her own disgust. She looked up at her reflection with a scowl on her face. And the scowl returned to her—on the face of the perfect-looking girl she remembered from the photograph.

What? Doreen couldn't compute what she was seeing. The beautiful mirror-girl had on the purple flannel pajamas Doreen's mother brought back from Nashville that time, the same pajamas Doreen had worn to bed. When Doreen moved her hand, the girl also moved her hand. The surface of the mirror was hard and smooth as any mirror, but her own skin, when she touched it, was soft and creamy. She watched the girl in the mirror touch her own face, her lovely mouth agape, her perfectly arched eyebrows furrowed in confusion.

Slowly, slowly it began to sink in. She'd made a wish, hadn't she? She wished she could be the girl in the picture, the stunner Biz made out of pixels and light. She stood staring at the image of herself in the mirror, afraid to look away and make it all go back to the way it was. She wanted to hold on to that moment, to make it stretch on for the rest of her life. She put her hand against the glass and took it all in.

——————●●——————

By nine o'clock in the morning, Heidi had run four miles, showered, exfoliated her skin, and blown out her hair to perfect, glossy straightness. She had also baked a pan full of pot brownies in the small efficiency kitchen of the dorm. The brownies were for Miss Jenkins, the dean's secretary. Heidi wrapped the treats over with cling wrap on a paper plate and tied a pink ribbon around them. She carried the platter across the still-empty quad toward the dean's office in the warmth of the September sun.

Heidi knew from experience that Miss Jenkins could not resist chocolate. She also knew that marijuana loosened her lips—though Miss Jenkins may not have been aware of this latter fact herself. Whenever Heidi wanted to uncover a useful, dirty secret about one of her classmates, she baked a baggie of weed right into her brownies. After she delivered them to Miss Jenkins with some excuse, she had only to sit around and wait for answers.

"Why, Ms. Whelan!" Miss Jenkins exclaimed from behind her cluttered desk on the morning after the arrival of Doreen Gray. "Classes have not even begun and here you are, bearing chocolate. And so early in the morning. You are a terrible influence," she said with a playful wag of her finger. Her clothes were dreary and shapeless, her glasses unfashionably round and ill-suited for her face, and she wore her light brown hair half up and tied with a scrunchie.

But Miss Jenkins's clean complexion and enthusiasm made her seem youthful despite her tacky presentation.

"Good morning, Miss Jenkins. Did you have a good summer? I am sorry for barging in like this. You see, I made these brownies for my roommate, Elizabeth Gibbons-Brown. Do you know her? She asked me to make them to assist in her efforts to woo some science nerd, but apparently his affections turned elsewhere. Poor little Bizzy is so distraught she can't eat a thing, and she says that seeing the brownies is painful to her. I ate as many as I could, but I was hoping that you might take them off our hands. Would you mind, Miss Jenkins? It would be such a favor." Heidi set the plate down on the secretary's desk, nudging them toward Miss Jenkins's nose.

"I understand that, of course. Boys will have their own whims, won't they? You're a good friend. Please have a seat, Ms. Whelan." Miss Jenkins gazed at the plate of brownies. "You know, normally I would never indulge in something so rich this early in the day, but I did happen to miss breakfast this morning." Miss Jenkins raised an eyebrow at Heidi, looking for approval.

"Oh, go on, Miss Jenkins," Heidi encouraged. "Have one! Have a couple. They're practically muffins anyway. What's the difference? My mother always said, breakfast like a king, lunch like a prince, dinner like a pauper. That's the key to a slim figure." Of course, it wasn't her own mother she was quoting, it was Biz's. Mumzy had a million pithy little sayings.

"Wise woman," said Miss Jenkins as she unwrapped the plate and helped herself to the largest brownie. Heidi leaned back and waited for the marijuana to have its effect.

Not surprisingly, Miss Jenkins spilled the whole story. An acrimonious divorce and a power lawyer left Doreen and her mom penniless. In desperation they moved back to the Midwest while Roland settled in with the new, shiny model wife (Heidi remembered her well) and their shiny, new children. Why had it rung so familiar to her? She made slow progress across the quad, her mind replaying the facts. Heidi's parents had never abandoned her. If anything the opposite was true. They loved her, told her so often, awaited calls that never came. But to have to live in the muck of regular life while Roland plucked goodies off platters and made cutting jokes about debutantes, it was so unfair! Doreen should have been taken in by him, given the easy life he enjoyed, but she had to be beaten down, made to feel worthless and ashamed.

And then Doreen's mother had barged in—good for her! At a society event. Heidi had been to one of those, too. In a long, silk chiffon, apple-green dress with a giant floral pattern Roland had borrowed from his sister, Heidi mixed with the wealthy and the renowned. The dress had a halter top and a cinched waist. Heidi couldn't help stealing glances of herself in every mirror she passed, and there were many at the mansion in Bridgehampton where the party was held. Now, even years later, Heidi could still close her eyes and recall the softness of the rich silk when she ran her fingers along the edge of the garment. It was so beautiful, and she'd been beautiful in it, more elegant and alluring than she'd ever looked before. He said the cut showed off her clavicle, a body part she had not previously known to be worthy of showing off, but once she did she could not stop running her fingers along it as she engaged in conversation with the beau monde.

Roland introduced her as his "little protégé." He said he found her behind a desk at a hotel like a sad, caged bird.

"And weren't you so kind as to hear my song and free me," said Heidi with a smile, concentrating on the refined accent Roland had taught her. "It was very charitable of you."

"Charity had nothing to do with it," said Roland. People laughed. They were charmed. She was witty. She said funny things, cutting things, she thought, what he would say if he were a woman in a gown. She imitated his laugh, his manner of speaking. Everyone sipped champagne and there was crab and lobster and fish. People looked wonderful. She looked wonderful. Her fingers danced along her clavicle.

"You see?" he whispered in her ear. "Do you see how easy it is? Everyone here is half-moron." His voice in her ear was like a torch she carried. Never in her life had she felt sharper or more powerful.

Later, as Roland drove them back to the hotel in his Porsche (she doubted the law would consider him sober enough to drive, but who was she to question?), he asked her what she thought of everyone. He wanted specifics. With whom did she speak? What did she say? What did they say back to her?

"I guess I always thought that rich and famous people were smarter or more interesting than the people I knew. But they're not—or not necessarily," she said. They cruised down Highway 27. Outside it was so dark, darker than anything Heidi knew from her city life. She wished the top were down so she could see the stars.

"Aha," said Roland. "Now you're starting to understand what I've been saying to you. You can have whatever you want, Heidi, I believe that. And it's not because you're beautiful, or not only because of that. There are plenty of beautiful girls, my dear, but none of them have what you have."

"And what's that?" she asked breathlessly. "What do I have that's so special?"

He adjusted the rearview so he could look at her. Hope filled her heart as she waited for him to assess her offerings—her spirit, her grace, her goodness—what would he choose?

Turning the car onto West Lake Drive, he said, "You have nothing to lose."

A mother lugging a desk lamp and a bag of golf clubs clipped Heidi on the shoulder, jolting her from her daydream. The quad was now teeming with activity. Expensive cars lined up around the periphery of campus. Parents and siblings unloaded plastic crates and bulletin boards, giant duffel bags filled with tailored clothing in khaki and blue stripes. It was so easy for them! She balled her hand into a tight fist, then let it go. Jealousy, she well knew, would get her nowhere. She was smarter than all of them, better than all of them because she'd made it this far on her own, made a life from nothing.

A boy who loved Heidi carried a fan into Smith Hall. He waved at her and she deigned grant him a tiny smile. He was so happy he crashed into a wall. She walked on.

Roland was wrong. They were the ones with nothing to lose, not her. You couldn't fall from on high when you were inside—not when you could sit on your grand settee and gaze down at the world from the safety of your penthouse. No. The ones on the inside did not risk falling. It was the outsiders, interlopers, window-washers, people like Heidi who had only a toe in the door while the rest flapped in the breeze, ready to be sent spinning back toward earth the second they were discovered. People like Heidi didn't get to take the elevator down, either. They crashed, splattered on Fifth Avenue like meat scraps.

Heidi had everything to lose, and just as he'd had the power to give it, Roland could take it all away, on a whim. No. Doreen was entirely too risky. It was stupid. Heidi needed to stay focused, get into college, Ivy League, the best. Forget about Roland, forget about Doreen and move on. That was all there was to it.

But she was so lonely. No matter how far she'd come, Heidi didn't really belong at Chandler—or in Yonkers. That was Roland Gibbons's legacy in her life. He made her into a person apart. And he'd done it to Doreen, too, hadn't he? If ever a girl belonged nowhere it was that poor, lost soul.

She's like my sister, Heidi thought. We are sisters

in his rejection. We will survive him. We will be not alone, but together. Heidi and Doreen. I will make her the way he made me, she thought, but better, because I will not abandon her to fend for herself. I will be there: friend, sister, guide. She felt weightless, filled with purpose. Worthy. Heidi felt sure that if she could make Doreen, she would cleanse herself of Roland forever. She would find the girl's beauty and poise, and the position that Heidi had worked and struggled for would mean so much more because she would have someone to share it with.

Heidi hurried back. Doreen thought she was going to be introduced around at the cafeteria that afternoon, but it was far too early for that. They had a lot of work to do before then.

———— ◦◦ ————

Heidi found Biz still padding around the suite in her pajamas.

"Sleeping in, are we? How unlike you," said Heidi.

"Yes, well. Listen, Heidi, I wanted to talk to you."

"I don't suppose I need to remind you that Doreen will be coming by at eleven." Heidi busied herself around the room, straightening furniture and replacing books.

"Yes, I remember. And that's what I wanted to talk to you about. Doreen—Heidi, she's not like you."

"Oh, no?" said Heidi with an amused smirk. "I suppose she's more like you, huh?" She fluffed the pillows of the sofa.

"No. Well, yes, I mean, she is my cousin. So, you know, genetically speaking—"

"Yes, Elizabeth, she is. And she may have some long-ago memories of scooting around your family's Amagansett estate, but that's where your similarities end. You see, darling, Doreen is an outsider. You don't know what that's like, having been born on the inside."

"What? Me? An insider? Is that a joke?"

"Hmph."

"Still singing the same old song, huh? I'm a Gibbons-Brown so I've obviously got it made. Life of Riley and everything. Sure, sure." Biz looked hurt. Money or not, the girl had not had the easiest time of it.

"Not an insider, maybe. But at least you knew where you belonged. Doreen and I—"

"All I am asking," Biz said slowly in a firm voice, "is that you don't ruin her, Heidi. Okay? Be careful with her. She's innocent now and she should stay that way. I would like to see her stay that way. Do you hear what I'm saying? Keep your claws to yourself."

"Or what?" Heidi said, hand on her hip. "You're going to give me a piece of your mind?"

Just then they heard a knock at the door. "Speak of the angel," Heidi said with an ironic curtsey as she crossed the room to open the door. Biz collapsed on the armchair, her forehead creased with worry.

Heidi gasped. "Doreen! Oh my god, what happened to you?" Biz rushed to the door to see what the matter was, and when she caught sight of Doreen, she, too, cried out in surprise. But Doreen accepted their shock with a smile.

"May I come in?" she asked softly.

"Of course!" Biz said, stepping aside. Open-mouthed, the two roommates watched Doreen walk into the room and take a delicate seat on the sofa.

"Aren't you going to close the door?" Doreen asked with a light laugh.

Overnight, the girl had transformed. No longer the awkward, lumpy person from the day before, Doreen was lithe and graceful. Her patchy skin had become smooth and lustrous and the frizz had gone out of her hair, replaced with gorgeous black curls. She blinked up at them, staring through long lashes with her piercing violet eyes: an exact replica of the girl in the picture Biz had touched up the previous evening.

"Well, I'm here to be outfitted," Doreen said. She stood up and spun around. "Do you have a vision, Heidi?"

Regaining her composure, Heidi broke into a wide smile. This was going to work! Even the same army-green knit dress from the day before looked great on her. "Doreen, you look wonderful. Really. Let's get you into some clothes, dear. Biz, close your mouth."

Doreen smiled with her strawberry lips and let Heidi lead her into the bedroom. Biz stood frozen in her pajamas, unsure of what she had just seen.

"A vision," said Biz, shaking her head in disbelief.

6

"It wouldn't be lying, would it, if I didn't mention certain things about my past?" asked Doreen. They'd managed to keep the conversation light for most of the walk to the cafeteria, but now their destination was in sight and Heidi could practically hear the sound of Doreen's heart beating.

Heidi had some misgivings herself—they might be rushing things along a bit, but it was only lunch and they had to start somewhere. And the girl looked awesome. They'd chosen a simple sundress from Heidi's own closet that made her look simultaneously girlish and sexy, nothing like the high school disaster from the night before. Heidi did not know how Doreen had managed it, but she felt confident that her own influence bore much of the responsibility for the transformation.

"I wouldn't want to make something up. Or should I? I don't know. Do I need some sort of story?"

"No need, my dear," said Heidi reassuringly. "Your family is a known quantity around here. Everyone remembers Addison, and though Biz is strange, she is acceptable because of her name. Keeping your home life to yourself will only make you seem appealingly mysterious. That's what I've done. I have never told a single lie about myself or my upbringing—I have simply kept mum. Reticence implies grandness, Doreen. You'll see." It was a lot for Heidi to admit. She hadn't said anything specific, of course, but it was so unlike her to make even the vaguest reference to her modest background to anyone. She would admit that and more to Doreen if she would only ask. But the girl was too caught up in her own story to bother with Heidi's.

"I'm sure you're right." Doreen squeezed Heidi's hand. "Oh, thank you so much for everything."

No matter, thought Heidi. There would be time.

"Here goes nothin'," said Doreen.

"Noth*ing*," said Heidi.

———— ◦◦ ————

"Now it's time for everyone's favorite back-to-school game, who got a nose job! I can't help but notice something different about your face, Misha."

"Lay off, Gordon."

"I think she looks great. You look great, Meesh," said Miyuki.

"I didn't get a nose job, okay?"

"Sure, sure. Maybe your nose is just smaller than we all remember it."

"Maybe it is!"

"Or maybe her face grew, but her nose stayed the same size."

"Shut up, Frankie!"

"Yeah, Frankie, leave her alone. She's obviously still recuperating."

"Ugh! I hate you guys."

"What do you think, Doreen? Oh wait. You didn't know Misha before. Well, picture the same girl, with a less refined central canal."

"Gordon, I am going to kill you."

"Save me, Doreen! She's fierce! Help! Help!"

Heidi was right. When they heard that she was a cousin to the Gibbons-Browns, no further questions were asked about Doreen's background. They were tired of one another now, in their final year, and boys and girls alike regarded Doreen with enthusiasm, happy for fresh society. The boys were especially keen—suntanned, with new muscles from summers spent on boats, they were keyed up around the new girl like wind-up toys come to life.

"Misha, don't be embarrassed. You look great. Truly! We've been waiting for you to do the snip for years. Doreen, she looks beautiful, doesn't she?"

"What? Oh." Doreen smiled and touched Misha's hand. "You do. You are beautiful."

"Huh? Thanks." Misha blushed.

"See, Meesh? And Doreen here knows a thing or two about beauty." Gordon held Doreen's gaze for a moment. "Don't you?" he said quietly. Then he returned to Misha. "Anyway, you needed something to go with your new rack!"

"That's it. You're dead."

"Doreen! Help! She has the nose of an angel but the devil's inside her!" He hid behind Doreen's back, his hands on her shoulders, while Misha pelted him with bread. Doreen giggled.

Slight of build, Gordon Lichter had a lovely, almost girlish face with long lashes and blond hair that was always falling in his face. He was pretty and nonthreatening, like a boy pop star, and though he was not exactly a genius, he was not an idiot, either, and the family was lousy with dough. They had homes around the world, a private jet, a Park Avenue penthouse. A girl could certainly do worse, Heidi thought. She had briefly considered making a play for Gordon herself, but she was at least two inches taller than he was, five with heels, and neither would want to look ridiculous.

But Doreen was smaller than Heidi, and look at how flushed he was to be near her!

"That's enough," said Heidi. "Gordon, sit down. Misha, you look phenomenal. Besides . . ." She paused. She had the attention of the entire table. "Now you can finally drink from a mug!"

Everyone laughed, even Misha. Heidi stood up and gave Gordon a signal to sit in her seat beside Doreen, and he did her bidding. She moved to the other end of the table, engaging in limited conversation while watching Doreen out of the corner of her eye. She looked gorgeous, an absolute natural! What had happened to that awkward, pimply girl from the previous night? Look at how Gordon hung on every word, every gesture. *Very promising*, Heidi thought, encouraging him with her eyes.

And there was something else. The scene in the cafeteria was such an old one. Heidi might have closed her eyes and imagined it all ahead of time, like an old movie she'd watched too many times. But Doreen changed that. Just having her there introduced a new level of interest for Heidi. And it was such a relief. Heidi ate her salad, she watched

Gordon flirt with her new friend, and she felt awake to her surroundings as if it was her first day, too.

Later, when they were safely outside the cafeteria, Doreen embraced Heidi. "That was the most wonderful time I ever had in my life! Thank you! Thank you so much!"

Did Heidi notice that where there had been rolls of fat only one night before there was now muscle and bone? Did she wonder how such a remarkable transformation was possible? If she did, it was for no more than a moment. She'd seen something exceptional in Doreen from the minute she laid eyes on her. That it was more available for everyone to enjoy, why would Heidi question that? Why would she want to? Her thoughts were not of the past, near or distant, but of the future.

"I have a good feeling," said Heidi. "I think we are going to have a lot of fun together this year."

With a smile, Doreen threaded her arm through Heidi's and leaned her head on her shoulder. They walked like that, side by side, all the way back to the dorms.

7

The introductory lunch had gone better than Doreen could ever have imagined. The Chandler Academy elite had smiled at her warmly, accepting her into the fold as Heidi's friend and natural participant in the upper echelons of East Coast society. Like she belonged there all along! How unexpected! Returning to her room, Doreen's happiness bubbled into laughter.

Doreen remembered the pride on Heidi's face as she introduced her to one handsome boy and then another, to a flock of elegant, long-limbed girls. Life, so dark and hopeless to her once, seemed suddenly sweet and full of possibility. And she was beautiful now, too. She, Doreen Gray, was lovely. Was it still true? How? Certainly this must be a dream. But the full-length mirror reassured her. There she was, the stunning girl from Biz's photograph, staring back from the glass. It was a miracle!

After she left her room that morning, she assumed she would never see that exquisite mirror-girl again. But the shock on Biz's and Heidi's faces when they saw her confirmed what she'd seen in the mirror was no temporary hallucination. They saw it, too. And at lunch the kids treated her differently. Of course, traveling beside Heidi had its benefits, but this was something deeper than that. When you were beautiful, people wanted to be near you. You could be interesting without saying a word. When you were beautiful, the world stepped aside to let you pass. How marvelous life would be now, Doreen thought as she admired the way her borrowed dress came in at her waist. Sad little Doreen

Gray was a thing of the past; replaced by this resplendent thing, a lovely girl, a beauty.

But she didn't have all day to stare at herself; she had to get ready for Gordon Lichter. He'd invited her for a tour around campus. Gordon looked like a boy from a movie! A boy like that would never have smiled at the old Doreen. He would not have studied his own lovely fingers, embarrassed to be in her presence.

"Good riddance," Doreen said aloud. She plucked the photograph of her former self off her desk and was about to rip it up, but then something made her want to keep the picture around—as a reminder of the pathetic creature she had once been. Carefully, she replaced the picture in the nightstand drawer. Knowing how far she'd come would make her glory even sweeter. She would keep the picture for herself, and only herself. It would be her delicious little secret.

8

"A shopping trip? In New York?" Doreen blinked, trying to comprehend the suggestion. Heidi's perfectly done face loomed over her bed. It was early enough to seem like it might still be night. "Right now?"

"Why not?" said Heidi. "It's Saturday. If we leave soon we can just go for a day and be back by tonight." She tossed a Diane von Furstenberg wrap dress onto the bed. "Put this on. I'll do your hair. Up, I think. You need to look older and comfortable and sophisticated."

"But Heidi, I don't have money for that."

"You think you can scrape together bus fare?"

"I suppose."

"That's all you're going to need, my pet. Now up and at 'em. I want to get to the shops by eleven if we can."

The two girls spent the bus ride huddled together studying fashion mags. Once they arrived at Port Authority, Doreen blinked into the bright lights, disoriented by the complexity and tumult around her. She had not been to New York since she was a girl, but Heidi was a sure guide. They made quick passage through the station and down into the subway.

"Where are we going? Uptown?" Doreen asked, squinting at a map.

"Naturally," Heidi said with a wink. "Come on!" She pulled Doreen through the turnstile on a single swipe of her card and they hopped on a train.

The shops Heidi referred to were not of the department store variety, nor designer boutiques or chain stores. They were thrift stores—charity shops on the Upper East Side.

"You see," she explained as they walked arm in arm down Third Avenue, "Upper East Side ladies have the most luxurious clothes and the largest closets and the most attentive staff, probably in the universe. They spend gobbles of dough, wear everything once, then toss it to make room for next season's must-haves. These foundation stores are here to help the ladies feel worthy for discarding their barely used designer duds. It's win-win."

"But Heidi," said Doreen, "even if it's cheaper than the stuff in the stores, I really don't have any extra—"

"Don't worry about it. Look." Heidi pulled Doreen away from the center of the sidewalk. She stopped and, looking into the rearview mirror of a parked Mercedes, reapplied her lipstick and fixed her hair. She gave Doreen the lipstick and gestured that she do the same.

Heidi felt the adrenaline rush through her. As many times as she had made the rounds through the Upper East Side charity shops, she had always been alone. She hid her familiarity with things like thrift stores and buses and subway systems from normal Chandler society. But she would share it with Doreen. She would show Doreen everything she'd learned.

"All you have to do is seem moneyed and bored, like you're not impressed. I've got the honking Louis Vuitton and you've got my giant fake Chloé. If you see something you like, just be quick-wristed and unafraid. I'll show you. It's easier than you think."

"This bag is a fake?"

"What? Yeah. But a good fake, isn't it? Tell anyone and I'll have you eliminated. Now be cool and follow my lead."

"Okay."

Heidi resumed her quickstep toward the first stop.

"Wait. Wait! Heidi!" Doreen called.

Heidi stopped and waited for Doreen to catch up.

"Sorry, I don't mean to, but . . ." Doreen pulled Heidi aside. "So are we stealing from charity shops? Is that the plan here?"

"Ha! Charity shops? No! That's outrageous. These aren't really charity shops. See that place right there? The Arthritis Foundation?"

"Yeah."

"Their gala is next week. Just getting in the door costs over a thousand dollars a person. Famous people go. There's a silent auction. Sting played last year. What I'm saying is, it's not like we're taking food out of the mouths of the needy."

But Doreen just shook her head. "I don't know. It seems wrong."

Doreen shifted from foot to foot and looked around at the passing traffic. She was uncomfortable, that was plain. Heidi had not considered the possibility that Doreen would not have what it took to participate in her innermost inner circle. And now it was too late. She'd exposed herself. Clueless, naïve Doreen would now be armed with information—about who Heidi Whelan really was and what she was capable of, namely shoplifting, posing, acting as if. Deployed to the right channels, that information could prove very detrimental to Heidi's social position. Doreen had to participate. That was the only way. Otherwise Heidi could lose everything.

An elegant woman clicked by in skinny jeans and a glittery top, led by three Pomeranians. Doreen stepped aside to let her pass, and Heidi saw her straighten her posture slightly. She even turned and watched the woman after she'd gone by. Heidi smiled, exhaled. Anyone could see the longing in Doreen's face. That woman had stepped right out of Roland Gibbons's world. But it could be their world, too. Doreen and Heidi's.

"I hear what you are saying, I do," said Heidi, taking Doreen's arm. "But, Dorie, you want to excel at Chandler. Socially, I mean. Don't you? That's what I thought. The unfortunate truth is that all entrances into high society are very closely guarded. That's the bad news. The good news for you and me, Doreen, is that the guards are superficial, but stupid. It is easy to get past, the only requirement is that you look the part. So, the way I think of it, the Arthritis Foundation is making a kind of unknowing investment in me. By giving me the trappings of wealth, they are making it possible for me to join the ranks of high society. So that one day, when I'm an adult, I can spend the five grand or whatever may be required to don a designer gown and help the suffering millions. Make sense?"

"I guess."

"Plus, it's fun. Trust me."

"But, wait, sorry, just one more question. If we are just going to steal the stuff, why come here? Why not just go to Bloomingdale's or something?"

Heidi sighed. "First of all, I would never go to Bloomingdale's. Second, these places have the same designer labels as the best stores, but everyone in there is a volunteer. There is practically no security at all. It's so easy, Doreen, you'll wonder why everyone doesn't do it. Now let's go. We have a lot to get to today."

Doreen resumed her pace beside Heidi. "Hey, you know what? I'm happy to go along. Seriously, you'll get no judgment from me. But maybe I'll just observe for a while. Would that be okay? I'll just browse and not, like, take anything."

The girl's resolve had shaken, but she would go along with the program, all right. Heidi was sure of that.

"Do what you want, Doreen. Just be quiet about it, cool?"

"Yeah. Right. Cool. You got it."

The clothes. The shoes. The scarves. Everything was so, so tempting. And Doreen looked perfect in everything.

"We'll donate, won't we? When we're older," said Doreen as they walked between the Cancer Foundation and AIDS Research, her step swinging from the mint-condition Roger Vivier heels she'd worn out of the store.

"Oh, we'll save the world, Doreen," Heidi said. "We just need a little boost first."

———•○•———

"Doreen, you are a natural. Better than I ever expected. You see," said Heidi, "when you look and act like you are in your rightful place, you are treated accordingly. It is simply the difference between feeling grateful and feeling entitled."

Doreen and Heidi sat at a little table in the lobby of the Ritz-Carlton hotel. Their haul of stolen clothes surrounded them, in shopping bags from real designer boutiques. Heidi had brought the bags along to transport their loot and add to the overall effect. And it worked. The girls looked exactly like a pair of society ladies relaxing after a tiring day of shopping.

Heidi leaned forward provocatively and lowered her voice. "Do we have a room here? No. Can we afford a meal or a cocktail? No. But for a couple of dollars we can sit here all afternoon, drinking Diet Coke and feasting on free snacks. We can speak intimately with one another about things nobody else will understand, we can allow ourselves to be admired. And mark my words, when you are young and lovely and well groomed, you do not often have to wait long to receive the generous attentions of—"

"Pardon me," said the waiter, setting two glasses of champagne before the girls. "But the gentleman at the bar wishes to—"

"Oh no, I'm sorry, please send it back," said Heidi with a wave of her hand.

"Yes, madam."

"Heidi! Are you sure?"

Heidi shot Doreen a reprimanding look then returned to the waiter, all smiles. "We are having a nice time, you see," she explained, "and we do not wish to be interrupted. Please thank the gentleman, whoever he is, and give our regrets." The waiter nodded. He disappeared with the two flutes.

"Do not turn around," Heidi commanded in a whisper before Doreen could locate the mystery man.

"But I don't understand. You were just saying—"

"Veuve Clicquot. A nice touch. Young, though, not much older than we are, I would say. An older man would approach. This is an old-world gesture, a movie gesture. Either he's a geezer or he's a young man putting on airs. Let's hope for the latter, shall we?" Heidi said with a wink.

Sure enough, almost as soon as the words escaped Heidi's mouth, a young man approached their table. He was tall, with an athletic build. His clothes were a sharper version of the Chandler look: starched pink shirt, khakis, blue blazer. His hair was deep black and charmingly rumpled.

"Too early in the day for champagne?" he asked. "You don't look like the kind of girl who watches the clock. Peter Standish. This is my compatriot, Coburn." Another young man stepped up from the shadows, the same age and type but blond with watery blue eyes and a general dimness of expression. "Coburn Everbock. He, like myself, is a Harvard man. A crew man. We have come to Gotham in search of distraction. Unfortunately, we have had no luck."

"What a shame," said Heidi dismissively. "Have you tried Broadway?" She rolled her eyes at Doreen, but the girl seemed altogether too fascinated by the two boys. Heidi hoped she would catch on soon.

"You see, our studies up in Cambridge are quite immersive—fascinating stuff, really, from the minds of giants. Distraction, for that reason, does not come easily. We require beauty, wit, charm—but mostly beauty," he said with a twinkle in his eye. "We were sure that our country's cultural center would have much to offer us in this regard, but as I have recently reported, wheresoever Venus may lurk in this fair city, she has eluded us."

"Until now. Oh, sorry, was I meant to wait for the punchline? How rude of me to interrupt," said Heidi.

"Ah, but it is your privilege! So you were right after all, Coburn. Grace and intelligence have not abandoned the city. I was sure we had wasted our time." Peter pulled a wallet out of his blazer and decorously passed a bill—one of many, Heidi could not help but notice—to his friend. "Your winnings, my friend. I give them to you happily and you have Ms. . . . ?"

"Whelan," said Doreen. "Heidi Whelan. And I am Doreen Gray." Heidi made a show of appearing irritated at Doreen for encouraging the boys, but flashed an approving glance, undetectable by the hovering suitors. A tiny smile of recognition appeared on Doreen's lips as she began to understand the game.

Peter nodded at Doreen, allowing his gaze to linger.

"Well, Coburn, you have Ms. Whelan and Ms. Gray to thank for your victory."

"Thank you," said Coburn.

"Please sit," said Doreen. Heidi expressed overt displeasure with her friend while continuing to give silent approval. They were working as a team now, communicating in wordless, imperceptible looks. Heidi had felt from their first meeting that Doreen could read her. And clearly, she'd been right.

"How kind of you, Ms. Gray, but I'm afraid your friend would prefer that we be on our way." He raised an eyebrow to Heidi.

"Sit if you must," said Heidi, "but if you insist on discussing yourself or your studies, I'm afraid I will require something stronger."

"Of course! Shall we have the champagne back? Or how about a round of martinis? It's after three, isn't it?"

"I suppose," Heidi said, and Peter disappeared to locate the waiter. Coburn walked around to sit beside Doreen. He reeked of salt and soap and money. Doreen turned toward him.

"So . . . did he say you were at Harvard? I wasn't really listening."

Heidi could not have said it better herself.

———◦●———

Naturally they moved from drinks to dinner. The portions were miniature and artfully presented. There was raw beef and living oysters and seared duck liver and wine, of course, wine for days. Remarkably, Doreen said yes to everything—she was game to taste it all, to be exposed to delicacies the likes of which she could not possibly have imagined.

Heidi remembered what that was like, to experience everything for the first time, and watching Doreen made her enjoy her own meal even more. Dessert was a pear tart and chocolate mousse and they had sweet wine and coffee and when it was time to get up from the table, Heidi was afraid Doreen might swoon.

"Are you okay?" she whispered to her friend.

"Oh, yes, yes. Just happy," said Doreen, and Heidi could see it shining in the girl's dewy face.

"Nightcap in our room?" asked Peter. "Don't worry, we are gentlemen."

"Oh, I hope not." Heidi held out a hand to him so he could help her around the chair and gestured that Doreen do the same.

"Would you mind taking these, Coburn?" Doreen waved a hand over the shopping bags. "I hate to be bogged down."

The girl is a quick study, thought Heidi, grinning despite herself.

"Coburn was trying to convince me to stay at one of the newer places—a boutique hotel or something with a single name. What? The George or somesuch. The Ted, I don't know. He's very interested in being hip. Aren't you, Coburn?"

"Not very," said Coburn. He leered at Doreen.

Heidi hoped she didn't mind taking the dumb one. He

was good practice, like playing a new card game open-handed.

"But for me, nothing beats the classic elegance of the Ritz. I mean, look at this view! Can you beat it? I guess I'm old-fashioned," said Peter, making it seem like being old-fashioned was the most wonderful way to be.

There was a light knock on the door. "Room service!" A cart with scotch and four glasses was wheeled into the room. Peter popped up to sign the check. He pulled a few more notes from his billfold and handed them to the waitress. The guy was obviously loaded. Heidi gave him a look that she hoped seemed simultaneously alluring and thankful.

"Thank you, that will be all," he said to the waitress.

But the girl wasn't looking at him. For some reason she was looking at Heidi, practically staring at her.

"Heidi?" she said. Heidi froze. She looked down at her nails. *Oh no oh no oh no oh no.* How could she have missed *this?* She didn't know what to do. "Heidi Whelan! Oh my god, it's Nicole Goswami from the Montauk! I thought that was you. I haven't seen you in a couple of years. How have you been?"

"Oh, uh, Nicole. Sure, yes, hello," said Heidi. Nicole pulled her in for a tight hug.

"Yeah, I bet you didn't recognize me! I bet you didn't know I was workin' here! I still go down to Montauk in the summers, but the bills need to be paid all year round! You know what I mean."

"Of course," said Heidi. She felt a flush burn from her face down into her bust. Nicole just stood with her hand on her hip, shaking her head like what a small world.

"So, what have you been up to? You're lookin' good. Nice. You here, what? Traveling through or somethin'?" Nicole said.

"I'm, uh, well." It was awful. Nobody did anything. What could they possibly think? She'd blown it. Heidi had blown it for herself and Doreen. It was all so humiliating. If there was a hole she could sink into, she would. "I'm here, I'm just—"

"It's so nice to meet you, Nicole," Doreen said sweetly, reaching out a hand to shake. "I'm Doreen. And thank you so much for bringing the booze. These boys were getting restless. Weren't you, boys?" Doreen swung open the door to the suite and waited for the girl to exit with her cart. Quick, confident, persuasive without being rude. The execution could not have been more perfect. Heidi shot her a look of gratitude.

"Oh. Oh, sure, yes. Uh, no problem." But Nicole just stood there, looking at Heidi and then at the rest of the party.

"It's no good when the boys get restless," Doreen added. She looked out into the hallway. "Thank you."

"Oh! Yeah, sure. So, uh, if that is all, I'll just . . . please let us know if there is anything else you might require."

"We won't hesitate, will we?" said Doreen.

"Thank you, Nicole," said Heidi, finally finding her voice. "It was nice seeing you."

"Yeah? Well. Likewise," she said. She wheeled her cart out of the room and Doreen closed the door behind her. There was a long silence.

"I knew you looked familiar!" said Peter jovially. He poured out the scotch. "My family has been staying at the Montauk for years. Nice to make friends with the staff, I think. The doorman, Manny? He sends us a Christmas card every year!" He raised his glass. "To Manny and that nice lady and all the other people who work hard to make our lives comfortable."

Heidi and Doreen exchanged looks. Heidi had said it herself a million times, when you looked the part and acted like you belonged, nobody would ever question your origins.

"To Manny and Nicole!" Heidi echoed. She clinked Peter's glass, then Coburn's, then Doreen's.

"To their hard work and loyalty," Doreen added. Where in the world did she come up with that? The girl had talent.

"Here, here!" said Coburn. They drank. The booze trickled hot and slippery down Heidi's throat. Peter kissed her on the mouth and she thought, *now this. This! THIS!*

Autumn came. It swept the leafy hillsides of New Hampshire like a change of heart. Like falling in love, Doreen thought, and that is exactly what she did. She fell in love.

It all began one afternoon, when Doreen emerged from her Japanese class to find Gordon Lichter waiting for her. He seemed to lurk around every corner these days—appearing after every class, hovering nearby during every meal. At first she had enjoyed his attentions. After all, a boy with Gordon's looks and affluence would never have given the old Doreen a first glance. But it grew irksome to have him forever on her tail, seizing every opportunity to guide her to a table somewhere so he could ply her with trinkets and brag about his family's money.

Plus, his infatuation with Doreen had changed him. When they met that first day in the cafeteria, he'd been confident and full of fun. But now he seemed to be standing in shadow all the time, with a dark expression despite his adorable face. So he was a drag. And so ubiquitous! When Doreen saw him leaning against the languages building after her class, his hands deep in the pockets of his Barbour coat, it irritated her.

"Doreen! Hey! I mean, hi. How are you? Did you, I mean, was Japanese, like, good?"

"Hello, Gordon," said Doreen. She continued to walk and he scuttled off the wall to keep up with her.

"I've been wanting to see you. I called. Did you get my message? There's something I wanted to—"

"I'm sorry, but I'm running late."

"Doreen. Doreen! Will you stop for a minute? I want to ask you about the Fall Dance."

"Mm? You know I love talking to you Gordon, but I have an appointment in town that I can't be late for. You understand. Can we pick this up later?"

"In town? Right now? Can I come with you? Or let me give you a ride."

"No, no. Thank you, but I have to go by myself. It's, uh, it's a private matter."

"But . . . okay. Yeah, okay. Fine. Go. We'll talk later." Gordon stood by a pillar and watched her walk away. He was really very miserable over her. It was wonderful in an annoying way or annoying in a wonderful way, she couldn't be sure which. In any case, when she turned the corner, away from his line of vision, Doreen felt remarkably free.

Of course, there was no appointment in town. Doreen walked without a destination. It felt like stolen time—to be away from campus with nowhere to go and to be totally alone. She was content to wander, to allow her mind to do the same. After all, she had experienced so many changes in just a few short weeks, she often felt like it was all happening without her.

She walked and walked, letting whim be her guide, rejoicing in the brisk fall air, the precious freedom. Her mind churned away and the afternoon turned to dusk. She found herself standing before a field where local kids were gathering on bleachers to watch a football game. She heard band music and cheering. Without thinking, she followed the throng into the stands and settled into a seat on the away side.

The scene was harrowing. Doreen recognized the crowd—not individually, but as a force that had caused her so much pain in her previous life. She sat among kids who would have been her enemies, who would have mocked her, made her feel worthless. Now all had changed. In the chic red coat that had been a gift from Biz, she still didn't fit in, but rather than feeling inferior, she felt the opposite.

You poor thugs, she thought, looking around at the crowd of face-painted, pennant-waving idiots. *You poor, sick souls who think this is the best in life. I know the best. I've seen it, tasted it, worn it. You don't know anything but this, you cretins. You will never have power over me again! You will never be able to make me feel anything but grateful for having escaped your ugly little world.*

The cheerleaders flip-flopped and cartwheeled and threw one another in the air. Doreen had been jealous of the cheerleaders at her old school. But now she saw how vulgar they were, volunteering their bodies for ogling in the name of school spirit. They were nothing but flesh for the eyes. It was delightfully horrible. And then there was the band. The band! They were insufferable! Could they be playing their instruments wrong? Trying to blow from the wrong side? It was all so deliciously bad, she sat on her hard seat grinning, unable to pull herself away.

But then there was a change on the field. The home team, Hamilton High, had taken possession of the ball and a reverent hush came over the crowd, as if they were not on bleachers, but on pews. Doreen spotted the source right away. It was the quarterback. Number Ten. He was some kind of genius, a physical genius. Doreen had never seen anything like it. Masculine, with an impressively built-up body, he had the grace of a dancer. Quick and light on his feet, he moved deliberately, fast but unhurried, even when chased by a defensive line. And despite his lightness he possessed a deep center, a gravitas, as if his body was in communication with the earth's core.

It was masculine beauty the likes of which Doreen had never experienced. She sat and watched like she was witnessing a miracle.

Hadn't she felt compelled forward all afternoon, like a force had guided her wandering? Now she understood. The force had led her here, to see him, this quarterback, Number Ten. It was fate, she thought, as she watched the boy make his first run for a touchdown. She fell in love with him before she even knew his name. And she knew somehow that he would love her, too.

She waited for him in the parking lot near the buses. There was a lot of commotion and Doreen fought the urge to leave, to find the boy some other way. Heidi's voice in her head reminded her that it was important to be waited for, waited upon, but never to wait for anyone. It made a woman seem desperate, like less of a prize. But she could not leave, she had to see him, she had to have him see her.

She stood under a streetlight, away from the crowd. Kids roughhoused around her and she leaned against the school in her light, waiting for Number Ten, trying to appear comfortable and aloof.

Even when he finally came out, looking as godlike in jeans and a sweatshirt as he had in a uniform, even as the crowd tightened around him, basking in his promise, his talent, still she did not move from her light. *Waiting here, that is as much as I will do*, she thought. *I will not make myself ridiculous. He must still come to me.*

It did not take more than a minute or two before he looked up from the adoring mob to see her. She let him catch her eye for a moment. Her heart! She thought it must be visible through her coat! But then, to her dismay, he returned his attentions to his rambunctious fans. All was lost. She was wrong, wrong. How could she have thought? She was only Doreen Gray, not Heidi Whelan. She could never win the attentions of a boy like that.

She ducked out of her light and fled the parking lot, speeding up the hill toward Chandler. If she hurried, she might catch the last hour of dinner. No one of consequence had seen her pathetic display—and she would never mention a word about it to anyone. Ugh. It was awful to feel embarrassed.

"Excuse me. Miss! Miss!"

The voice came from behind her. She turned to find him—him!—racing to catch up, waving at her. How elegantly he moved! She was so happy to see him, she thought she could cry.

"Please, I . . ." He pressed something into her hand. His touch was electric. "Your glove." He smiled at her, looked deep into her eyes, their hands clasped. "You dropped it, over by the school." Slowly, she comprehended his meaning. She looked down to find a glove in her hand.

"How nice of you! Only, this isn't my glove." It was a grimy, greenish thing. "This must have been dropped by someone else—and some time ago, by the looks of it." She laughed. He blushed and smiled sheepishly. It was the most meaningless exchange and yet it felt positively momentous.

"That's what I get for trying to be chivalrous. I end up stealing some poor girl's glove! But anyway, I only wanted to meet you, even if it isn't your glove. I'm Simon Vale."

"Simon, I'm Doreen. Doreen Gray."

"Good to meet you," he said. They stood looking at one another for a moment, then, without a word, began to walk together, side by side.

"I saw you play. You were wonderful!"

He blushed again. His humility was pure and irresistible. "Aw, well, thanks. Just football. You know. Nothing important. But how did you end up at the game? You don't go to Hamilton."

"You sound so sure! You can't possibly know every single person at your high school."

"No, I don't. But I never saw you before. I know that. Because there's no way I would forget seeing you. And no way I'd let you get away without talking to you. That's how I'm so sure. Are you from Chandler?"

"I am, in fact. Brand-new. Transfer."

"Oh yeah? Where from?"

There are some people who have everything in common, yet cannot find a word to say to one another. Other people can be as different as day from night, but their conversation flows easily, naturally, without haste or embarrassment. Doreen and Simon spoke like that, effortlessly revealing themselves to one another, so that by the time they arrived at Chandler Academy they felt as if they'd known each other all their lives.

Simon's story was not typical of a high school quarterback. His father was an academic who had run off with a student, leaving his mother to raise Simon and his sister all on her own. Simon got his first job when he was only twelve, working in the hardware store where his mother was the cashier. The store owner was a former college football coach, and he saw how strong and graceful Simon was, even as a boy, and took him under his wing, teaching him to throw and other fundamentals of the game. Then the man died, leaving the store to Simon and his mother.

"It doesn't make much, just a little place in a small town. Everyone goes to Home Depot out on Highway 1. Sometimes I think my mom should just sell the place. I don't know. If I could just get a scholarship, go to a good school so that I could go out and make some real money for her."

"You are a good person," said Doreen. "The way you worry about her." They stopped and faced one another near the entrance to campus. She wondered what time it was. Surely she had to be getting back.

He brushed a hair from her eyes. "Nice of you to say that, but I'm not that good. It's selfish, really. I want to be a hero, you know, come back and save the day."

Doreen nodded. Her body's intense reaction to his closeness made a verbal response impossible. She was beyond words now. She closed her eyes and felt him lean in to kiss her.

It was the kiss of a lifetime. A kiss that promised joy in life the likes of which neither Simon nor Doreen had experienced before. It was a kiss of mutual discovery, of unity, of change and growth, and a brighter, better future. They kissed themselves out of their present, the hardship, the loneliness. It was the joining of souls, a meeting of hearts.

And just like that Simon Vale and Doreen Gray were hopelessly, miraculously in love.

10

"There's ribs in the fridge from last night. You can heat those up before you go. Or you can order a pizza if you want." Linda Vale poured herself a cold cup of coffee from the morning's pot and stood by the ancient microwave while it heated. Since the death of Mr. Hopper two years earlier, Simon noticed that his mother always seemed like she was running late for something—whether she had something to do or not.

"You're not going to stick around?" Simon asked.

"I think you're old enough to heat up your own leftovers." The microwave dinged and his mother popped open the door and fetched her favorite pink mug. She leaned against the counter as she sipped her old, sour black coffee. Watching her, Simon felt a sympathetic pang in his own stomach.

"Not for me, for Jane. You're not even going to say good-bye? She'll be gone for a long time."

"I know that, Simon. You don't have to tell me that." She was in her going-out makeup and a shabby red dress that she tried to spruce up with jewelry she bought from TV in the middle of the night when she stayed up brushing the dog. She insisted that the coffee had nothing to do with her sleeplessness. "You don't have to tell me what's going on with my own daughter." She wiped under her eye with a long nail and looked out the window.

Simon used to think his mother was pretty. She had a long neck, deep-brown eyes, and dark skin that always looked tan. He watched her check her reflection in the glass of one of the kitchen cabinets. Maybe she was just getting old and tired, or her clothes were getting old and tired. But having seen Doreen, the whole world seemed duller and uglier in comparison.

"What are you grinning about, huh? Seems to me you been grinning a lot lately. You can't wait for Jane to get out to Bolivia, can you? Get herself killed out there, that's what's happening. Drug dealers run around out there like it's a free-for-all, you know." Simon's mother crossed her arms over her chest like a petulant child.

"Mom, she's going to the Peace Corps, okay? It's not like she's joining the circus. Can you stop trying to make this about you?"

"Excuse me if I find it difficult to understand why your sister needs to run down to a country a million miles away to help a bunch of strangers, when her own family needs her right here! I know that working in a hardware store isn't the sexiest job in the world. Believe me, I had different plans myself!"

"I know you did, Mom," Simon said softly, trying to be reassuring. He wondered what Doreen would think of the house. She would love it, of course, for being his. She would love his mother, too. She would see Linda Vale for the kind, well-intentioned woman she was. Simon was sure that Doreen could see the whole world as if they were looking through the same set of eyes.

"I was an actress, you know. And a good one. That's why your father even noticed me. He came and saw me do Juliet at the O'Neill. He found me after the show." It was hard to imagine his mother as a young ingénue, and equally hard to imagine his father—who was polite and distant and seemed to do everything according to some choreography he thought it his duty to carry out—as a man so moved by a performance that he sought out his mother, wooed her, married her. Like Doreen in her red coat the first time they met. Her face, when she saw him, was like a person found.

"I know, Mom. You don't have to tell me that."

"I'm just saying that I know everything that hardware isn't." She sighed and placed her coffee cup on the counter, next to the many-ringed reminders of coffee cups past. "But it's everything we have right now. It's irresponsible."

"You know I can hear you. But I don't care." Jane came down the stairs looking scrubbed and ready, her dark hair brushed back into a ponytail with a little band around her head to keep the strays back. In her khaki pants and boots and a fleece pullover, Simon's sister looked prepared for an adventure. He admired her bravery.

Jane kissed their mother on the cheek, but Linda remained in her sulking position against the counter.

"I'll miss you, Mommy. You know I will. But this is something I have to do right now. For myself. I know that's probably hard for you to understand."

"Don't treat me like an idiot, Jane Vale. I'm *your* mother, don't forget," Linda growled. "I understand precisely what it's like to want to do something for yourself. What I don't understand, young lady, is choosing to do those things when the family needs you. That's not how I've lived my own life, and I guess I'm just a little disappointed that I didn't raise you to think the same way."

Jane's smile descended. "I'm sorry, Mom. I just—look, if you really need me here I won't go, okay? I thought—"

"You didn't think. Not about your brother and me."

"You're right. I guess I didn't. I thought I did, but I didn't. I'm sorry." She looked down at her hiking boots, appearing to be near tears. Her mother's expression softened.

"Hey, it's okay, Baby, it's all right. You're young, you should go out in the world. Never mind me, Janie. I'm just going to miss you, that's all." Simon watched them embrace, the two women in his life who, until recently, were his entire world. He was sorry that Jane would be going before she could meet Doreen. He was sure they would love each other.

A horn sounded in the driveway. "That's my ride!" Simon's mother managed through her tears. "You know I hate good-byes, my favorite girl. Be careful. Okay? You promise?"

"I promise. And I'll e-mail all the time. We can Skype!"

"Just call me on the phone. How about that? Call collect, okay? We'll manage. Good-bye, my darling girl," said their mother, leaving a hand on Jane's cheek. After one final hug she grabbed her purse and coat and raced out in her heels to the awaiting car.

Simon and Jane watched their mother from the kitchen window.

"Which one is that?" Jane asked. "The guy from bowling?"

"I think he's the one from church. But I don't know. Wait! No, look, it's what's her name—"

"Fat Beth." Their mother's friend waved from the driver's side of her Caprice.

"Bye, Janie!" Beth called out, her fingers flapping through the open driver's-side window. "Have fun in Mexico!"

Their mother gave a final wave over the car before getting in. Jane waved back and watched the car drive away.

"She's bad at good-byes," Simon said.

"I know. It's okay. Anyway, it gives us a little time, little brother. So."

"So. All packed?"

"Yep." Jane flashed a wicked grin and stared hard at Simon. "I'm on to you, you know."

"What?"

"What do you mean, what? I'm on to you. I just thought you should know that." She jutted out her chin with know-it-all satisfaction.

"I don't know what you're talking about."

Jane wagged her finger at him. "Please, you can't fool me. Just because I'm getting ready to get out of here doesn't mean I haven't noticed the way you've been floating around this house with a goofy grin on your face."

"I have not," Simon protested, but just hearing the effect that Doreen had on his disposition, he could feel his mouth widen into an unwanted smile.

"There! That's the one! That's the grin I'm talking

about. Now 'fess, little brother, or I'll beat it out of you."

"Uh, I'm a little bigger than you now, Jane. I don't know if you've noticed."

"You may be bigger, but you're probably still . . . ticklish!" Jane attacked Simon with the secret knowledge that can only come from growing up with someone—tickling him mercilessly, for maximum impact. Simon flew off his chair and landed hard on the linoleum floor. He swung his body, kicking and begging her to stop. "Never! Not until I know the truth!" Jane screamed.

"Mercy! Mercy! I'll tell you anything. Anything! What do you want to know?"

Jane stood up, her tiny hands still clawed and ready to attack. "Who is she, Simon?"

"Who is who?"

Jane raised her arms as if threatening to pounce again.

"Okay, okay. Her name is Doreen Gray," Simon said, the warmth of the name filling his body.

Seeing the change come over her brother, Jane lowered her arms. "A girl from school?"

"Yes. Well, not from my school. From Chandler."

"Chandler Academy?"

Simon hopped onto his feet. "Janie, you have no idea. I've wanted to tell you about her, but I guess I wanted to keep her to myself, just for a minute. I never met anyone like her in my life. She's beautiful—so incredibly beautiful, but that's not it. That's not all there is to her. See, I met her after the homecoming game." And Simon proceeded to tell his sister everything. About how he saw her standing in the parking lot and then she disappeared like a ghost. He told her how he picked up some disgusting old glove and ran after her—just for an excuse to talk to her, to stay in contact. He told her about their walk, about the way they talked, about this feeling of *inevitability* about it all.

"Janie, I don't know. It just feels like everything's different now. I feel hopeful. Really hopeful in a way I haven't in a long time. She said she was going to try to get me into Chandler. A football scholarship to help me get into a better college. But I really don't care about that anymore. I know I should. I am sorta the man around here, even if I am the youngest. And with you heading down to Bolivia for two years, Mom's gonna need me to really step up and take charge. But ever since I met Doreen, she's all I can think about. Everything else—school, the store, even football—seems like a distraction from what really matters."

"And what matters, then?" Though Simon was too wrapped up in the affairs of his own heart to notice, Jane was worried about him. She had never seen her brother so unguarded. He always had a firm grasp on the practical aspects of life. But now, just as she was leaving, doing something for herself for the first time in her life, some little harlot had come around and derailed him from his path. "This girl is all that matters to you now? Do I have that right? You're going to throw it all away for this girl?"

Simon wrinkled his nose. "Don't say it like that, Jane. Don't say 'this girl' like she's someone I picked up at the

movie theater. Her name's Doreen, okay? And she's . . .
she's . . . she's magnificent! Can't you be happy for me?
Come on, Jane, I thought you'd understand. You're the one
who's always telling me that I can't let other people rule
my life, that I have to do something for myself. Isn't that
what you say? 'Don't let Mom tell you what to do all the
time, Simon.' Right? Well, I found something for me—someone for me. And I'm happy! This is what it is to be happy,
Jane! Oh, I should have known you wouldn't understand."
Simon huffed out of the kitchen and threw himself on the
couch in the family room. Jane followed close behind.

"Now, don't pout. I was just asking. Of course, I don't
mean to begrudge you this . . . whatever . . ."

"Love. We're in love."

"Both of you? Has she expressed the same feelings?"

"God! Yes, Jane. For crying out loud, I'm not seven anymore. I know how the world works. She loves me. A lot.
More than anyone has ever loved me. Doreen Gray is in
love with me and I with her. We found each other. We're
lucky. That's why you've seen me floating around this ugly
house. Because for the first time in my life I feel so, so lucky."

Jane sat down beside Simon on the small space left on
the couch. She looked at her brother, so strong and beautiful, even with that ugly scowl on his face. Of course, any
girl would fall for him, how could they resist? It was his
goodness that always struck her, and the ease with which he
coasted through life. No matter how tough it got, he knew
the right thing to do and he always did it. Their deadbeat

father, crazy mother, the loss of Mr. Hopper, none of that had taken away Simon Vale's inner goodness. And now he was big and grown and handsome, too. Doreen Gray, whoever she was, didn't stand a chance.

"Don't be mad, rhymin' Simon. I didn't mean her any disrespect. I'm only looking out for you."

"You can cut that out now, okay, Janie? I'm grown-up. And you're leaving, so if I couldn't take care of myself before it's about time that I learned."

"You're right, you're right. I'm sorry." This was not how she wanted to leave things with Simon. She would miss him the most of everyone. "And really, I'm happy for you. Truly, I am."

Simon sat up on his elbows. "You are? Really?"

Jane smiled. Out in the world she did this rarely—most people thought of her as humorless, cold. Because she was small and cute, she had to fight to be taken seriously. But for Simon she could smile all day long. "Of course I am. If you're happy, I'm happy. And I trust you. If you say the girl's magnificent, I have no reason to doubt that she is."

"I knew you'd understand!" Simon flung his big arms around her tiny shoulders, squeezing the air out of her. "Anyway," he said, hopping up from the couch, "we better get you to the airport, huh? You don't want to miss your plane! I'll go up and grab your stuff." He ran a few paces toward the stairs.

"Simon! Wait!"

"What is it?" He stood looking at her with his hands on his hips, his forehead furrowed in dumb concern. Janie stepped up to face him. He was a foot taller and twice as wide, but he was still her little brother.

"Simon, honey, I want you to know something. I'm sure the two of you will be very happy together, that there will be nothing but love and joy from here on out, but I want to make it very clear." Jane grasped Simon's wrist tightly and looked deep into his eyes. "If this girl Doreen Gray does anything to hurt you, I will kill her, do you understand? I'll murder her with my own hands if I have to. I will find her and kill her."

"Got it," said Simon. He yanked his wrist from her grip. "Now don't look so serious, Janie. You're going on an adventure! Lighten up!" With that, he popped up the stairs to retrieve her bags.

"I mean it, too!" Jane called behind him. She looked out the kitchen window onto the ugly suburban block. Leaving Place—what a street. Soon this would be a memory, just one forgettable house in a forgettable town. She was determined to find something for herself out there, away, out in the world. And she could really leave, too, if it weren't for Simon. Simon would keep a part of her there, in Hamilton, no matter how far away she might travel.

"All set!" he said. Simon came down the stairs with two duffel bags slung around him and a backpack in his hand. Still, he seemed light, unburdened. "Let's get you to your plane!"

11

To Heidi's annoyance, Doreen suddenly had one thing on her mind: Simon Vale. Every chance she got, she ran off campus to watch Simon practice, or meet him at Bread the News Café on Main Street. And when she couldn't be near him, she talked about him. Nonstop.

Heidi knew better than to express her disapproval openly since Doreen, like most people, believed herself to be autonomous. A negative word from Heidi would only make them closer. So she said nothing, hid her eye rolls, and hoped the whole thing would blow over—soon.

Heidi's objection to the boy had nothing to do with him personally. She was not so far removed from her roots that she could pass judgment on someone because they were without the means to attend private school. In fact, she had no doubt that he was as handsome, kind, and athletic as Doreen went on and on and on and on about. And on. And on.

Walking to their afternoon class:

"Did you see what Juliet Goldberg did to her hair? I can't believe she thought she could pull off a pixie cut with her face! She just doesn't have the bone structure," Heidi said.

"The person who loves her won't care," said Doreen dreamily. "Simon told me he would love me if I had green skin and a carrot for a nose. He said that even if I gained a thousand pounds and doused my skin with castor oil, his love would be undiminished."

"I wouldn't test it."

"What?"

"Nothing. You're lucky to have found him, Doreen. Juliet, on the other hand, is single."

"I am lucky, aren't I? Everyone should be as lucky as I am. Everyone should find true love in this world." Doreen plucked a leaf off a tree and took a whiff with her eyes closed.

"Watch out for that bench!" said Heidi, though part of her hoped to see the girl tumble over it and back down to earth.

"Thanks!" Doreen flicked the leaf away. "Anyway, I think you're being too hard on Juliet. She's beautiful on the inside."

Heidi turned away and tried not to gag.

At breakfast:

"You know, it's funny, I never liked sports before I met Simon."

"Waste of time, if you ask me," said Biz. "I really don't understand the appeal at all." She had helped herself to a little of every single cereal on offer. Cereal suicide, she called it.

"I'm with you," said Heidi as she loaded up her coffee with skim milk and Equal.

But Doreen did not seem to have heard them. "I never knew why girls wanted to be with athletes. Girls who don't particularly like sports, I mean. Why would someone who doesn't watch football want to date a football player? But now I am starting to understand." She took a thoughtful nibble of whole wheat toast. "Here's what it is—"

"You don't have to explain," said Heidi. "Really."

"When I watch Simon play football, he's so much better than everyone else and it makes me feel like a winner myself, naturally. But I also feel very safe. Because Simon loves me and he would kill anybody who would want to hurt me. And he could do it, too. With his bare hands. He is so, so strong."

"Anyone could do that," said Biz in between bites of cereal sludge. "I mean, I could kill someone with my bare hands. Truly. It's easier than you might think if you're familiar with human anatomy. All you have to do is—"

"I was thinking," said Doreen. Heidi made an involuntary cluck with her tongue. *When you interrupt you seem overly eager, and stupid. Civilized people wait their turn.* Roland had taught her that. "Do you think that Simon could get a football scholarship? To Chandler? I know you haven't seen him play, but you have to believe me when I say he is remarkably good. He would be a huge asset."

"Sorry, did you say football scholarship?" asked Heidi.

"Yes. Chandler does have a team, don't they?"

"Sure. I think we do. We do, don't we, Biz?"

"I have heard that we do."

"Why wouldn't they want to win? And with Simon leading the team, they would win. Wouldn't they be willing to cough up some tuition for the bragging rights? Biz, what do you think?"

Biz and Heidi exchanged a look. Chandler was not the sort of place that gave football scholarships. "Uh," said Biz.

"He will achieve such greatness. But he needs help. Just a little nudge in the right direction. Wait until you see him play! You will see what I mean."

"Here comes Misha. Let's change the subject, okay?" said Heidi.

"But why should I—"

"Doreen! Just trust me. Keep it mum for now all right?"

"What are we talking about here?" Misha slid in next to Heidi.

"We were . . ." Doreen looked at Heidi, who subtly shook her head. Simon or not, Doreen still wanted to be popular, didn't she? "We were talking about that cute top you're wearing, Meesh. Where is it from? It's adorable."

Bullet dodged, Heidi thought. For now.

———◦◦———

As Misha reported on some half-true piece of gossip she'd heard from Wes Sylvan, Heidi became even more convinced that the Simon Vale business had to be kept under wraps. If it got leaked to the Chandler gossip mill, Doreen would be finished. Doreen had not even finished a single semester at the school, and she'd already decided that the boys on offer were beneath her consideration? Boys and girls alike would not take kindly to that. Add to that Doreen's worthy attitude about Simon's "goodness," and soon enough people would turn on the girl.

If she had to, Heidi would take action. It wouldn't be the first time she'd broken up a couple she deemed unsuitable or inconvenient, though she hoped it wouldn't come to that. Better to try and talk some sense to the girl, remind her of their larger project. She watched Misha try to impress Doreen and felt a wave of pride. They had come so far already, there was no saying what they might accomplish together if they stayed focused. And Heidi was thinking beyond Chandler now. Two girls from the outside win at high society? This was a partnership that could be mutually beneficial for the rest of their lives.

The thing to do was to loosen up a bit, reestablish their bond with a little one-on-one fun. Heidi made a plan to meet Doreen in the shed behind the stadium an hour before curfew. "Just us," she said with a wink, and Doreen grinned. She still had some influence over the girl, Simon or not.

————●●————

"How's that?" asked Doreen. Heidi examined the sad-looking joint.

"Um, a little better I guess. But you have to roll it tighter. Here. Like that, see?"

"I'm hopeless at this. You should just roll these."

"But rolling a joint is a great skill, Doreen. Very sexy." She sparked the joint with a lighter she'd "borrowed" from Ad-rock two years earlier.

"Really?" They'd laid out Heidi's raincoat to protect their little tushes from the wet earth. The dank smell of the ground mixed pleasantly with the armpitty weed stink. It felt very natural, something Heidi felt infrequently.

"It's one of those things, like playing pool. Working a socket wrench. Men like a girl with skills." She exhaled.

"What's a socket wrench?"

"I have no idea."

Doreen burst out laughing and Heidi joined, their giggles muffled by the shed's wet wood.

"Stop it," said Doreen, wiping away tears. "Oh my god. I'm going to pee my pants. Wait. What did you say? Now I can't remember what was so funny."

"Me neither!" They fell over themselves laughing.

"How long do you think kids have been getting high in this shed?"

"About a century. Give or take."

"And they never get busted?"

"Who knows?"

"I bet my dad smoked pot in here." Doreen looked around as if trying to picture it. "He went to school here, you know."

"Yeah," said Heidi, trying to keep her tone relaxed. "Sure, you said that. It's funny though, you never talk about him. Uh, so, what's he like?"

Doreen drew lines in the dirt with her finger. "I don't know. I don't really know him anymore. He picked me up from the airport in Boston. But before that I hadn't seen him since I was little."

"What did he say when he picked you up?" Heidi was doing her best to seem caring and interested, not nosy. She drew in another hit.

"I guess he was afraid that I was going to embarrass him. At Chandler. He said something about how it was his turf and he had certain expectations, whatever that means."

"Oh, Doreen. I'm so sorry. What a jerk."

"What? No, I don't know. He has a reputation to protect." Doreen's face fell, and she was once again the bullied, lost child. Heidi felt a rumbling in her heart. She knew what it was like to feel like you deserved to be treated badly.

"Nonsense. You have as much right to be here as anyone else. No offense, but that guy sounds like an asshole."

"You're right." Doreen clenched her fists. "He is an asshole! HE IS AN ASSHOLE! He kept going on and on about how I was lucky to get the opportunity to attend Chandler, that he'd pulled strings for me. Like I was a stranger, you know? Not his own kid."

"Oh man. If he could see you now, right? He probably never expected you to be so popular. Gordon Lichter is fawning over you, any number of boys would love to get their hands on you."

"Well, they are out of luck. Because I only have eyes for Simon."

"Yes. Right."

A darkness fell across Doreen's lovely face. "Sometimes, when I watch him play football, I like to think of how small my dad would look next to him. How weak and unmanly compared to Simon."

"Your father would probably hate him," Heidi said encouragingly.

"I know. Isn't it grand?" Doreen gave Heidi a savage grin. "Don't think I didn't think of that." Doreen resumed the sweet tone of a young innocent. "None of it matters now. When I bring Simon to the Fall Dance—"

"Sorry?" said Heidi as she coughed out her hit. "Did you say . . . ? Hold on." She was afraid she might choke. To the dance? That was *unacceptable*.

"Didn't I tell you? He's going to be my date."

"No. That's not . . . What about . . . Gordon will be there."

"I don't care about stupid, little Gordon Lichter! He's nothing but a version of my father. Not Simon. You wait, Heidi. Wait until you see him play football. You're coming to the game tomorrow, aren't you?"

Heidi rubbed her eye. Okay. She could fix this. She would think of something. "I said I would, Doreen, so I will. A real lady always fulfills her obligations."

"Good. You'll see. You'll understand it all when you see him play." Doreen leaned her head back against the side of the shed. She breathed deep into her chest. That little lost girl was gone now, replaced by a fearless, powerful woman.

Had Simon done all this for her? If so, how could it be anything but good? But it didn't seem good, not at all. Something new had come into Doreen, a coldness Heidi had never seen before. It took an absolute hold on the girl, sending a chill through Heidi.

But then, just as suddenly, the old warmth returned. "Trust me," Doreen said and patted her friend on the leg, "it will all work out. You'll see."

Heidi scraped the joint against the wall and buried the roach. She wanted to be far away from that place. "Okay, lovergirl, we better jet."

———◦◦———

Later that night, Heidi tried to focus on her AP Chem homework, but was distracted by thoughts of Simon and Doreen. It was bad enough for Doreen to go off-roading so early in her time at Chandler, but to shove it in everyone's face at the Fall Dance? It was a disaster waiting to happen. Heidi hoped that whatever Simon and Doreen had between them, it was worth losing everything for. Or worse. Chandler kids were not above dishing out the kind of cruelty Doreen had faced at her old school. Sure, she had gained some standing on campus, but she was still an unknown, with few ties and no history. Her status was hardly guaranteed. The girl was setting herself up for some heavy retribution, especially where Gordon Lichter was concerned.

But she was Heidi Whelan! She could protect Doreen, couldn't she? The periodic table swam before her eyes and she closed her book. Heidi felt off her game. When she focused on her own desires, she always knew what to do. But this new effort to use her powers for good was leaving her more confused than anything else. Leave them to their happiness and hope she had enough clout to keep Doreen safe from the wolves? Or break them up and sacrifice what Doreen swore was true love? She certainly did seem to have very strong feelings for the boy. But how long could that last? They were just kids, after all.

Heidi munched a pistachio. Was it really Simon that had her so out of sorts? Or was it something else? The way Doreen looked in the shed tonight had frightened her. Her cold expression, as if she had no feelings at all–Heidi had seen such a thing before, not from Doreen, of course, but from *him*. She was his daughter, wasn't she? And she hated him.

Doreen hated Roland. Heidi had seen it in her face. She loathed her father for what he'd done to her and her sad stewardess mother in the Great Plains. It satisfied Heidi tremendously. Maybe he loved Doreen when she was little. Maybe he shined his attentions on her, just as he'd done on Heidi. And then he took them away, pushed her out of the light, into the cold. He'd made Heidi feel like she could do anything, like she was beautiful and special and gifted. And then he tossed her out like one of his wet, burned-out cigars.

We hate him, Doreen, Heidi thought. *And we will make him pay.*

12

A football game! Doreen scampered across the bleachers, making easy passage through the crowd to her favorite spot. Heidi and Biz tried to keep up, but their progress was slow. Heidi hoisted herself over each bleacher as delicately as she could on her high-heeled boots, attempting to remain dignified with her fuzzy, yellow-gloved hands upraised for balance. Beside her, Biz kneed and elbowed everyone they passed.

"Hey! Heidi! Biz! Down here!" Doreen called from near the bottom of the stands, waving an arm back and forth. Heidi waved back. Biz waved, too, kicking some kid in the ribs as she did. Slowly, apologizing to every human obstacle in their path, they caught up to their friend.

"Well!" Heidi exclaimed with a warming shake of her shoulders. "I didn't know there would be a physical challenge involved. How fun!" She snuggled in close, threading her arm through Doreen's elbow.

"Metal bleachers to view a winter sport—uh, interesting choice!" Biz made a show of seeming comfortable on the bench while maintaining the rail-straight posture that had been drilled into her by Mumzy. "I might have chosen a material that doesn't conduct the cold so readily. Wood, for example. Or hard plastic." She brought her camera to her face and snapped a few pictures of the crowd.

"Hush, Biz. And be a good sport. This is Doreen's day. Anyway, I brought a little something to take the edge off your cold buns." Heidi fished through her Louis Vuitton tote and pulled out a small mother-of-pearl flask. Taking a quick snort, she passed it to Biz.

"Yes, I believe this time I will take you up on it," said Biz, emptying a sizable deposit of booze into her gullet. "For warmth."

"Of course, of course. Doreen?"

"Huh?" said Doreen.

"Schnapps?"

"Oh, uh, no. No, thank you." The marching band conductor scrambled onto the field and the band made their way to their feet. A large sound emerged. It sounded not unlike music, but not totally like music, per se.

"Wow!" yelled Biz, smiling through her obvious misery. "An impressive volume, don't you think?"

"What!?"

The fans around them began to sing enthusiastically. "It's the fight song. They're about to come out. Look! Look! There's Simon!" Doreen pointed and jumped up and down, unable to contain herself. Heidi could imagine her as a child, her bright purple eyes wide and hungry for experience. "Heidi, do you see him? He's the one in front. Oh my god! He's looking for me!" Doreen waved. "Simon! Simon! I'm here!"

Heidi felt a pang of embarrassment at the sight of Doreen's blatant eagerness. She seized Biz's camera.

"Hey!"

"Shhh!" Heidi slapped Biz's hand away. She found Simon and zoomed in the powerful lens to get a better look.

The boy was looking up toward their seat, helmet in hand. Heidi watched him search for Doreen and when he found her, he grinned madly, with an almost insane joy. He was certainly handsome—more than that, he was resplendent. Leading the team of musclemen onto the field, Simon had a broadness about the chest and solid legs with a long body he carried upright, making his movement seem effortless. His complexion was dark with black, short hair and a meaty mouth. Though—and it may have been the uniform or the shoulder pads or the crazy glee—Heidi thought he looked like he might be an imbecile.

"Wow," she said. "Well done, Dorie! He looks like a movie star."

Doreen blew a kiss out onto the field. Simon pretended to catch it. Heidi winced. "And he's so good! Wait until you see him play," said Doreen, breathlessly.

"Can I have my camera back now?" asked Biz.

"No," said Heidi. "Stop asking."

"Look at him smile at you." Biz strained over Heidi's shoulder at the camera's display. "I'm afraid he's going to fall down!"

"Who, Simon? Never!" said Doreen. "Just watch. I've never seen him do anything that wasn't deliberate." Meanwhile, Biz kept nodding and smiling, nodding and smiling, staring out at the proceedings without a clue as to what she was meant to be looking at.

"Here we go! Opening kickoff. Ooh, this is so exciting!" said Doreen, clapping. "Go, Hawkeyes!"

"It certainly is exciting!" Biz said to Doreen. Then, in Heidi's ear, "What are the rules of this game, Heidi? Do you know? I should have read up on it before."

Heidi lowered the camera. She happened to know that the pilled, filthy, baby-blue hat that Biz wore over two greasy braids was Italian cashmere and that it had come with a matching scarf that Biz had lost. Just lost somewhere, left behind. It was a splendid scarf, too, soft and long enough to wrap and wrap around an appreciative neck. Heidi felt the loss of that scarf physically, as if it had been hers to cherish—which it would have been, eventually. Contempt and jealousy bubbled up from her guts. But she swallowed it. Poor Biz looked panicked.

"Don't fret, dollface," Heidi whispered, passing her the flask. "Just follow my lead." Biz nodded. "Woo!" Heidi screamed. "Let's go, Hamilton!"

"Yeah!" Biz tried. She stood and waved her arms. "Hurrah for the team!" She sat back down with a thud. "How was that?"

"Good." Heidi patted her friend on the knee. "You almost sounded like a teenager there. A teenager from Mars, but that's not nothing."

"Thank you," said Biz proudly. She took another shot of schnapps. "Minty!"

"Careful there, sport." Heidi screwed the cap on and dropped the half-empty flask back into her purse. "We don't want you to get sloppy."

"Don't we? Where is Simon? Is he out there?"

Doreen clicked her tongue with irritation. "No, Biz. The defense is out now. He's the quarterback. See? He's there on the sidelines. He's number ten."

"Ah, yes. He's a wonderful ssssitter, isn't he?" Biz stared longingly at the camera in Heidi's hands.

"He's wonderful at everything," Doreen replied. Heidi hid her rolling eyes by peering through the viewfinder. She saw Simon sitting on the bench, but instead of looking at the action on the field, he was staring right at them. A teammate was trying to say something to him, but he wasn't listening. Heidi lowered the camera and turned to Doreen, who was cheering on Hamilton's defense. If she noticed Simon's unfaltering stare she made no indication. Heidi had enjoyed her share of admirers, but Simon's possession was beyond what even she had experienced.

"Fascinating," said Heidi, resuming her spying gaze through the camera.

"Indeed!" Biz said boisterously from her hunched-over position near Heidi's knee as she poked through the Vuitton.

"Hey! Can I help you? It's not polite to rummage through another girl's handbag, Ms. Gibbons-Brown." Heidi kicked away Biz's prying hands and fished out the flask that she knew was her object of desire. She raised it high above her head. "I would expect better of someone with your upbringing."

"I wasn't! I mean, technically it's *my* handbag." Biz reached for the bottle, but Heidi had longer arms than she did. "Technically."

"Right, well. Still."

"Don't be stingy with the bottle, Heidster. Pass 'er over! Schnapp me, baby!" With a resigned sigh Heidi handed Biz the flask. Meanwhile, some activity on the field had fired up the crowd. Doreen whooped and hollered.

"That's right! Don't mess with the Hawks!"

"Doreen is, like, a sssuperfan!" said Biz with a giggle. "Go sssports!"

"Here he comes," Doreen whispered. She grasped Heidi's hand. And though as a policy Heidi did not tolerate hand-holding, especially from another girl, she let it slide. Her friend's excitement was palpable—her pale, lovely skin flushed from the cold and the thrill of anticipation, her eyes sparkly and wide. "Heidi, just, you won't be able to . . ." But the girl's emotion was too much; she could not even finish the sentence.

"I know I will," said Heidi, her heart filled with tenderness for her friend. The Hamilton offense took their positions at the line of scrimmage.

"Simon's the one with his hands up that other guy's bottom?"

"Biz, hush." Heidi raised the camera to watch the snap. He looked magnificent, Heidi had to admit, as he caught the ball from the snapper and hustled back to make the pass. But he was strangely listless. His position with his arm behind his ear was all strength and grace, but there seemed to be no fire behind it. When at last he let his pass go, the ball came out in a soaring, lazy trajectory that bounced on the line and dribbled out of bounds, beyond the reach of any receiver.

Heidi felt Doreen's body tense beside her. Doreen shook her head. "I don't under—"

"He's probably just warming up," said Heidi. "It's only one pass."

"Yes, I'm sure you're right. Although . . ." Doreen didn't continue, but Heidi knew what she was thinking. Out on the field, Simon seemed not just unapologetic, but triumphant. His upward gaze toward the girls' position was proud and sneering, as if the bad pass was part of his own secret victory. Against whom, Heidi had no idea.

"Second and ten!" Heidi yelled with a rallying clap. "Go, Hawkeyes!" But Simon continued to perform as woodenly in the subsequent downs as he had in the first. Play after play, as the game wore on, the Hamilton offense failed to convert a single down. And after every lob, bad handoff, sack, interception—of which he threw no fewer than five in the first half—he repeated the same strange triumphant smirk up toward Doreen.

"I'm speechless. I—oh, you probably think I made it all up, but I promise you this is not like him. It's just so disappointing!" Doreen cried bitterly. "What could he be thinking?"

Meanwhile, the crowd began to boo. They called Simon out by name, yelling nasty, cruel things at him.

"Hey! Hey! Leave him alone!" Biz yelled back. "What have you ever done in your life? Huh, Fatty? How about you, Ugly Shirt? Go, Simon Vale!"

"Shh, Biz, don't bother. Let them yell. They have a right to. Boo!" she yelled, using her hands to magnify her voice. "Simon Vale, you suck!"

"Doreen!" Biz pulled on her friend's coat. "He'll see you! He's looking right up here."

But Doreen would not sit down. She hissed and jeered at her beloved as he maneuvered mechanically on the field, failing to make any gains. At long last the half ended and he trotted into the locker room, waving with the same dumb rapture he possessed when he first entered. Doreen sat down hard on the bleacher, her face frozen, her trembling lips slightly open. The band struck up what may have been a medley of disco or popular Ukrainian folk tunes or movie songs from the future. Fans began to file out of the stands, grumbling and incredulous.

"He'll be better, Dorie, don't dessspair," Biz slurred. "Maybe he was nervous!"

"I don't think so. I was so wrong about everything." Doreen buried her face in her hands.

"But football—is it really that important?" Heidi asked.

"Of course it is! It's everything! Without it he's just a boring public school kid from Leaving Place. So conventional. So utterly unexceptional. Oh, this is a mess. I'm sorry I wasted your time. Why don't you go? Yes." Doreen wiped away her tears. "Yes, there's no need to stick around and freeze to death in order to witness this embarrassment."

"Normally I would insist on staying," said Heidi, "but I'm afraid that Biz might have overserved herself."

Biz was waving her hat over her head and shaking her hips. "Macho macho man. La-la-la-la-la macho man!"

Heidi lay a hand on Doreen's shoulder. "He's obviously very handsome. There's no reason that shouldn't be enough. After all, there won't be any football at the Fall Dance."

"There won't be any Simon Vale, either."

"Really?" Heidi hoped Doreen couldn't hear the pleasure in her voice.

"Can't you understand? He disgusts me now! Oh, it's revolting. I couldn't stand to be held in his arms, I'd rather die. Go, go. Let me wallow in this humiliation for the rest of the game. Please. I want to do it alone. I will come by your room tomorrow. Please."

"Poor Dorie," said Biz. She took her camera from Heidi and aimed it at Doreen's despondent face, but Doreen immediately grasped the lens and pushed it away.

"If you put that thing in my face one more time, Elizabeth, I am going to sock you. I mean it. And shatter your precious camera into a thousand pieces."

"Sorry," said Biz. "Doreen—"

"Don't." Doreen shrugged off her friend's touch. "Just leave me alone! Go on, get out of here! Can't you see my heart is breaking?" Doreen shoved her hands into her pockets and closed her eyes until her friends had gone.

———◦◦———

So it was over before it began, without Heidi having to meddle. Lucky break!

As Heidi hauled Biz home and put her to bed, she thought of Gordon Lichter. With the right trinket he might be able to lure Doreen to the dance as his date after all. Something pretty but not too flashy, something that said there was more where that came from. And there would have to be a dress, of course. The promise of a dress could do wonders.

"Hello, Gordon? Listen, I know Doreen hasn't been around much of late. . . . No, no! She hasn't been avoiding you. She's been sick. . . . Oh no, nothing serious. Some kind of something, but she's better now. Listen, I think you and I should talk Fall Dance, okay? . . . I know you were, but you don't have to give up. I think there are ways to make her, uh, *amenable*. But you have to be quick, the store is only open for another hour."

In downtown Hamilton, the second half of the homecoming game wore on much as the first. Even the visiting team seemed bored with its own easy victory. The crowd became thinner and thinner, until, when at last the clock wound down at the end of the game, the bleachers were mostly empty. From the lips of the few fans that remained, the name Simon Vale emerged like a curse. Doreen could hear it and feel it in her body like a lashing. A hero fallen is a disgrace, Doreen thought, an abomination. Better to be ordinary your whole life than to so recklessly squander genius. Simon's performance insulted all who had glorified him, including Doreen.

Oh, how she used to cherish every step that brought him nearer to her, how she would skip and rush through the empty high school, unable to control herself. To see and be seen by him, to hold and be held by Simon Vale—that was all Doreen had wanted then. But on this evening she could neither skip nor hurry. If her shoes were made of lead, it would require no more effort than it did to inch herself through the abandoned halls of Hamilton High, her heart heavy with shame.

By the time she arrived at the door of the locker room, everyone had already left. Only Simon remained, looking scrubbed in his sweatshirt and jeans, his expression dreamy and—could it possibly be? Happy.

"Doreen!" he called, pulling her rigid body into his warmth. "Wasn't I awful?"

"Horrible," Doreen agreed. She could barely look him in the face. He took her hand to walk her out, but she pulled away.

"Are you angry? Ah, you don't understand, yet. That's okay. I'll explain it all, little Dorie. First, come here. No need to be so serious. Let me kiss you."

But Doreen wouldn't let him get near her. "Understand? How could I possibly? You were an embarrassment, Simon. My friends were bored—I was bored. And the crowd! Are you sick? Have you got a fever or something? Maybe you should have stayed on the bench for this one. Really, I never saw anything so humiliating."

"Sick?" Simon laughed aloud, flicking the locks on the

lockers as he passed them by. "Doreen! I've never felt better. Listen." He stopped and grabbed her by the wrists.

"Ow! Simon, let go of me."

"Baby, don't you see? Football . . ." He wrinkled up his face as if grossed out by the word. "Football was all I had before. It was my escape from this blech, sorry excuse for a life I had. Leaving Place, remember? What kind of name is that for a street?" He chuckled to himself. "But once I had you, once you told me you loved me, oh, Dorie! Who needs football? Who needs to throw and run and jump around? What for? To win the adoration of regular people? Who needs them? I already have the adoration of someone so much better! Doreen." He held her by the shoulders. "Why should I want to escape from life now? Now that I have everything I ever wanted?" He leaned in to kiss her, and she rolled out of the way.

"No! Don't touch me!"

"Baby, don't be mad at me. Is it because of your friends? Yep." He nodded. "I can see that might have been embarrassing for you. But hey, I'll meet them at the dance, right? I'll make it up to 'em then. Doreen, babe, why aren't you looking at me?"

In fact, Doreen had huddled against the wall, her face buried in her hands. "You ruined it," she whispered bitterly.

"What? Sweetie, I can't hear you." Simon laid a big paw on Doreen's shoulder. The feel of his hand repulsed and enraged her. She flipped around and pushed him away.

"You ruined it!" she screamed. "You killed my love!" Despite his size, the thrust of Doreen's rebuff sent Simon reeling backward. When he regained his stance he stood blinking at her as if she was speaking another language. Finally, he smiled.

"That's not right," he said, coming to some kind of pleasant conclusion. "Nope. No way."

"You don't get it. You idiot! I loved you because you were exceptional. Because you had brilliance in you—specialness. But the way you lumbered around out there. Ugh! I can't bear to think that I ever let you come near me! You're just some lame public school nothing! Some *boy!*" And this last came out of a mouth so pinched with disdain, in a screeching voice so heavy with spite and violence, that it wounded Simon like a shot to the gut.

"But you can't mean—"

"I never want to see you again! The sight of your face makes me want to vomit. Do you hear me? Don't call me, don't come find me. I wish you were dead! Just so I could be sure that I would never see you again!"

Simon crumpled down to the floor, the great athlete reduced to a cowering, quivering thing. "No, no, it's not true. It can't be," he moaned. "I love you, Doreen. I need you. Please! Don't you understand? I won't make it without you!" He crawled over to her and threw his arms around her legs. Seeing him like that inspired no sympathy in Doreen Gray. All the warmth and affection she'd felt only that morning was gone. She felt nothing for him now, and his dramatics did not lower or raise her estimation of him—she had only one feeling left, and it was the desire to be elsewhere.

"I don't care," she said, and kicking him away, she walked out of Hamilton High School forever. She slammed the door behind her, shutting out the sound of his pathetic sobbing. The cool autumn air on her face smelled like relief.

"Good-bye to all that!" she said. She huddled into Biz's beautiful coat and hastened her pace home to Chandler Academy.

13

Cutting the dead weight out of her life lightened Doreen's step and her mood. The quad was lit up for the evening and crossed at intervals by students traveling in pairs and packs between the library or the dining hall to their dormitories, laughing in a way that Doreen herself sometimes laughed now—comfortably, as if the possibilities for the future were endless.

And weren't they? Only that morning, Doreen's fantasies had been so caught up with Simon that she had barely thought of her own future except insofar as it pertained to him. And at what cost? Her grades had been getting steadily worse, she'd spent so much time away from campus—physically and mentally—that she had failed to make more inroads with the popular kids, disappointing Heidi and herself. Doreen had simply allowed herself to become distracted, to take this amazing opportunity for granted. But now she had to get serious. She had to make the most of her two short years at Chandler, to set herself up for the glittering life Heidi always talked about, the kind of life she deserved.

A towering pile of books greeted her in the dorm. "Time to hunker down," she said to herself. She might not have been as good a student as Biz, but she was clever enough, and she would have to improve her grades if she wanted to get into a good university. "Yes," she said. "No more distractions." As blissful as it felt to float around with her mind only on Simon and memories of their kisses, it was nice to feel more like herself again. It was like returning from some magical vacation in a tropical paradise, only to find herself surprisingly happy to be home. At least, Doreen imagined it was like that—she'd never been on a vacation.

Doreen sat on her bed and passed her hand over her comforter. It was soft white eyelet. She'd had it since she had been a child, and feeling the nubby cotton under her fingers made her feel grounded, like she knew who she was after all these changes. And here she was, changed again. Truly, she felt an internal shift, as if the confrontation with Simon had made a mark on her. She looked up at her reflection in the closet door mirror, however, and saw the same porcelain-skinned girl with the black flowing curls that she had become accustomed to seeing.

"Just one peek," Doreen said to her stuffed elephant, Mopey, who seemed to give her a chastising look from his position near her pillow as she reached across to the drawer in her nightstand. "Then I will hit the books, I swear." Earlier in the semester, she would look at the photograph almost daily, when she was first learning to navigate the perks of her new face and body. But ever since she saw Simon Vale play quarterback at Hamilton High, she'd forgotten all about it. Now she slipped the paper out from the drawer with giddy anticipation.

"Mopey, let's see what Mama used to look like, shall we?" she said with a wicked little giggle.

At first glance, the picture seemed just as she remembered it. Her flesh protruded unflatteringly from the red dress, her expression meek and ill at ease. But then—it was strange, but she thought she saw a difference, a slight tonal shift. She took the picture over to her desk and studied it under her lamp.

It was there, in the eyes. A disturbing glow had come into them, as if she was lit by some kind of internal, sinister force. Her mouth had also changed, ever so slightly. The corners of the smile had receded, sunk, turned into a sneer. What could it mean? Doreen looked from the image to her reflection and back again. Her own face remained unchanged, but the difference in the picture could not be blinked away.

A tap came from her window and Doreen screamed. She put her hand on her heart, trying to regain her breath. "It's just a tree," she told herself. "It's just the wind. You're being hysterical." But then she heard the tap again and she could hear the sound of her name being called through the small opening in her window.

"Doreen," someone whispered. "Doreen Gray. Come to the window." Should she run to get her RA? Call campus safety? But what would she say, that the trees were calling her name? "Doreen!" said the voice again, even more urgently.

Doreen closed her eyes and took in big, deep breaths, feeling her heartbeat begin to slow down. Another tap came at the window. "Dorie," said the voice, "Come on! I'm freezing my balls off out here!"

Doreen rushed to the window and saw Gordon Lichter standing under a tree in the mostly dark. He was rooting around in the grass, probably looking for another pebble to throw. She hoisted up her window and stuck out her head. "Gordon!" she whispered as admonishingly as she could. "What are you doing here?"

"Doreen! There you are. Come down, okay? I want to talk to you."

"I can't, Gordon. It's after check-in. You want to get me kicked out of here? And shouldn't you be back at your dorm, speaking of?"

"I'm a senior, remember? I have until ten." He looked around. "Fine. I'm coming up." He wiped his hands on his khakis. "Screw it. All those years of gymnastics should be good for something, right?" And with that he jumped up and pulled himself up the drainpipe, using the trellis as a ladder to climb his way toward her second-story window.

Doreen quickly slipped the picture into the top drawer of her desk, hiding it under a notebook. He was coming to ask her to the Fall Dance. She'd been dodging him for days, and now here he was and what could she say? What would she do? She would turn him down. She'd have to, it was the right thing to do, wasn't it? She didn't give a whit about him, and her breakup with Simon was barely an hour old.

Gordon came flying feetfirst through the window, landing with a light thud on his feet. He was no Simon Vale, she thought, but he was impressively nimble.

"Huh?" he said with a little bow. "How you like me now? Bet you don't know a lot of guys who would shimmy up a drainpipe just to talk to you. Do you?"

"No. I don't suppose I do. Here." Doreen plucked dry leaves from his hair with a laugh. "You're a bit of a mess."

"Oh. Thanks," he said, bending at the neck and closing his eyes as she picked through his hair and clothes. He was barely taller than she was, but his hair was glorious. It was shiny and white-blond, like corn silk—the sort of hair one might expect to see blowing in the headwind on the bow of a yacht.

"There. I think I just about got it all." Gordon opened his eyes, gazing directly into hers. She saw pain in his eyes and need, a kind of hunger unique to men.

He reached out and grasped the edge of one of her curls. "Not fair. Shouldn't I get to touch, too?"

Doreen escaped from his grasp. "If I ever have dead leaves in my hair." She walked over to the waste bin near her desk to throw out the detritus.

"You're so cruel! How can you be so cruel!" Gordon cried. He buried his face in his hands.

As she saw cocky Gordon Lichter reduced to sniveling, she wondered if he could be right. Could she be cruel? After all the cruelty she'd suffered in her life? The change in the picture seemed to suggest at least that much. But how absurd. She must have imagined the change in the photo. Of course! It was some sort of trick her mind was playing on her. A little leftover guilt from her breakup with Simon. Doreen was a nice girl. It wasn't her fault that Simon wanted something from her that she couldn't give him. Staying with him when she didn't love him, now that would have been wrong.

"Me? Me cruel?" she said. "What about you?"

"Me?" asked Gordon. "I've been nothing but kind to you. I dote on you, Doreen. I'd do anything for you, you know that!"

"And what about Samantha Brooks? Huh? I've seen the way she follows you around. And you won't even condescend to say hello to her. The poor thing obviously just wants you to acknowledge that she exists." Doreen had noticed chubby, unloved Samantha Brooks on Gordon's tail like a bad stink. She'd never spoken to the girl, but she would. She would do it soon. Tomorrow! Tomorrow she would be so good!

"But she's . . . I'm not . . ." Gordon sighed deeply, with resignation. "You're right. You're right." He sat down on the edge of her bed and grinned up at her. "The amount I've suffered because of you, Doreen. I probably have it coming to me. But I don't care. I don't care how much you hurt me. And you do hurt me, Doreen. But I'll take a punch in the gut from you over some other girl's kiss any day of the week. Doreen Gray, you know I love you, right?"

"Hush now, Gordon," she said, though it pleased her enormously.

"I won't. I won't hush. Doreen, look. I bought you something. Here, come sit next to me, okay? I'm not going to bite. Please? After all I did to get up here?" Doreen sat beside Gordon on the bed. It amazed her how little his closeness affected her. With Simon, every centimeter closer he came to her she could feel all over her body.

"Doreen?" Gordon said. "Are you listening?"

"Yes, of course, Gordon. What is it?"

"Here." He pulled a black velvet box from his pants pocket. "Open it."

Doreen took the box. It had a pleasant weight to it. Whatever was inside (a necklace? Earrings?) would certainly be more elegant that anything she'd had back in the Midwest. Gordon was so rich. And popular. And he clearly had very strong feelings for Doreen. So her own feelings for the boy weren't the stuff of rock songs, so what? He would get her a dress, wouldn't he? And a hotel room.

"Oh! Oh, Gordon," she said breathlessly when she saw the ring—rose gold, with a single, perfect pearl beset with two small diamonds on either side. "It's beautiful."

"I thought you would like it. Listen, Doreen, why don't you go to the dance with me, okay?"

"Mmm?" said Doreen. The look and feel of the ring had her completely transfixed. How it relaxed her, to see such beauty beam up from her own hand.

"Earth to Doreen!" said Gordon with a laugh. He grasped her bejeweled hand and turned her chin to look at him. "To the dance, Doreen. I want you to come to the dance. Listen, we'll get you all decked out, okay? Whatever you want. And you'll go, we'll go together. What do you say? Me and you, Dorie. Please. It would make me so happy." Gordon looked at her with pleading, pitiful eyes. The poor kid couldn't be accustomed to the sort of runaround he'd received from Doreen during these past months. Life for him had been nothing but open doors and green lights until he'd met her, and now that kind of life would be hers, too.

She slipped her hand from his grasp and moved a pesky strand of hair away from his eye. "Of course, Gordon. It would be my pleasure to attend the Fall Dance with you."

"Oh, Doreen!" Gordon leaned over to kiss her, and she let him. He should have his fun, she thought, as he moved himself around her mouth like it possessed some necessary nutrient of which he'd been long deprived. "I love you! Oh god, I love you so much!"

14

It wasn't hard. To keep her eye on what counted: the work, the vision, the realization of an idea. Youth mattered only because it gave Biz time and energy. Not like her mother, a beautiful dancer once, who allowed herself to become distracted with the business of society and all its attendant obligations. For Biz, the only obligation she felt was to her art. Her family, her few friends, even her own heart came second to the daily grind of learning the language of expression in pictures.

And so she remained locked in her own world, closed off from the inane teenage dramas unfolding around her. She took care of herself, and when her work was going well, nothing could hurt her. But lately the work was not going well. The pictures, her flying carpet over the banalities of everyday life, had lost all their magic dust. She sat alone in the basement photo lab of the Carver Arts Center one Friday evening in late October desperately paging through her most recent batch, but not a single shot had liftoff. With her face inches from her Mac monitor, Biz clicked and clicked and clicked, but nothing made her feel as she knew she could, like she had contributed something meaningful to a meaningless world.

Biz turned off the monitor and leaned back in her chair. The Gryphters, a coed a cappella group, rehearsed a familiar pop ballad in one of the rehearsal rooms on the floor above. Normally she was too wrapped up in her work to hear anything—even, on one occasion, a fire alarm. But her photos had betrayed her, or she had betrayed them. In any case, she was no longer protected. Not from the saccharine music or the clanking pipes or sorrow or loneliness or memories or hope.

Biz squeezed her eyes shut. Her mind played, loudly, a memory from childhood. They were at the Connecticut house, preparing to move out to the beach for the summer. In the playroom, Biz had her little pink-and-yellow toy suitcase open while she studied the bookshelf. Maria had promised to help Biz choose the books to take with her to the beach house. They would be there such a long time, more than a month, and so Biz had to think hard about what books she would want to read, not just now, but in the future. She tried to imagine herself one month older. What would future Biz want? How could she be sure not to disappoint her? She put one book after another in the suitcase, then took them all out. She could not decide.

She needed Maria. Maria always knew the right books to pack. They would go through, one by one, and together they would finish the job. Only Maria knew how to say words that made the sticky sensation Biz felt, the feeling that she was going to make the wrong choice, go away. But Maria never came. Biz waited and waited. Finally, she padded down the back staircase, the one with the blue carpeting that led to the kitchen. She found her mother there with her assistant, Frederick. Her mother had her red leather planner open and her reading glasses on. As she spoke, Frederick wrote furiously in his notebook and nodded.

". . . and make sure that my husband is on the early train on Saturday. He will want to drive, but please try and dissuade him. There are plenty of cars in Amagansett already, and I don't need him arriving in a foul mood from sitting in traffic all day—oh, there you are, Elizabeth. Are you finally ready? Addison is waiting out in the car. Why don't you join him and I will be out momentarily."

"But where's Maria? She said she would help me pack."

"Maria? Oh, she's not coming, I'm afraid, my darling. A family emergency. Her son—"

"Daughter," said Frederick.

"Are you sure? I thought she had a son. Oh well, no difference. Her child, my dear, has had some sort of medical, uh, happening. And so she had to go. Anyway, you're too old for a nanny now, don't you think?" With a wave of her hand she turned back to her planner.

"But she promised me," said Biz, trying to comprehend what her mother had told her. Maria had a daughter? How old was she? Where did she live? Maria lived here in their house. She had a room upstairs where she kept her things like her Bible and lotion that smelled like peach ice cream. But she never said anything about her daughter. She said she was born in Honduras, and that she was the youngest of seven children, including one sister who died. Was Maria's daughter going to die, too? Biz's eyes welled up. "She promised to help me pack." Her voice came out in a wail.

"Oh, sweetie," said Mumzy. She slid her reading glasses on top of her head. "You don't need to pack. Frederick made sure you have everything you could possibly need. Okay? It's all folded up in a suitcase in the car, ready to go."

"But my books. Maria was going to help me pack my books."

"Elizabeth." Biz could see that she was wearing down her mother's patience. It was easy to do. Which is why it was better not to bother her at all. Better to take all her concerns to Maria. But Maria was gone. She had a dying daughter and so she had to go. "Just pick a few books and let's go, okay? There are bookstores in the Hamptons. There's even a library. Anything you forget we will get for you, or we can tell your daddy and he can bring it over the weekend. Sound good? We are going to Long Island, my dear, not to war. Provisions will be made available."

Frederick giggled. Mumzy crouched down in front of Biz and took her hands. "I'm sorry about Maria. I know that you were fond of her."

"She didn't even say good-bye."

"Now don't be selfish, Elizabeth. You can't expect her to put you before her own daughter, can you? That wouldn't be right. Maria is not your mother. I'm your mother. And I am not going anywhere except to the sanitarium when you finally drive me over the edge. Now run upstairs and pack your books. I expect you to be in that car in the next ten minutes. Understand?"

The Gryphters switched to a dance song. Through the floor vents Biz could hear the rhythm section spitting out percussion sounds while a white girl attempted melisma. Since Doreen had reappeared, useless memories, things she hadn't thought about in years, seemed to haunt her at every corner.

The picture of her cousin in the red dress was the last Biz could say she was proud of. But she could not even look at it for comfort. As she had promised she would, she'd destroyed all digital evidence of it. It was a shame, really. Thinking of that picture gave her a sinking feeling. A grief, a loss without closure—just the way she felt when Maria went away. Was that the summer that Doreen came to the beach? It was undoubtedly that summer when her mother informed her father that Elizabeth had spent far too much time indoors, moping about.

And so her father brought a camera for her. He said, go out and take some pictures. Let's see what you find out there, little Bizzy.

The fluorescent overheads flickered on in the lab, giving Biz a jolt.

"You will go blind. You know that, don't you?" said Seth Greenbaum. He was a film guy, with film guy facial hair and glasses and black jeans. He clocked in a fair amount of time in the lab, too, editing. He made short films around campus with names like *The Delinquent Exterior* and *What Everyone Says about Hester.*

"Wait, your monitor isn't even on. What were you doing in here, Biz Gibs? Thinking?"

"Something like that." Although Seth's posturing could grate her nerves when she was deep into her work, Biz was happy to see him now. Without photography, she craved the company of others. How strange it was to need people. "What are you working on? A new opus?"

"Oh yeah, this one is going to be epic. It's a love story between a young man and a teacher. They have a fiery, sexual connection they cannot deny. But she's a moral person who loves her job. So he has to seduce her. It's called *Another Morning in Tomorrow's End*. Shooting over fall break. Incidentally, are you going to be around? Man, I would love you to be DP. I'm going to be in it, see? So I could use someone with your eye."

"What's a DP?"

"Director of photography. You know, the cinematographer. Like, you'd shoot the camera. I tell you what to shoot and you just aim it, hit Record. That sort of thing. The way you take pictures, man, except it's video." Seth started up a computer station across from Biz. "Yeah, since I gotta act, too, I'd love to have someone I can really trust in the trenches with me, you know? Granted, you're more of a lone-wolf type, but maybe it will be good for you to engage in a little artistic collaboration. See what that's like for a change."

"I don't know." The prospect of making someone else's vision come alive instead of agonizing over her own was tempting. But what could she offer Seth? Nothing she made had any value anymore.

"Think about it. I'd really love to have you on board." He smiled at her.

"Seth! Oh my god, there you are." Miyuki Moto swept into the lab, and without any acknowledgment of Biz's existence, she headed right for Seth. She kicked a high-heeled boot over his legs and straddled him in his desk chair. With a flick of her purple hair, she gave him a long, deep, pornographic kiss. When she detached herself, the boy was practically panting.

"I've been waiting for you," she said in a pouty baby voice. "I don't like to wait. Even for geniuses." The girl's fingers danced on his chest.

"Sorry, Miyuki. I told you, I have to get this screenplay in tip-top shape before go time. I'm worried about the second act and—"

"Se-eth," said Miyuki. She leaned in to whisper something in his ear. Her fingers crawled lower on his body. Biz looked away.

"Okay, okay. Just give me a minute."

Miyuki sprung up from Seth's lap and huffed across the room, disappearing down the hall.

"Miyuki! Miyuki, don't be mad! Shit. Okay, dammit. All right. Can you shut down for me? She's my star, you know. And she's hot as hell. But it's all for the movie and everything. I mean, it's for the good of the movie." Seth raced after Miyuki. "Think about what I said, Biz Gibs."

Biz shut down her own computer and Seth's and turned off the lights. The Gryphters were calling it a night. Nothing was happening, so Biz figured she may as well do the same. With nowhere in particular to go, she took the long way back to the dorms.

She felt embarrassed for Seth, and angry on his behalf. Miyuki obviously didn't really like him. She was just using him to star in his movie. Why that could be important to anyone, Biz could not imagine. But it gnawed at her, to see him so quick to turn his back on his work to appease a pretty girl.

But she would do it, too. She would love to. For the right person, she would turn away from everything, she was sure of it, though it was easier to contemplate now that there was nothing to turn away from. Biz considered the notion of spending fall break shooting Seth and Miyuki. They would have something, a movie and something else, a secret between them, sex, intimacy. And Biz would stand by filming, a witness to someone else's life. What would she have? A document. But of someone else's time. Where would she be in it? Where was her time?

Maybe the moment had arrived for her to step out from behind the camera and live her own life. Isn't that what people always told her? It had been so comfortable for her there, shielded by her camera, bearing witness. But she didn't want to be a bystander anymore. She wanted to feel something, too. To live.

Look at Doreen. She had come to the school as a wounded victim. But she'd found love. In the face of whatever social hierarchy nonsense Heidi worried about, Doreen had gone out into the world of the living and uncovered someone who could matter to her.

Yes, Biz decided. I want to live. The only question was: How?

———◦●———

Biz arrived at her dorm room to find Doreen sitting comfortably on the chesterfield with a magazine on her lap.

"What's up with you?" asked Doreen. "You look flushed. Coming from a rendezvous with your muse?"

"She didn't show up," said Biz with a grin. "The bitch." She was not surprised to find her cousin so cozily laid out. Doreen had a key to their room and was often there without them. Biz liked it. Even if she knew that it was Heidi, and not Biz, whose company Doreen sought, finding her there made Biz feel like part of a tribe for the first time in her life.

"Oh, I'm sorry, Bizzy." Doreen gave her cousin a sympathetic frown. "Still blocked? That sucks. That must be so hard. I know how important it is to you."

Biz could feel her insides unstick. Like Maria, Biz thought, Doreen had the power to make her into a believer.

"I don't know, I think something is going to change for me. For my work. I don't know how to explain it." Biz sat at her desk chair, allowing the collage of images to swirl in front of her. "I just think this may all lead somewhere, somewhere great but also a little scary."

"You sound excited." Doreen tilted her head and studied Biz. "Yes, I can see it. I can see something different."

"Really?" Biz looked at herself in the full-length mirror on the bedroom door.

"You're not going to see it in the mirror, silly." Doreen flipped the magazine onto the coffee table and walked up to Biz, bracing her by the shoulders with both hands and turning her slightly from one side to the other. "Something tremendous is going to happen to you this year, Elizabeth."

"You really think so? Like what?"

"Who knows?" Doreen returned to the chesterfield, snapping her fingers. "Maybe you'll fall in love!"

"Like you and Simon."

Doreen picked up her magazine. "Simon Vale? Oh, that's already old news, I'm afraid. No. That is over. Way over."

"But I thought—"

"After his pathetic display at the football game?" Doreen grimaced. "I couldn't. I could barely look at him after that. You must understand in some way, Biz. You're an aesthete, aren't you? He was so clumsy and graceless. Ugh! No, I've decided to go to the dance with Gordon. I know it seems early to make the transition, and I considered turning him down, but he is so keen on the idea. Anyway, it's just a dance, it's not like I'm engaged to the guy." Doreen stretched her hand out in front of her, her eyes on a pearl ring.

"Is that new?"

"Hmm?" Doreen dropped her hand. "Anyway, that's what I'm doing here. Heidi and I are journeying to Manhattan for a frock. Care to join? I know shopping is not exactly your passion, but you are entering this new phase."

"Uh, I don't know." Was this the sort of thing Biz was meant to do in order to feel she was living? But it all seemed so seedy. For Doreen to cast aside Simon so readily, and for what? A dress and a ring. That was not the kind of bite she was hoping to take out of life.

Also this: *Heidi and I are journeying to Manhattan for a frock.* It was exactly something Mumzy would say.

"I think I will stick around here for now," said Biz. "The muse may show up after all. But maybe next time."

"Suit yourself." Doreen returned her attentions to her magazine.

15

Valentino. Dior. Versace. Armani. McQueen. In the dressing rooms of New York's finest department stores, the labels offered themselves to Doreen like ripe fruit to be plucked and devoured or tossed away on a whim without a second look. Scuttling, name-tagged employees hauled and hung and offered their wares, and though it was only Gordon's money that gave Doreen access to the silks and sequins of haute couture, to the obsequiousness of salespeople, Heidi noted how quickly the girl had become accustomed to being doted upon. Where was that awkward, bullied schoolgirl who until recently had never eaten duck or sipped wine? Doreen frowned and gave orders like it was her birthright.

At Saks, their third stop, Doreen emerged from the dressing room in a new dress. She stepped delicately onto the platform and spun around in the three-way mirror so the women could ooh and ah over her. Gordon's charge card shined on her like a light from her borrowed fake Chloé bag. Yes, Heidi thought approvingly, Doreen seemed very comfortable indeed.

The gown was a lavender, lacy, plunging wisp of a thing that clung to her chest and waist and hips as if it was unwilling to share her body with anyone. Doreen turned and gazed at herself from every angle. The color of the dress brought out the purple in her eyes. She was breathtaking.

"What do you think?" she asked, though her face betrayed her new confidence.

"It's a perfect fit," a saleslady said approvingly. "And the color—"

"I wasn't talking to you," Doreen snapped. "Heidi? Do you like it? Do you think Gordon will like it?" She had her hands on her hips with her backside to the mirror. The diamonds on her new pearl ring sparkled. Heidi commended herself for the choice.

"Doreen, the kid will not know what hit him."

"I'll take it," Doreen said to the saleslady, without removing her admiring gaze from her own reflection. "Please wrap it carefully. We have a long trip."

No bus would take the girls back to campus at this time. After a few additional stops—for manicures and waxes, some tastefully lurid underwear—Gordon's man drove them up in the town car. They cleared the Midtown traffic on the West Side Highway and pulled onto the Saw Mill. The car passed directly through Yonkers before nosing up to Connecticut.

While Doreen narrated the girls' day to Gordon on the phone, Heidi gazed out at her hometown through the tinted window. She clocked the detour to her parents' house at ten minutes. They could stop in and see Heidi's mother. She would serve them liver mousse and crudité and feel very grand, maybe play them something on the old upright. Her father would come home, smelling of refuse, but thrilled to see her and meet her friend. What would Doreen think of them? Would she be charmed? Embarrassed? Heidi knew perfectly well what Doreen's father would think of the Whelans. Roland would be disgusted. He would see nothing but filthy mediocrity.

But Doreen was not Roland. She came from nowhere,

too. Maybe Doreen would laugh at Heidi's father's stories and find her mother's singing sweet. Maybe Heidi would be able to look at them again, freely, without disdain. She could love them again, then. If she could just see through the ugliness to the beauty that Roland Gibbons did not know enough to look for. She couldn't seem to get there on her own. She could never seem to forget.

About a week after she'd been fired from the Montauk Inn, when she was up late flipping through the channels on her parents' old TV, she found *The Wizard of Oz* on cable. At first she thought of skipping past. Everything she used to love had become awful to her since she got back to Yonkers. Her father's howling laugh, her mother's bizarre insistence on formality, her sister's moonfaced ignorance. The house was ugly! The block was ugly! Her friends and boyfriends were nothing but airheads and buffoons. Even the kindly librarian whom she'd known since she was a kid, the one who saved books for Heidi, seemed dowdy and small-minded now. She saw everything through Roland's eyes, and found it all utterly lacking. This was the cruelest thing he did to her: he made her see her tiny, meaningless life for what it was.

She wanted to preserve Dorothy, Scarecrow, and the Wicked Witch. She did not think she could take losing something else to the refinement of good taste. But there was nothing else on, so she watched. She watched the whole thing, even though it was late, and she was happy to find that she still loved the movie. Dorothy was so lucky! She got to escape dreary old Kansas and head over the rainbow. She loved all the scenes in Oz, the Good Witch, the Munchkins, the makeover. But then, at the end, after Dorothy clicked her heels three times and woke up back in Kansas, it struck Heidi for the first time that Dorothy got a seriously bum deal. Sure, she played the good niece, psyched to be back in Kansas, returned to Auntie Em and friends. But she couldn't have been, not really. Once she'd feasted her eyes on a world more colorful than any she had ever known, how could she settle back into boring old black and white? How could she ever be satisfied again? Heidi had been over the rainbow, too. And Kansas? Sucked.

She would never be content again until she found a way back to her Oz, to that luxurious, leisurely, Technicolor world she'd seen for only a flash. On the old couch her mother had reupholstered by hand in horrible salmon-colored toile, Heidi resolved to do whatever it took to hoist herself up over the rainbow again. If she had to run into the eye of the tornado? So be it.

And she'd done it, hadn't she? Whatever her methods, she had found a way to Chandler, to the elite world of the rich and privileged. Here she was being chauffeured around by an employee of one of the richest families in America. And it had cost Roland, too. But not enough. Not nearly enough. Money he had by the truckful. She wanted to see him lose something dearer than cash, something irreplaceable.

"You seem pensive. What's on your mind, lady?" asked Doreen when she clicked off with Gordon.

"Hm?" Heidi hadn't said a word for miles. Yonkers was now far behind them. "Oh, nothing. Well, actually it's about your father."

"My father? What's he got to do with anything?"

"Nothing. Or everything." Heidi checked her friend's reaction through the corner of her eye. She would have to proceed with care. "I was thinking that maybe the whole Simon Vale affair was a way for you to seek revenge."

"On my dad? That doesn't even make sense." Doreen typed away at her phone.

"Doesn't it?" Heidi turned to face Doreen. "You said it yourself when we were in the shed. It delighted you to think of how castrated your father would look beside Simon."

"I'm sure I didn't say castrated. Anyway, I was high as a kite at the time. Are we still liking this nail color?"

"Okay. So maybe it was feminine. Simon's manliness appealed to you because it would, hypothetically, make your father feel emasculated."

"Could you not with the AP Psych right now? This sounds like the time you diagnosed Biz with autism."

"It was mild Asperger's. And I still think there's a case to be made, but listen, about your dad—"

"I don't want to think about him, okay? We were having a good day. I just want to have a good day!" Doreen threw her phone into her bag in exasperation. "You don't know my dad. I don't even know him. He's just the guy who writes the tuition checks. That's it. Now can we drop it?"

"Of course. I wasn't trying to upset you."

Doreen crossed her arms and slouched into her seat. For a while they rode along in silence. Heidi knew she should let it go, but she couldn't. "Doreen, don't be upset. On the very first evening when we met, we talked about liberty. About delivering yourself from ties to live spectacularly. Remember?"

"Yes," said Doreen sulkily. "I remember."

"That's all I'm talking about. If you rise, make yourself glorious—Chandler is just the beginning. He didn't believe in you, right? Well, I believe in you, Doreen. You are already on your way. All I was saying is that Simon Vale has no currency for someone like your father. What he cares about is this world, the one with livery cars and American Express Black cards, unmarked doors in the back for members only." Heidi grasped her friend's hand. "If you can elevate yourself to the top of that universe, you'll threaten his little fiefdom. And that will really show him."

"Show him what?" Doreen looked at Heidi directly now, her eyes pleading. The poor girl was still a lost child seeking a guiding hand.

"Show him that he's nothing special. That he's ordinary. And irrelevant. Because you will be a beautiful, young girl in the spotlight, the darling of high society—no thanks to him. And what will he be? Just an old, drunk, worthless playboy. A cliché. And that will kill him, Doreen. I just know it."

Doreen turned toward the window. Heidi wondered if she'd given herself away. How could she know so much about Roland if she had never met him before? But Doreen just sat in quiet contemplation, staring out at the highway.

"I would like that," she said at last. Traffic was clogging up around them, but what did it matter? They had nowhere to be but together. "I would like that very much."

Heidi let her eyes glaze over the dull landscape, stunned by her own behavior. She'd injected Roland into their friendship, had done so intentionally, and there was no going back now. The story she'd told herself, about how Roland had nothing to do with her relationships with Biz or with Doreen, had been a lie. She saw that now. Sure, she was bored, she was looking for a noble project, but to claim her intentions with Doreen were pure charity was laughable. Heidi had a Roland jones. She wanted to see him suffer. And Doreen was her ticket.

One afternoon, at the Montauk Inn, Roland was teaching her about wine. They sat on the terrace, away from the concierge desk, where five or six tastes had been poured from the hotel's cellar. She picked up a glass, sniffed, and swirled as he had taught her to do. But she could never get it right. Her assessments were off, her taste uncultivated. He laughed at her and commended her for her impressive talent for bullshit.

Then he received a call. Predictably it was from Benedict Ruehl, his art dealer. Since Roland had begun these sessions with Heidi, they were interrupted almost daily by Benedict—never by his wife, which struck Heidi as odd. Her own parents couldn't eat lunch without telling the other what was on the menu. This time, the news from the art dealer was good. A painting had been sold for an exorbitant sum. Roland called over the waiter to replace the wine with martinis. They drank to art and, emboldened by the liquor, Heidi asked him about his family. Did they miss him? Did he miss them? Did he get updates on their whereabouts?

Roland cleared his throat. He wore a white linen suit that day with an open-collared shirt. Everyone wore white in the Hamptons, but nobody wore it like him. "Constantina lives her own life, my dear, and I live mine. We are independent people. Our children, too, have their own circle of nannies and playmates that occupy their time. We prefer to keep our own space. I'm sure this is hard for you to imagine. I've never seen your parents', uh, home, but I can imagine that the quarters are rather more cramped than ours. And so you are *involved* with one another. We prefer a bit more air between us."

"But you still love each other, right?" Heidi asked. "Because it doesn't sound like it. I mean, not the way I think of love."

Roland's mouth turned down. He looked at her with rage in his eyes. "One should not discuss things one knows nothing about. That does not leave many subjects open for you, I realize. But I would think even you know when to keep your opinions to yourself."

"Sorry. I didn't mean—"

"I will let this slide, my dear. But please try to use your head. I would not like to be intruded upon again."

Heidi cringed at the memory. Until that point, Roland seemed to have endless patience for her mistakes. But to ask him if he loved his wife? Even a garbage man's daughter should know better than that. He had every right to be angry. Thankfully, he seemed to forget all about the incident the next time they met, and they never discussed his family again.

But there was something else there, too. In that moment, Heidi saw pain in Roland Gibbons. Whatever feelings existed—between Roland and his wife, Roland and his children—they were not satisfactory to him, she was sure of that. Here was a man who knew everything except how to be loved.

Heidi looked at Doreen, who had leaned her head against the window and closed her eyes. Her lips remained slightly open, in a half smile. She was perfect, absolutely perfect, more beautiful than any work of art or fine automobile. Roland would want her for himself, to show off, to love. Heidi knew it.

There was a hole in that man's heart. Why else would he have paid any attention to her that summer? Alone, his family elsewhere, his wife just months away from leaving him for good, Roland plucked Heidi from behind the desk at the Montauk Inn because he wanted to be adored.

When Heidi became inconvenient, he tried to make her disappear. He thought it would be easy to do, and cheap. In the end it was neither, Heidi made sure of that, but she was a stranger, a kind of servant, actually. She meant nothing to him.

But Doreen was Roland's daughter. A fresh chance for something real. If they played it right, they could make him care deeply. Doreen could make him feel like he had everything he always wanted. And then, with Heidi's help, Doreen would take it away. Like that. No warning.

They would present Doreen to Roland as his own Oz, his paradise. They would give him a glimpse and then snatch it away, send him back to Kansas alone and unloved. Then he would know what it feels like to have to live without color, in a world of black and white. And Heidi could finally be the one to laugh at *him*.

16

When Gordon saw her coming out of the dorm on the night of the Fall Dance, Doreen was afraid that he might start weeping.

"I told him not to blubber. But it was not displeasing," said Doreen. "In the limo on the way over he kissed me, and I think I almost felt something."

"That sounds like progress. Anyway, you look *wicked*," Heidi said, mocking their New England classmates who were always going on about wicked awesome, wicked fun.

"You look totally awesome, too. I, like, love your outfit," Doreen drawled.

"What? This old thing?" Heidi twirled around. She'd chosen a black tight-fitting Versace embellished with bodacious black ostrich feathers around the hem and sleeves and accessorized with insanely yellow Louboutin platform pumps. Her lips were shiny, luscious and red, and her hair was piled on her head just like it was nothing at all for her to look like that and be like that.

"Honestly," said Doreen, "I don't think I've ever in my life seen anybody look so incredibly cool."

Heidi felt her heart flush. Doreen's praise came less easily now, so it meant more. She was surprised by how much it gratified her. *Careful there, kiddo*, said the voice in Heidi's head. *Trust no one.*

"There you guys are. I looked for you on the bus. But I should have known you would find your own means of transportation." Biz approached the twosome. Heidi recognized the red strapless dress Biz wore as the same Carolina

Herrera from the picture they took on the day they met Doreen.

"Why, is that Elizabeth Gibbons-Brown at a school dance? I never thought I'd see the day."

Biz hiked up the dress under her armpits. "I decided I should make at least one of these things before I graduate. Rite of passage and all that. Memories, et cetera."

"All dressed up like a lady! And I can't help but notice a certain accessory missing from around your neck. Why, Biz, could you have come all this way without your camera?"

Biz smiled. "I thought maybe I'd try taking mental pictures this time. You know, like a participant."

"Mumzy will be ecstatic."

"Say one word, Heidi Whelan, and you'll lose handbag privileges. For life."

"Oh, calm down." Heidi couldn't help grinning. She was glad to see Biz at the dance. Sure, the outfit seemed like an afterthought, accessorized, predictably, with Biz's sad wire glasses and makeup-free face. But at least she'd bothered to tie her hair back and trade in her beat-up All Stars for a pair of prim ballet flats. And to travel without her camera. What was going on with little Bizzy? Heidi would have to get to the bottom of that later.

"Wait! I can't believe it. Are those *earrings* in your ears, Elizabeth? I didn't even know your ears were pierced! Jesus, where have you been hiding that set of sparklers? Wow-ee."

"Claws off, vulture," said Biz, swatting Heidi's hand away. "These belonged to Grandmère Kiki. They are off-limits to the likes of you. Anyway, you look nice. Doreen, you're looking really nice, too. Hey, Doreen? What's wrong?"

Doreen's face had drained of all color. She seemed afraid, as if it wasn't her friend Biz who had approached, but some sort of otherworldly creature, a demon or spirit.

"That dress," she said.

Biz looked down at the three-thousand-dollar dress as if it was a bedsheet. "It's the one you wore. In the picture I took for your GryphPage profile."

"I know what it is. What I don't know is why it is on your body. Why did you wear it here? Are you trying to make fun of me?"

"Huh? No! Of course not! I just, I had to wear something. And this one, I remembered about how we got reacquainted that day. I actually thought you might like—"

"Well, it looks terrible. Really awful." Doreen clenched her fist like she was ready to sock Biz in the kisser.

"Doreen!"

"What? Heidi, you know it's true. You look ridiculous, Elizabeth. You look like you're trying to dress up as someone else. Me, I guess. Is that right? Are you trying to copy me?"

"No! No, I just . . . I didn't mean . . ." Biz's voice shook and her eyes misted. "I didn't realize . . ."

"Stop it, Dorie!" Heidi put her hands on Biz's hunched shoulders. "You don't look ridiculous, Biz. You look nice. Sweet and girly, for once, and the dress fits *you* perfectly. I can't think of what has come over our friend here. I imagine it's nerves? Is that right, Doreen? Are you nervous? Or has some devil possessed you?"

"What? I—" Doreen shuddered, as if recovering from a bad dream.

"We save our venom for outsiders," Heidi scolded. She did not even attempt to hide her disappointment.

Doreen looked from Heidi to Biz and then back again. "Oh, Bizzy, I'm so sorry!" She threw her arms around her cousin. "Forget what I said. It's all a bit much for me here, I guess. You look fab, really. Maybe I'm a little jealous is all."

"Jealous? Why?"

"You look much better in that thing than I did. Look at you! Where have you been hiding that figure?"

Doreen kiddingly tickled her ribs. Biz blushed. Heidi felt herself release tension. All seemed right with the world again.

"Forgive me?" said Doreen.

"There's nothing to forgive," said Biz.

"Good. Now since you don't have a camera, I will have to do the honors for once. We need some photographic evidence of you in a dress!" Heidi and Biz posed head to head as Doreen snapped a picture with her cell phone. Biz even smiled a little.

"I'm in the picture." Biz looked down at the image on Doreen's phone.

"Now you know how it feels," said Doreen.

"You really look beautiful, Biz," said Heidi. Bad hair, no makeup, no natural gifts to speak of, and it was true, Biz practically glowed.

"Thanks! So! This is a school dance."

The three friends turned and gazed into the party. The grand ballroom of the old Hamilton Colonial Hotel was graceful and elegant, and the lighting and decorations equaled the scale and taste of the space. Even the band was surprisingly hip. This was a party designed for the sons and daughters of the East Coast elite, kids who had seen it all. Dolled up in their finest, the Chandlerians danced and munched and performed the awkward rituals of teenage seduction. Deep down, in a part of her that she let nobody see, not ever, Heidi was impressed.

"Ah, well, here come our dashing gentleman callers," Heidi said with a flick of her head. Gordon Lichter and Peter Standish approached the girls bearing glasses of punch and identical goofball grins typical of the recently stoned. Tieless, in a gorgeous bespoke wool suit, Peter looked as comfortable at a high school dance as he did at the Ritz. Heidi's insides fluttered.

"Welcome back." Heidi accepted the punch that Peter held out for her. It had been spiked, of course, with—what was that? Scotch. Single malt. She would have preferred the booze straight, obviously, but one had to at least attempt to maintain appearances. "How was your foray in the parking lot?"

"Very, uh, refreshing," said Gordon.

Peter grinned and pulled Heidi in by the waist. He smelled wonderful. "Sneaking in a joint in a high school parking lot, spiking the punch with booze. I feel like a kid again."

"Listen to you, the wise old man," said Heidi.

"Cradle robber." Peter gave Heidi a deep kiss that was shorter than she wanted by an hour.

"Biz, you know Gordon, right?" said Doreen.

"Ha! I've known Gordy, like practically my whole life."

"Our mothers are bridge partners," Gordon explained.

"Of course," said Doreen. "Well, this is Peter Standish. Peter, my cousin Elizabeth."

"What's up, Biz?" said Peter.

"Hiya. It's been ages."

"You guys know each other?" asked Doreen.

"Ad-rock," Biz explained. "Harvard. You came to the house for—what was that? Memorial Day?"

"Something like that." Peter had Heidi in the crook of his arm. "Biz here whooped my ass in chess."

"It's what I do."

Heidi could not believe it. Biz was actually socializing, engaging in witty repartee with the boys. She could not have been prouder of her own daughter.

"Everybody knows everybody out here," Doreen said to Heidi under her breath. She looked embarrassed.

"Welcome to the aristocracy," said Heidi with a subtle wink. "The houses are giant, but the world is small."

Gordon rested a hand on the lowest part of Doreen's back, tucking a finger under the lace of her dress. "Let's dance, Doreen."

"Not now, Gordon."

"Come on, please! Please dance with me."

"Okay. Okay, okay! Please excuse us. Gordon seems to have boogie fever."

On the dance floor Gordon was all hands and eyes and hunger, pawing at Doreen, whispering in her ear. When he did look around it was to see if anybody saw him—proud, like he'd won an important prize—and Heidi wondered when or if anybody had ever felt like that about her.

Peter refreshed Heidi's punch with a shot of booze from a flask in his pocket. He gestured with his head at Gordon and Doreen. "When Coburn heard I was coming out to this thing, I think he was hoping he'd also get a call. The kid was a bit sprung on your friend there."

"Yes, well, he's going to have to get in line. Look around! Everybody is looking at her."

"She certainly is something," said Peter.

"Uh, hello?"

"But she's got none of your style."

"There it is. Anyway, do you want to dance?"

Peter smiled, his eyes crinkling up in the corners. "It isn't called the School Stand, is it?" He held out his hand for hers. Nice guy, Heidi thought, smart, wealthy. And a grown-up. She let him take her hand. He was warm to the touch.

But before they could make a move, a great commotion came from near the entrance. "Lay off me! I was invited to this thing, okay? Step off, son, or I'll pummel you!" A deep, male voice penetrated the crowd. "Out of my way! I was invited, I told you."

Heidi had never heard the voice before, but as soon as it reached her ears, she knew to whom it belonged. She peered over the crowd on her towering heels without any doubt as to the source.

Doreen knew it, too. Before she could open her eyes and raise her head from Gordon's shoulder, she knew who the crazed boy pushing and grunting his way toward the bandstand was and what he was after.

Even Biz looked up from her awkward conversation with a girl in her French class, with every expectation that it was Simon Vale who had burst through the doors of the ballroom. Poor, forgotten Simon Vale had come to pry his beloved from the lily-white hands of the ruling class. But he was too late. The hapless quarterback would leave empty-handed. Heidi knew it, Doreen knew it, Biz knew it. The only one who didn't know it was Simon himself.

"Doreen!" he roared. "Dorie!"

"Oh shit," said Heidi.

"Who is that person?" asked Peter, but before Heidi could answer, Simon plowed past them and charged toward the dance floor. With the strength and grace that had first sent Doreen into raptures, he seized Doreen bodily from her dance partner, taking her into his arms and practically carrying her away. Murmuring her name, he kissed her over and over again—on her neck, then her cheek. When Simon went for her mouth, Doreen held up her hand and pushed his face away.

"Simon! Let go of me, please. You're making a scene."

"Ha! As if we care what these preppies think." Simon looked terrible. Scruffy, desperately in need of a haircut, at least he'd had the wherewithal to rent a tuxedo. Heidi elbowed her way through the gathering crowd to get a closer look. What did he think? That he could just show up and become Doreen's date simply by virtue of being there? Doreen stood frozen in her purple lace gown, her lips frowning in disgust. Through it all she remained perfectly calm, with cold, pitiless eyes. Simon tried to nuzzle his face in her hair.

"No, Doreen. We don't care what anyone thinks—all we care about is each other!"

"What *we* is it that you are referring to, Simon? If it's you and I, then let me assure you that such a *we* no longer exists. You have no claim on me, on what I do or don't care about. You are simply you, and I am me, and since this is my school I hope you will make a respectful exit before I have you ejected." The hush in the room was eerie. Doreen gestured to the band to start up again.

"Oh, Doreen, you don't fool me." Simon forced her hand against his cheek. "I know you, Doreen Gray. I know who you are."

Heidi found Gordon Lichter standing at the edge of the dance floor. He watched the confrontation in a silent fume. "Hey," she said.

"Hey." His eyes remained fixed on Doreen. "So I'm wondering if I should kick this guy's ass. Do you think I should?"

Simon was twice Gordon's height and built like a lumberjack. Humiliating as it must have been to witness an unknown kid in a rental tux manhandle his date, it would be more humiliating still to get thrashed in front of the entire senior class.

"Seems, uh, that might get messy," said Heidi. Gordon nodded. Of course, he had no intention of doing anything. Gordon had inherited his slightness of build from his ancestors, but he had inherited something else, too: smug, entitled contempt. As Simon Vale begged and pleaded and bargained with Doreen, Gordon relied on the hundreds of years of his family's dominance over its competitors. Confidently, without panic, he simply stood with his arms crossed. And smirked.

By this time, Simon had grown even more desperate. He dropped to his knees and forced Doreen's hands onto his forehead as if he were praying to a mountaintop guru. It was painful to see.

"Who is that guy? How does Doreen know him?"

"Maybe he's from her old school."

"He looks like a psychopath."

"I wouldn't kick him out of bed, psychopath or not."

"Look at those biceps!"

"He's pathetic!"

"Jesus, is this what happens when you hook up with Doreen Gray?"

"Don't be such a creep, Wes."

"Don't be such a prude, Claire."

"Heidi, who is that? Do you know that guy?"

"Uh, no, but . . . Shut up, okay?"

"Heidi probably knows him."

"She probably hooked up with him, too."

"That's a rental tux. No way Heidi Whelan is touching that with a ten-foot pole."

Heidi plugged her ears. She tried to think of what, if anything, to do. Surely it was a good thing to command so much attention, right? But for how long?

"There you are," Biz said breathlessly. "Should we do something?"

"Honestly? I have no idea," said Heidi. And the comments kept churning.

"Maybe Doreen put a spell on him."

"Yeah, she's like a witch or something. A beautiful she-wizard."

"Gordon Lichter is lucky as shit."

"So you know this guy?" asked Peter over the din.

"He's a quarterback," said Heidi. "An ex-flame."

"I don't think he got the message about the ex part."

"Clearly not."

Biz hopped on her toes. "Can't we help her in some way? Isn't there something you can do? I'm afraid he might hurt her."

"I don't think he has it in him. I mean, look at the poor guy!"

Simon grabbed the hem of Doreen's dress as she tried to escape.

"Yikes," said Peter.

"Oh shit!" said Frankie Cavalieri. He pushed to the front of the crowd, his phone raised up in front of his face. Heidi knocked the cell phone out of his hands before he could take a picture. "What the hell, Heidi!"

"Show some respect," Heidi snarled. "All right, this is ending now."

"Where are you going?"

"No pictures. Okay?" She narrowed her eyes and scanned the crowd. That shut them up. Then, smoothing her dress and throwing back her head, Heidi stepped up to where Simon lay prostrate on the ground. "Simon Vale!" She extended an arm down to his spot on the floor as if they were being introduced at a society function. "How wonderful to finally meet you! I am Heidi Whelan, a dear friend of Doreen's." Simon looked up at her with red eyes. He gazed at her extended hand as if unsure of what it was, and for a moment Heidi was afraid that he might try to bite it off with his teeth. But somehow he got a hold of himself and made his way to his feet.

"Nice to meet you," he said, and even managed a polite smile as he shook Heidi's hand.

"Heidi was in attendance at your last home game. It was my intention to introduce you after the game, but after your abysmal performance, she did me the great favor of leaving at halftime so as not to prolong my embarrassment." Doreen's eyes showed no mercy. Her perfectly glossed upper lip curled in revulsion as she spoke. "Of course, I believed that would be the last time you would embarrass me, Simon Vale. I believed I had the good fortune of never having to see you again."

"Oh, Dorie. Please don't talk that way to me."

"What choice do I have, Simon? I don't love you. Leave me alone."

Heidi cleared her throat. "Yes, well. It is marvelous to meet you at last, Simon. But I'm afraid the time has come to say good-bye now." The poor wretch was so hunched over with defeat he had to look up at Heidi in order to nod in hangdog compliance. An Adonis, a Thor, and look at what little Doreen Gray had done to him. Heidi held out her hand and, like a child, he allowed her to lead him toward the door for a few paces.

"Go on!" someone yelled. "Get the hell out of here."

"Go back to where you belong!" A giant boo emerged from the throng. Heidi tried to silence them with her eyes. But it was too late.

Simon looked around as if awakened from a trance. "Wait! Where are you taking me? You're trying to pull us apart? That's not going to happen, do you hear me? This is bigger than you. Doreen! Doreen!"

He shook out of Heidi's grasp and lunged at the dance floor. He reached out his arms and hurtled his body toward Doreen, and was stopped by a swift, unerring punch in the face. He dropped to the floor.

"Ouch," said Peter, rubbing his hand.

"Oh, thank god," said Heidi. "My hero!" The crowd

burst into cheers and applause. Peter grinned and pulled Simon up off the ground.

"You all right? Sorry about that, man."

Simon nodded, finally giving up hope.

"Okay, we're going now," said Heidi. "For real this time. You ready?" With her arm on the poor kid's back, she walked with Simon toward the exit.

"Did you see that?"

"That was crazy. Ho-ly crap."

"Oh man. I should've taken a picture. That shit would go viral in like a second."

"And cross Heidi Whelan? Are you out of your mind? Don't you remember what she did to Tatiana Wang that one time? That girl had to *transfer schools*."

"Yeah, man. Why do you think I didn't do it?"

When Simon and Heidi slipped out of the ballroom, nobody noticed.

———◉◉———

It was quiet and musty in the lobby. Simon dragged his feet toward the door. Heidi felt almost sorry for the guy, despite his wildly inappropriate behavior. "You need to forget all about her," she said. "I'm serious. She's not going to come around, so you may as well move on. You'll be better off."

"She destroyed me," said Simon Vale.

"You'll be okay. You're a football star! There are plenty of other girls."

Simon stopped and looked at Heidi. His eye was bruised and bloody. "Not for me." He managed to smile a little, but it was a smile so heavy with sorrow and pain that Heidi couldn't imagine that a sob or a scream would seem sadder. "Thank you. I know you're just trying to be helpful."

"Take care of yourself," Heidi said, but the quarterback had hunched into his tux jacket and disappeared into the empty autumn night.

Heidi was happy to see him go. Wasn't she? She'd wanted them to separate since the moment they got together and there was no question of that now. But still it felt wrong, the way Doreen had treated him. Did it have to be so humiliating? Did she have to be so cruel? Though, undoubtedly, she had done wonders for her social status. Doreen made herself into the talk of the dance.

Heidi stopped in the bathroom to freshen her lipstick. She told herself to put the image of the fallen quarterback out of her mind. "He'll be fine," she told her reflection. "It's nothing but a high school crush." But somehow it seemed like more than that.

Heidi heard the band strike up a fast dance number, but when she returned to the ballroom she saw that nobody was dancing. All eyes were on Doreen, who stood in front of Gordon on the dance floor. He was saying something, but before he could finish, Doreen had his mouth with her lips, her teeth, her tongue. She pressed herself against him, kissing, kissing, deep and long and hard. People whooped and whistled. Heidi could see Doreen performing for the crowd, giving them a show. When they separated, Gordon was dough in her hands. She whispered something in his ear and took his hand.

All in attendance at the Fall Dance watched as, hand in hand, Doreen Gray and Gordon Lichter made their exit. Heidi found Biz and Peter by the punch bowl and together they witnessed the triumphant gleam in Doreen's eye, the light that shined from her as she led her besotted date toward the fulfillment of his fantasies. What a fantastic bitch, thought Heidi with some awe.

"She looks so beautiful," Biz said. "I wish . . ." Her hands twisted around themselves.

"What?" asked Heidi.

"I wish I had my camera."

17

"There you are. Aren't you cold?" Peter stepped out to join Heidi on the terrace of their suite. Even though it was dark outside, Heidi could see the hotel's gazebo on the lawn, a small, manicured lake beyond it, and the distant hills. It all smelled clean, like change. Peter wore a salmon-colored bathrobe with the hotel's initials embroidered on it, and the effeminate getup made him seem even more virile and masculine by comparison. He handed Heidi a glass of red wine.

"Where did you get this? Oh, I don't care. Thank you. How is your hand?"

"A little stiff, but on the mend."

Heidi could only imagine what that meant for Simon's face. "I was impressed. You were pretty brave."

"I don't know about that. It was more or less a sucker punch, but I was happy to be of service. That Gordon character didn't exactly seem up for the job."

"No. I'm sure you're right about that." Heidi leaned over the railing and breathed in the crisp night. Peter did the same.

"It's warmer than I thought," he said.

"It's lovely, isn't it? You know, I'm from the city."

"I didn't know that," Peter said with a smile. "Which city is that? Wait, you don't have to tell me. Anybody who refers to their hometown as *the* city, as if there were only one in the world, could only be from New York."

"Yes, well. Nature always surprises me. It's so busy, in its own way, like a city, but for plants and animals."

"That's a way of thinking about it, I guess."

For a minute they stood in delicious silence—private and yet comforting.

"Heidi Whelan from New York," Peter said at last. "So that's two."

"Sorry? Two what?"

"Two details about your life." Peter turned his back on the landscape and leaned his elbows on the railing, gazing with amusement at Heidi. "In addition to spending time at the Montauk Inn, you are from New York City. Other than that I know only that you attend Chandler Academy."

"So that's three."

"And have very sensitive ears." He leaned forward and nibbled on one to demonstrate and Heidi giggled. "See?"

"I'm a private person, I guess."

"Private? No. This terrace is private. As a person you are like Fort Knox. I'm not criticizing—I'm only observing. One might think, sugarplum, that you have something to hide."

Heidi could feel her face flush. She was happy for the cover of night. "I will say that my reticence gets remarkably little attention from most gentlemen."

"That's because you distract them. By being so sexy."

"And by keeping the conversation on them. Speaking of, other than the unfortunate walloping, did you have an okay time at the dance? It must have been sort of silly to play high school again at your advanced age of twenty."

"Oh, no. Not so fast. We aren't done with you yet."

"No?" Heidi took a sip of wine.

"So you are from New York City. East Side? West Side? What? Tribeca?"

"Me? Oh. I grew up in Yonkers." It was amazing. The fact came right out of Heidi's mouth as if it was the most natural thing in the world. Why couldn't she find a way to skirt the issue? Or, barring that, simply lie! Here was this blue blood—handsome, interesting, intelligent. She never let anyone know who she was or where she came from, so why start now?

"Yonkers? That explains it then."

"Explains what?" Heidi's heart was rattling against her rib cage.

"Explains why nobody I asked had ever heard of you—and why you are so much more exciting than the other girls that my mother is forever flinging at me. Yonkers, Yonkers. My mind is a blank. What's it like there?"

"It's very nice."

"Oh, come on! Very nice. Who are you? Who are your folks? I want to know everything about you! Let me guess, your family is in real estate. No? Uh, doctor-lawyer type guy? No. Let me think."

Heidi sighed. "Sanitation. My father is a garbage man. Good? Speechless? That's not unexpected. Let me know when you recover from the shock."

"Me? Not at all! I mean, it's not what I expected to hear."

"Okay, shall I go on then?"

"Please do! Tell me everything."

"Everything? Well, my family is Irish Catholic. Especially my mother. She's a true believer—crucifix over her bed, Hail Marys on the subway, the whole bit. She says *drapes* instead of *curtains* and *sofa* instead of *couch* because she thinks it's classier. She is in love with France. When it came time to pick a language, I picked Spanish because screw her. Also, I told her I gave up piano but I still play secretly when she's not home."

"You play piano?"

"My father gets all of his news from the *New York Post*. He doesn't vote because he says all politicians are the same, full of malarkey. That's a word he uses without irony. He said he would vote for Derek Jeter, and that's about it." Was it the wine that made her so loose-lipped? And her accent was slipping. Where were those carefully trained *r*'s? The nice round *a*'s?

"I'm on full scholarship. And I'm eighteen. When I transferred from my piece-of-shit public school the dean made me repeat my sophomore year, though nobody knows that, not even my roommate. My sister, Katie, waxes lady parts at Roberto's International Hair Salon on South Broadway. Her boyfriend is an elevator repairman, which, in my neighborhood, is considered a high-status job because they have a strong union. His name is Donald and he is almost completely bald."

Peter giggled.

"I'm not in the least bit joking. Know what else?" Heidi felt electrified and alive. Adrenaline pumped through her. "That girl Nicole? From the Ritz? The girl who knew me from the Montauk Inn? She was my coworker. I worked a summer there as the front desk girl and then I got fired." And here she stopped. The truths had spewed out, like something she'd been holding back for too long, something her body rejected. Probably the boy would never speak to her again, never return a text or an e-mail. She may as well go all the way. "For smoking weed in the boiler room."

And with the last, single lie, the final upheld boundary, Heidi felt depleted, like she could sleep for a decade. She collapsed into a white Adirondack chair. She closed her eyes. For a minute nobody said anything.

"Wow. I mean, wow."

Heidi looked up at Peter Standish III. He stood in the peach robe, his hand on his hips and a big old grin on his face. Was this all somehow funny to him? This, her, her whole life. All at once the enormity of all she had admitted descended on Heidi.

"Oh god," she said. "Excuse me."

Heidi leaped up from the chair and escaped past the glass doors into their suite. She unfolded the luggage stand, unzipped her bag, and began to pack. Why? Why had she gone so far? Said so much? After everything she'd done—the careful misdirections, the intricate layering of ambiguities, the persona that she'd created for herself from nothing—why had she given it all away to this Harvard boy? She didn't know. But it had something to do with Doreen, of that she was quite positive. Watching her friend perform as she did at the dance had made Heidi feel invincible.

She threw her dress, shoes, and underwear into her bag. She went into the bathroom for her hair dryer and makeup bag.

"Where are you going?" asked Peter, the amused look still on his face. He slid the glass door closed behind him. "Wait, hold on now. What's going on?"

"It's fine, okay? Don't worry about it."

"Will you stop packing, please? It's the middle of the night! You're not going anywhere."

"Look, I know how this works." At least her accent slip had been temporary. The *d*'s and *t*'s came tripping off her tongue like any high-class broad. *What?* "I know I just wrote my ticket out. I can't for the life of me understand why the fu—why I did it, but there it is, and I'll be going now so you don't have to worry. I would ask you not to tell anyone, but I'm sure that's more than I can expect." She checked under the bed for stray objects. She saw the watch, thin gold band, delicate, the one Roland had given her in that other hotel, the one she told people had been a gift from her father. She thought of leaving it there under the bed for a maid to find, but she picked it up, wrapped it around her wrist. She buttoned a shirt on over her negligee and hopped into a pair of jeans.

"Just wait. Stop it. Heidi! Stop!" Peter grabbed her arm and gave her a shake. "You don't honestly think I care about any of that, do you? I don't know what kind of villain you think I am, but this isn't the seventeenth century. You think I want some fancy-pants Connecticut heiress? Some dull, overindulged, diamond-hungry socialite? Why? To protect the Standish name? No, thank you. No. I'll take this, us, you, over that. I'll take brilliant and witty and gorgeous. Was I surprised to hear about where you come from? Yes. But I shouldn't have been. I should have known from your quick mind that you were different than all those nitwits I grew up with." They were standing very close now. He grasped both arms above the elbow. Heidi could hear her own breath.

"You. You are an exciting person, Heidi Whelan." He slid a finger up her throat. He kissed her—*her*, the true, authentic Heidi Whelan, and it felt so different. She felt something unlatch within her, like a door opening after a long time, letting the light come in. It was just Heidi there, just Heidi and Peter. It was more than a kiss. It was a revelation.

"Talk to me. Talk like a girl from Yonkers," Peter whispered. "Talk to me, Heidi Whelan, like it's public school, like we're under the bleachers."

"I don't know what you are *tawkin'* about, okay?"

18

Heidi Whelan raced across the quad as fast as she could, threading through packs of kids bundled up against the cold, still buzzing from last night's dance. She did not slow down enough to listen to what they were saying, though she was sure that her friend was taking up a lot of real estate in the campus gossip. What were they calling Doreen? Heartbreaker? Man Eater? Fine. Good, even. But murderer? Heidi sped up her pace. They had to keep control of the story before it got out. She hoped it wasn't too late.

She scampered up the stairs to Doreen's room, but Doreen did not answer the door right away. Heidi had to bang and jiggle the handle, yelling out Doreen's name in desperation. Where could she have gone? Heidi's imagination reeled. Finally, after some minutes, Doreen opened the door.

"Oh, thank god," said Heidi. She burst into Doreen's room. "I thought—you don't know what I thought. You never returned my messages. I was worried."

"You sound like my cousin," said Doreen with a smirk. "Anyway, I'm fine. I've just been studying is all."

"Studying?" Heidi stood gaping as if unsure of the word's intended meaning. She looked at the pile of books on Doreen's desk. "That's unexpected."

"Yes, studying. And if you don't mind—"

"Listen, Dorie, the whole thing is terrible, of course. It's just awful and I wanted to be sure you weren't taking it all too hard. I was afraid I'd find you here, I don't know, pulling out your hair or sobbing, pounding your chest."

"What are you talking about?"

"Darling! Simon! Simon Vale!"

Doreen cringed at the mention of his name. "It's unfortunate, of course."

Heidi nodded gravely. "Doreen, I'm so sorry about the way things went down, but there's no point in blaming yourself."

"Blame myself? I have no intention . . . You see, I've figured the whole thing out. I'm going to fix it."

"Really? How?"

"Well, admittedly, I did wake up this morning with a bit of a bad taste in my mouth. Not literally—after all, the suite where I stayed with Gordon at Hamilton Colonial was exquisite and there were breakfast pastries and cappuccinos and tiny glass jars of French jam. But something about the whole scene last night, it made me feel rotten. I did love Simon and I never loved Gordon—I never could or will love Gordon. I love his power and his access, but there's more to life, I know there is. So I've resolved to be better. I realize that I've lost touch with the girl that I was back in Indiana. And I want to get back to that person, to make my insides more beautiful. I want to be good, Heidi, and that all begins with Simon."

"But Doreen—"

"Look, don't bother with your disapprovals. I don't want to hear it. I've tried it your way and look where it's gotten me! Sure, I got to wear a fancy dress and stay in a fancy suite, but for what? Simon is a good person, he has a good and giving soul. I should never have treated him that way. And so my plan is to make up with him."

"Make up with him?"

"Yes, Heidi. And you can skip the list of reasons why he is unsuitable or embarrassing. I just don't care about any of that. I am going to march up to Leaving Place and beg that boy to forgive me. I'll get down on my knees if I have to."

"Leaving Place? But, Doreen, didn't you get my text messages or e-mails? Haven't you seen? It's all over GryphPages!"

"I don't have a profile. I turned my phone off. What is it?"

Heidi pushed her friend aside and logged onto her own profile on Doreen's old laptop. She clicked a link to the *Chandler Times* homepage.

"I've been trying to reach you all day," she said as Doreen sunk into her desk chair.

HOMETOWN FOOTBALL HERO
SURVIVES SUICIDE STUNT

Simon Vale, 17, apparently threw himself off the Peabody Street Bridge early on Sunday morning. Vale was seen jumping off the bridge some hours after attempting to gain entry into the Chandler Fall Dance at the Hamilton Colonial Hotel on Saturday night. The extent of his injuries is unknown at this time, but onlookers claim that he was in stable condition, though obviously in pain, when the paramedics arrived to retrieve him from the bottom of the ravine. Until recent weeks, Vale was the star quarterback of the Hamilton High School football team. A series of bizarre performances on the field led the coach to bench him for the last game against the Manchester Wild Cats. "He's been acting wicked strange for a while now," says Coach McCullers. "I don't know what's been up with that kid."

"Stable condition, see?" said Heidi. "That means he's going to be okay. The Peabody Street Bridge is pretty small. I'm sure it was just a cry for help. Doreen? Dorie? Are you all right?"

But Doreen didn't answer. She groped her way to the bed and sat down. "So I killed him. I killed Simon Vale."

"No, Dorie, I told you, he's in stable condition. He's going to survive. It even says so in the headline."

"But he wanted to die, Heidi, didn't he? And it's all because of me, because I told him I didn't love him. I was so cruel to him. Didn't you walk him out of the dance? You did, didn't you?"

"Yes." Heidi thought of the hopelessness on Simon's bleeding face as he walked away in his rented tux.

"How did he seem then?"

Heidi was surprised to see that her friend's eyes were dry of tears. She seemed shocked, of course, but also somewhat delighted. Heidi was sure of it. "Oh, he was pretty low. I don't think the evening had gone as he'd planned."

"No. No, of course it didn't. He wanted me back. He loved me so much, and there I was with Gordon Lichter. To think! Heidi, if I saw this in a movie I'm sure I would cry my eyes out! But somehow, since it is happening to me, I feel more astonished than anything else. It's so strange. Simon Vale tried to end his life because he couldn't have me. But I'm still here and you're still here. People are eating. My biology test is still on Tuesday. Everything goes on just the same." A faraway look came into Doreen's eyes as she gazed out the window onto the darkened quad. "There's something sort of beautiful about it, the way time goes on, indifferently."

"Yes. And I think you should, too. That's part of the reason why I came by. I think we should go to the dining hall and make an appearance. Nobody knew Simon's name, but since the paper mentions his attempt to infiltrate the dance, people are definitely going to make the connection. This kind of scandal—we're in some unchartered territory here, Doreen, and I honestly have no idea how it will go for you. But staying holed up in your room makes it seem like you feel guilty."

"But I don't. Maybe I should, but I don't feel guilty. Do you think that sounds heartless?"

"The guy was disturbed. He wanted you to be much more than any girl could be to any boy. He wanted you to save him. What did I tell you about influence? Simon couldn't live without you to follow, or anyway, he thought he couldn't. Clearly that's about an emptiness inside him—it has nothing to do with you. Can you help it if you're beau tiful? And kind?" She added with slightly less conviction.

"But I was so mean to him after the football game. I never told you about it, Heidi. All of a sudden he seemed disgusting to me. Has that ever happened to you? One minute I was walking around on a love cloud and the next I find Simon Vale to be physically repulsive."

"It was a pretty pathetic football game."

"But I think what you said was right. He said he'd done it for me, played like that, embarrassed himself, because football no longer mattered. It was too much! It was weak! I didn't want a child; I wanted a man. You don't think I'm some sort of monster, do you? I couldn't take it if you did."

Heidi sat down next to her and Doreen rested her head against her shoulder. "No, Doreen. No, of course I don't think you're a monster. It's hard not to feel bad for Simon, but he made his own choices."

"And to think that I was going to make up with him! I can't decide if that would have been better or worse."

Their intimacy was like a warm blanket, securing them to one another, and despite the circumstances, Heidi allowed herself to feel comforted. She wanted Doreen to survive this scandal for a host of reasons—her own reputation could suffer by association, and then there was the Roland problem, the sense of failure if Doreen were to become an outcast so early. But overriding all of that was basic concern for her friend's well-being. She'd been given an unexpected gift of true friendship, and she would do what she could to save her.

"Listen, Dorie, why don't you get dressed and we'll go down to the cafeteria, okay? You'll have a nibble of sandwich or something, show your face. How does that sound?"

"If you think it's best, Heidi, I'm happy to." Doreen gazed at her desk. "Just, one thing. If you don't mind."

"What do you need, Doreen? Anything."

"I wouldn't mind a minute alone. Just to collect myself. Would that be all right?"

Heidi smiled. "I understand, of course. I'll just wait for you outside. I should call Peter anyway."

"I don't know what I'd do without you, Heidi. I've never had a friend like you—never in my life."

Heidi stopped at the doorway and winked at Doreen. "This is just the beginning, kid." And swinging Biz's maroon Ferragamo over her shoulder, she let herself out.

——◦◦——

As soon as she heard the door click closed, Doreen scrambled over to her desk. She couldn't wait anymore, she had to look. The truth was, she'd been obsessing about the picture all day. The creepy change she saw before was in her head, that's what she told herself over and over again, but still, she had an odd notion that the picture was tracking her every move. And after the way she'd treated Simon at the dance, she couldn't help wondering if the picture had gotten even worse. It was crazy, crazy! But she'd been too afraid to find out. Instead she had vowed to make up with Simon, study, improve herself.

And with Heidi's news that Simon had thrown himself off the bridge because of her, she couldn't avoid it any longer. She had to see for certain if she'd made up the change in the image and if the recent events had any additional effect. Better to know what she was up against, what the picture had in store. With shaking hands, she opened the top drawer of her desk and slid out the photograph.

This time, there could be no doubt. It was real! It happened! The change in the image she'd seen before was no product of her imagination; it was right there in front of her, only worse, more horrifying. The eyes blazed cruelly, the mouth had become redder, as if from blood. There were grotesque boils popping up in the skin. She gave out a cry.

"Doreen? Are you okay?" Heidi asked from the hallway.

"Uh, what? Oh, yeah, I just . . . I stepped on an earring."

"Oh, okay. Almost ready? The dining hall closes in an hour."

"Just give me one more minute!" Doreen paced around her room. What should she do? How could she fix this? She thought of ways to make herself better, to counteract the damage that had already been done, but she didn't know how to begin—or if it would even work. She'd have to be a nun, or even better than a nun! She'd have to be Biz! No more boys or distractions. No more manipulating or materialism. No more life.

"No more life," she whispered. A shiver went down her spine. What a sacrifice. She caught her reflection in the full-length mirror. That girl, the one with the skin of a doll and the face of a model, her hair flowing and soft, would she have to ignore all the perks of beauty in order to be good? It seemed such a shame.

She rubbed some lip gloss on her lips, tied back her lustrous hair. She watched herself do it—so gracefully. How could anyone who looked so perfect be bad? And then it dawned on her. Of course! Why didn't she think of it earlier? She didn't have to change a thing. Doreen Gray could act exactly as she liked. She grinned.

So the picture was getting worse. What of it? Doreen herself had never looked prettier. Look! Look at that girl in the mirror. The only thing that mattered was how she appeared, and her appearance was perfect. She slid the photograph back into the drawer. She'd keep it around for kicks, but she was free to live her life as she wanted, liberated from guilt! Free to stuff herself on the banquet of life! Almost skipping, she ran out to meet her friend.

A wind cut through the quad. Winter was coming, and it wasn't going to be nice about it.

"Brr!" Doreen took Heidi's arm. "Doesn't the cafeteria look warm and inviting? I hope there's soup tonight."

"Doreen, listen, you don't have to worry. Just be yourself in there, okay? I'm sure everything will just take care of itself. You are on the side of the angels now."

But Doreen wasn't listening.

"Marvelous, marvelous. To be young! Heidi, to live without doubts. Everybody should be so lucky!"

She was a fascinating person, that Doreen Gray.

19

Blue blazers and cashmere sweater sets clustered together between classes. The day was gray and overcast, but Biz had no problem spotting Doreen. In her red coat, huge sunglasses and a dramatic black scarf, she looked like a movie star on the lam.

"Doreen! Doreen!" Biz called out the window of the astronomy lab, but her cousin continued her diagonal path across campus.

Biz fled down the stairs of the science building and raced across the lawn to catch up with her. Since hearing about the Simon Vale tragedy, Biz had left countless messages on Doreen's voice mail, plus e-mails and text messages. She even waited outside Doreen's art history class that morning, but Doreen never appeared. It broke Biz's heart to think of her cousin so despairing. Biz called her name again from a few feet away, but it wasn't until Biz could reach out and lay a hand on her shoulder that Doreen noticed her.

"Jesus, Elizabeth. Do you have to paw me?"

"I tried . . . I saw you . . . I ran . . ." Biz panted, clinging to the wool of Doreen's coat and trying to catch her breath. "Are you . . . How? Is everything? I'm . . . I'm so, so sorry." She threw her arms around Doreen. "I can't imagine what you must be going through."

Doreen squirmed out of her cousin's embrace. "I don't know what you're talking about, but please let go of me. I'm not feeling well." Doreen resumed her quick pace, and Biz hustled along beside her.

"Of course, the whole thing is too grim. The poor guy!

Have you spoken to his mother? Do you know how he's doing? When I didn't see you at art history today I thought maybe you'd gone to visit."

"To visit? Who would I go to visit at nine o'clock in the morning?"

Biz could see herself blinking dumbly in the black glass of Doreen's Miu Mius. "Who? Well, Simon Vale! You heard, of course, of his, um, tumble off the Peabody Street Bridge after the dance?"

"Oh, *that*. Are we still talking about that? That was ages ago."

"Ages ago? Doreen, it happened yesterday! I'm sure Simon is still in the hospital. Do you know how he's doing? Will they let him out or will he have to be institutionalized? Do you think he really meant to kill himself or was it just a cry for help thing? Me, I thought maybe he was trying to get your attention, not that it's your fault or anything. Any more than Reagan's attempted assassination could be blamed on Jodie Foster."

"Biz! Please!" They'd stopped in front of Doreen's dorm. Doreen flipped back her sunglasses to rest on top of her head, exposing red, blurry eyes. She squeezed the bridge of her nose. "I have a terrible headache. I had a dawn visit from Gordon this morning, complete with champagne."

Leaving the dorm room after ten at night was strictly forbidden and could result in expulsion from Chandler. But at five o'clock in the morning, curfew was lifted. And since there was no faculty around at that hour and campus safety was no longer trolling for fugitives, many would-be paramours used that time to sneak into their lovers' beds. Breaking visitation was a far lesser crime than breaking curfew, though Biz always thought that setting an alarm to squeeze in a little sex before classes began was a disgusting way to go about courtship.

"Gordon? Champagne? But you couldn't have! Not while you knew that poor Simon Vale was in the hospital!"

"Lay off the righteous indignation, Elizabeth. Okay? You said yourself that what happened to Simon Vale had nothing to do with me."

"Wait. No, I said it wasn't your fault. Obviously, I mean it must have had *something* to do with you, Doreen. He did love you, right? It seemed that he loved you very much."

"That's his problem, isn't it?" Doreen sighed. "I'm sorry, Biz, I'm going on zero sleep here. I need to go up and lie down."

"So that's what you were doing during art history? Sleeping one off? While Simon Vale fought for his life in the hospital?"

Doreen sighed again. "Good-bye, Biz," she said, and marched into her dorm.

"Wait, Doreen!" Biz ran after her, following her into West Hall. "I'm sorry. Look, there's something else I wanted to talk to you about."

Biz had good news to share. The week since her realization in the photo lab had been the most productive of her life. Something clicked for the young artist. The art that seemed so out of reach only a few days ago seemed to bend to her every whim now. The work was good; it was better than good. In her best moments, looking at what she'd made, Biz allowed herself to believe that she was approaching the creation of something beautiful.

And she wasn't the only one who noticed. When Mr. Cameron saw what she was working on, he was speechless. On the spot he offered Biz her first solo photography exhibit. It would be in Douglas Hall during Parents' Weekend. There would be a group show in the gallery, but he wanted to give Biz her own space. He said that her work was on such a different level from her classmates that they would suffer by comparison.

"I know it's just a high school show, but at this school you never know who is coming for Parents' Weekend. This could actually turn into something big for me, something of my own." Biz followed Doreen up the stairs. "You should have heard what he said about my portfolio, Dorie. He was very complimentary. He was excited. He said, I mean, I don't want to brag, but he called the work brilliant. But I really feel my portfolio isn't complete. I know your relationship with that picture is complicated, but now that some time has passed, you must be able to see how strong it is, compositionally speaking. And since I destroyed all the files on my computer just as I told you I would, I thought maybe you still had a hard copy."

Once in her room, Doreen collapsed onto the bed.

"You do still have it, don't you?" asked Biz, looking around.

"Have what? What are you on about?"

"Wow, Dorie, you really are in a fog today. The picture that I printed of you in the red dress. I want to include it in the show. Is it in your desk?" Biz innocently slid open the top drawer of Doreen's desk.

"No!" Doreen lunged and slammed the drawer closed. Biz withdrew her hand just in time to avoid losing all her fingers.

"Jeez. What's gotten into you, Doreen?"

"I don't have the picture, okay? I tore it up. I destroyed it. Nuked it. Burned it. The point is it's gone, so I'm afraid I can't help you."

"But you said that you wouldn't do that. Remember? You said you wanted to keep it as a reminder."

"That was a long time ago, Biz. I don't know why I would keep a stupid picture you gave me months ago. Sorry I can't help you, but I really have to lie down. I am not feeling well at all."

"You do seem a bit, uh, piqued." Biz studied her cousin.

Doreen attempted a smile but it came out like a wince. "I am, really. Maybe I'm coming down with something. The flu maybe. Jessica Feinberg down the hall is practically tubercular. I think she has pneumonia, so I should probably, you know, rest. Lovely to see you. Kiss, kiss."

"Yes. Maybe rest is the thing. You've been through a lot these past days. It's probably affecting you more than you know. I'll go to the dean and tell him you're not up for your afternoon classes. It's a bit of a relief, actually. To be honest you seemed a bit coldhearted before."

"No, no. That was only a cover. Self-protection and everything, you know, trying to take it all in. The truth is you're right, Bizzy. I'm really very despondent over the whole thing." Fully clothed, Doreen climbed into the bed. "Yes, poor Simon. Poor, poor Simon Vale."

———••———

As soon as Doreen spotted Biz on the quad, she launched herself from the bed and paced around her room. Obviously, she couldn't leave the picture in her drawer. There were too many snoops around, constantly dropping by, nosing around in places they did not belong. She'd barely managed to avoid complete disaster with Biz. And what if Gordon was digging around for a condom? Or Heidi needed a pen? No, no. The desk was totally unsuitable.

She opened her closet. Maybe some shoebox? Or tucked into an ice skate or something? But still that did not seem far enough away. She would be constantly tempted to pull the picture out and check on her soul's progress—which would be bad for her well-being and completely catastrophic should someone catch her in the act. Suddenly her room felt unbearably small and vulnerable, as if every corner and every drawer had the power to expose her secret.

Okay, she thought, time for action. Doreen pulled out her American literature folder and dumped all the papers onto the bed. Without looking at the image, she slipped the picture from her desk drawer into the folder. Then she found a big manila envelope filled with family photos.

She added the photos to the pile of papers on the bed and dropped the folder into the envelope, securing the string enclosure and taping the flap closed with packing tape. The package seemed innocuous enough, but she could still feel the beating heart of the picture inside. The black plastic bag in which Gordon had toted the bottles of champagne that morning was still in her wastepaper basket. She retrieved the bag and dropped the envelope inside, using the rest of her packing tape to secure the plastic around it. She felt the size and shape of the parcel in her hand. It looked like nothing, like trash. The act of disguising the evidence of her shameful secret made her feel powerful and in control.

Next item on her agenda: long-term storage.

Every floor of West Hall had a garbage shoot. And if there was a garbage shoot, there must be a garbage room, some deep, smelly pit in the basement where few would venture and nobody would want to stay for long.

Doreen tucked the package under her arm and made for the stairs. She descended to the basement and pushed past the fire door, entering a dark concrete room with huge piles of garbage in stacks along the walls. The room had a wet, festering smell that reminded her of a weekend she spent with her mother at a bed-and-breakfast near Dubuque, Iowa, on the Mississippi River. There had been a recent flood, and as they drove to the inn from the highway, Doreen saw shards of broken furniture and drywall and other wood scraps in heaps along the side of the road. She could smell the mildew in the air from the rotten detritus, and they did not get a break from the smell all weekend—not in the cutesy little inn or in restaurants or in the movie theater.

Doreen shook herself. What a time to think of that, her mother and that long-ago trip! She needed to focus—time was ticking. The main room of the basement was unsuitable, but it opened up into two smaller rooms at the back. Doreen chose the one on the right first. She found an exposed light switch on the wall and a florescent tube flickered to life overhead, revealing a smallish workroom with power drills, metal tools, and extension cords scattered around the place. Here the rotten stink merged with the smell of paint thinner and machine oil.

The walls were open, with pink puffs of insulation packed between wooden beams. But the room seemed too active. Things were always breaking down, weren't they? Somebody had to fix them, and that somebody would come here. Doreen flicked off the overhead light on her way out.

The other room was smaller and darker, with only a dim incandescent bulb overhead. She spotted a flashlight and used that to assess the contents of the room. It appeared to serve as a storage area for electrical wiring, plastic tubing, and other seemingly worthless items. Extralong mattresses wrapped in plastic leaned against a wall. Doreen squeezed past some bed frames at the back of the room. Along the back wall she found a metal ladder coming out from the ceiling.

"This must go somewhere," she said, needing the human sound of her own voice in order to muster up the necessary courage. The ceiling looked closed, but nevertheless, with her package still under her arm and the flashlight tucked into her neck, Doreen climbed the ladder.

Sure enough, Doreen found a square opening cut out of the ceiling with just an unpainted piece of drywall laying over it. She slid the drywall aside easily, and climbing another rung on the metal ladder, shined the flashlight into a small, dark crawl space. There were a few dusty blankets and some filthy rolled-up butcher paper, but nobody human had been up there for a long time, probably years. Doreen envisioned the image of her soul sequestered in that dank, uninhabited space while the rest of her enjoyed the pleasures of her new social position out in the world. She smiled to herself at the perfection of the setting.

"You think that 'cause they're girls they'd be clean and sweet," a man's voice boomed from the front room.

Doreen hurled herself into the crawl space. She slid the drywall cover closed and clicked off the flashlight. Huddling her knees against her body, she crouched by the old blankets and tried to make herself as small as possible. The air was still and thick with dust and the smell of moldering wool. The darkness was impenetrable.

"But these kids are used to being picked up after. Something gets broke, I've seen it with my own eyes, it turns into instant garbage," the voice carried on.

"Mm-hm," responded another gruffer voice. "I know what you mean."

"You should see some of the stuff that gets thrown out around here. A computer missing a single key on the keyboard. Clothes. Televisions. Hey, I'm not proud. You don't want your father's fancy shit, girl? I got no problem taking that home. Or selling it. I sold a violin to some guy over in Radley? Guy gave me a hundred bucks for it. That's free money. Now, what's that light doing on?"

Doreen could hear that the men had come into the storage room directly below her. She tried to make her breathing as quiet and slow as possible, though she was finding it harder and harder to take in the stale air.

"Anyway," the man droned on. Doreen heard the scraping sound of things being kicked and moved around a few feet beneath where she sat. "Let's see now. Ah, here we go. This what you need?"

"Let me see," said the gruffer voice. "Hard to see in here."

"Thought I had a flashlight," said the first man. Doreen tightened her grip on the flashlight in her hand. "I could swear I had one right here."

"I think this will do it. Help me lug it out, will you?" said the second man. Doreen heard the men strain and direct one another as they moved something out of the room. She heard the freight elevator ding. And then, like a beautiful gift, she heard nothing at all.

Doreen sat in silence for some minutes before she dared to move. When at last she felt sure that she was safe, she clicked on the flashlight. She hid her package among the rotten blankets. The air, dense with trash and paint, smelled fresh as a new day when she slid open the drywall door to her cell. Carefully, she replaced the drywall and scrambled down the ladder. She thought she would leave the flashlight where she'd found it, then thought better of it. For all the man knew, he'd lost the thing somewhere.

Filthy, disgusted with her state, Doreen hustled up the stairs. *Let it decay there*, she thought as she ripped off her clothes and made for the showers. *Let it rot and stink and fester in that nasty crawl space.*

What she was referring to, of course, was her own wretched soul.

20

Biz tried to ignore Heidi's telephone chatter and focus on her calculus homework, but it was impossible. Heidi had been at it for hours, making one call after another from a prone position on the chesterfield.

"She generously agreed to a few dates. That's just the kind of person Doreen is, you know. Even coming from her family, she is not a snob. Anyway, they barely even kissed when the guy went bonkers. He called her constantly, came to campus to try and see her. Eventually, she didn't have a choice, she had to break things off with him. Love him? She hardly knew him!"

With each telling of the story Simon became more obsessed and crazy while Doreen became more and more of a passive victim.

"And the way he handled her at the dance! Didn't he seem a bit forceful? He is an athlete, after all. He is trained to push people around, to use his strength to get what he wants. Huh? No, I'm not saying he hit her. Well, she never said he hit her. Of course, victims of domestic abuse rarely say anything."

"Oh, for crying out loud," said Biz.

Heidi shot Biz a look. "What? That's nice of you to say, Miyuki. I'll let her know. Oh, she's strong, you know. Gordon has been a real comfort. Okay. Okay. Sure, you too. Bye!" She clicked off the phone. "What is your problem?" she fired at Biz.

"Problem? I don't have a problem. I have a math problem, is that what you mean?"

"You've been making little disapproving noises all day.

Look, I'm trying to help your cousin here. If you're not going to contribute, the least you can do is—"

"Help? How is this helping? You're lying! You are spreading lies about her."

"I am not!"

"Heidi, you are telling people things about Doreen that aren't true. That is the definition of lying. And I don't understand the point when she didn't do anything wrong."

"It's not lying. It's managing. If we let them control the story, they'll go negative. I'm telling you, everyone prefers a scandal that has the pretty girl going down. This way we are simply ensuring that they reach the right conclusion. Doreen did not owe Simon a date to the dance any more than she owed him a glimpse of her underthings. But people are not generous, Biz. Does her reputation have to go down with the ship in order to maintain your sense of integrity? Hasn't she suffered enough?"

"No. I mean, yes. I mean, grr! Who died and made you publicist of the year?"

"Look." Heidi knew what she was about to say because it had been said to her, back when she was nobody. She flipped back the curtain and gazed out the window onto the quad, remembering again the speech Roland gave her on the way to the party three years ago, as they sped along in the Porsche on the road to Bridgehampton. "The only currency in this world," Roland told her, and she repeated his words verbatim to his niece now, "is how you are seen by the people that matter. Perception is reality. Control your own story, manage the character of yourself as it is doled out to the public, and reap the rewards. The second you lose control, you lose everything."

"Do you really believe that?" Biz asked.

"Mmm?"

"Perception is reality. Do you really think that? Because if you do, I feel sorry for you."

Heidi's PR campaign paid off a thousandfold. After the Simon Vale incident, Doreen became the most in-demand girl on campus. She became a queen. And her court was the dining hall. At the center table, Doreen would sit between her most enthusiastic yes-girls, Misha and Miyuki (the Mi-Mi's, as Heidi and Doreen called them behind their backs), while the masses approached one by one to hear what she had to say. They hung on Doreen's every word. Like Chastity Thibodeaux, who came to Doreen one lunch hour. Her boyfriend had attended a family wedding without her. Doreen declared the offense unforgivable.

"Look, Chastity, it's obviously up to you, but in my opinion? You are selling yourself short. Graham Weaver is *so* not worth it."

"Do you really think so, Doreen?"

"Pass the salt, please," said Heidi. She wondered what Doreen was cooking up. Graham Weaver was the oldest of old money. His father was a senator. If he wasn't worth it, nobody was.

"Absolutely. He is small potatoes. And the whole thing stinks of racism. Break up with him, that's what I think. You— you are such a prize! I mean, with a little bit of a makeover. I'm thinking blonde. Platinum! What do you think, Miyuki?"

"Amazing idea."

"But I'm black," Chastity said with bewilderment.

"That's exactly what I'm talking about, Chastity. You think that because you're black you can't have fun with hair color? Look at Miyuki! She's Japanese and her purple extensions rock." Doreen slapped Miyuki five.

"You know it," said Miyuki with a demonstrative flick of her hair.

"But, I'm just, I don't see . . ." Chastity touched the edge of her straightened hair with a worried look on her face.

"You need to work on your self-esteem, Chastity." Doreen sipped her smoothie. "That's some serious self-loathing right there."

"Salt," Heidi repeated.

"But the last time I tried that my hair fell out. I mean, it's really dark."

"Unh-huh. Like I said, it's up to you. All I'm saying is that if you are looking for a higher-caliber boyfriend . . ." Doreen said with a vague wave of her hand, as if she was too exhausted to complete the sentence.

"You need high-caliber hair," said Misha. Heidi stood up and walked to the other side of the table to get the salt. By the time she got back to her seat, another girl was trying to get into it.

"Excuse me, do you mind? Scram."

Doreen stood up. "That's Heidi's seat, Cynthia! What the hell do you think you're doing?" Her face was red with rage and she slammed the table with the palm of her hand.

"Sorry, Doreen."

"Don't apologize to me, you knuckle-dragger. Apologize to Heidi."

"Sorry, Heidi."

"Ah, don't worry about it. I have a meeting with my counselor anyway." Heidi plucked her yogurt off her tray.

"Nice," Cynthia said as she settled into Heidi's seat.

"And so you think you can just sit here? After that? Out, Cynthia. I mean it! Go sit somewhere else. And that blush makes you look like a carnival worker." Cynthia walked away, a reprimanded child. Doreen turned to Chastity, her tone perfectly sweet. "Excuse me for a moment won't you, Chastity? I'll be right back."

Doreen pulled Heidi out of hearing distance. "I'm so sorry, these bitches, they are basically savages."

"It's fine." From the corner of her eye, Heidi saw Biz alone with her book and her turkey croissant.

"Really? You know that all you have to do is say the word and I'd tell them all to get lost." Doreen pouted pityingly at her friend while looking around the room.

"Um, no. It's fine." Heidi could not believe the implication. *Heidi* need *Doreen*? How ridiculous! "You know I could mash Cynthia Stern like hot lipstick if I wanted to. You know that, right?"

"No. Of course! I didn't mean to imply . . ."

"I just don't care enough. Anyway, you seem to have your hands full. Speaking of which, if Chastity bleaches her hair she is going to look ridiculous."

"I know, right?" Doreen said with a wicked grin.

"What are you up to here?"

"I'll come by this afternoon and explain it all. It's actually hilarious. And we have to discuss winter break. Wait until you see the amazing bikini I made Gordon buy me. It cost an absolute fortune! The poor slob still thinks he's going with us to Hawaii." She rolled her eyes and gave Heidi a double kiss. "See you later."

"Okay. See you."

With a wave to Biz, Heidi made her way past the back tables, through the exit, and out onto the quad.

It was all unfolding as Heidi had planned. Doreen was a superstar. She was beautiful, calculating, manipulative—a living embodiment of the tenants of Roland's tutelage. She had no way of knowing it, of course, but Doreen was becoming exactly the kind of girl that Roland Gibbons would admire. Heidi had made the daughter into the darling of Chandler Academy, using what she'd learned from the father. The circularity of it satisfied her tremendously. And she did not miss the daily grind of running the place. After two years at the throne, Heidi was relieved to leave the minions to a new master, as long as Doreen kept her in the loop on all her little subplots, which, of course, she did.

All blue had drained from the sky, leaving a cottony

whiteness the weak sun could not penetrate, even at midday. Heidi turned onto the path behind the half-frozen pond that led to the administrative offices. Once inside, she warmed the tips of her ears with her fingers. There was an elevator, but as always, she chose the calorie-burning ascent up the stairs. As she chugged up, she couldn't help imagining, as she'd done a thousand times before, what would happen when Roland saw Doreen. What would he say when the horror show he dropped off at the Chandler gates emerged, a model of physical perfection?

Heidi found her counselor's office and followed the secretary's directions to wait on a lone polyester chair near the door. She closed her eyes and allowed herself a brief indulgence, imagining the moment when Doreen would speak her mind to Roland. How delicious it would be when Doreen rejected him, just as he had rejected her—and Heidi. Roland Gibbons would be left alone, a sad glass of scotch in front of him, while Doreen told him what he could do with his tardy fatherly affection.

After a lifetime of disappointments, Roland would have to contend with the fact that the perfection he'd been seeking—in the wives, the children, the obsessive acquisition of art—was standing right in front of him, in the form of his very own first-born daughter. Then Doreen would tell him, in no uncertain terms, to go fuck himself.

Heidi giggled. The secretary told her to go on in.

"I'm very optimistic," her counselor declared. "I see great things for you, starting with a top-notch college.

What did you have in mind?" On the table he'd laid out several glossy brochures: Harvard, Princeton, Stanford, Northwestern. *This is it*, Heidi thought, *this is the beginning.* She felt like squealing! Dancing! Hopping up and down! She called Peter as soon as she left the meeting to tell him the good news.

"That's great, babe. I'd love to see you in Cambridge, though I fear for what you will do to the weak-hearted Harvard men. I'll have to install an electric fence around you that nukes anyone who comes close."

"Some girls may find that a little controlling, but I enjoy being treated like a dog."

"I'm not treating you like a dog, I'm treating them like dogs. You would be more like a house I own."

"How romantic."

"You know it. Anyway, gotta go. Heading into my metaphysics midterm."

"Are you really? Or is some creature zapping your brain with electrodes to make you think you are heading into your metaphysics midterm? No way of knowing, really."

"Is that philosophy humor? From a high school girl? You are a gift from God."

"Or from some godlike, brain-zapping monster. Good luck on your midterm."

Heidi clicked off, her heart full. Peter Standish knew almost everything about her and he wanted her anyway. He understood her. They laughed together, they made plans, and Heidi Whelan, who never really fit in—not in her family, her old school, at Chandler—finally felt like she belonged. She understood for the first time what it meant to be happy.

———◦◦———

The final weeks of the semester found Doreen enjoying the benefits of her newfound status. Her throat became accustomed to the cool swish of a fresh oyster, followed by a fizzy burst of fine champagne. Her shoulders were draped in cashmere and hand-stitched Italian leather. Her breasts were lifted by ingeniously crafted underwear and scented in rare French perfumes. She was waited upon, worshipped, pampered, flattered. On a private jet between New York and Hawaii, Coburn Everbuck fed her fresh toro and told her she was his miracle.

That poor, lost, chubby girl who ate her lunch alone in the choir room could not be this same exquisite creature stretched out on the sand of a private tropical paradise. That friendless sophomore who spent the evening of her homecoming dance making smiley-face pizzas with her mother could have nothing to do with this violet-eyed, raven-haired beauty who'd been pleasured in the back of limousines, the bathrooms of Fifth Avenue hotel suites, and here, on the shore of the Pacific Ocean. The sons of fortune had wept at her feet and begged her to stay. But she always left. She knew the power of being longed for, of leaving her suitors unsatisfied. Heidi taught her well.

The perfect, crystalline water lapped Doreen's manicured toenails. The Standishes' concrete and glass mansion hovered on a bluff above her.

"Look at the snake basking in the sun," said Heidi. She stepped onto the sand from the rocky steps that led down from the house. It was early. Peter and Coburn were still sleeping. She'd assumed when she left for her run that Doreen had been asleep as well, but she was happy to find her stretched out on the sand in her Missoni bikini. News had come from New Hampshire, and Heidi was anxious to share it with her friend.

"I tried to sleep in, but I couldn't resist the ocean," Doreen said sleepily. "It's too gorgeous, isn't it? Anyone who says money can't buy happiness has never had access to a private beach in Kauai. Right?"

"Coney Island it ain't, that's for sure." Heidi kicked off her sneakers. In her tiny running shorts and a sports bra, the rippled landscape of her midsection glistened with a thin layer of sweat.

"I don't know how you do it, Heidi. You must have sucked back ten mojitos last night, and you look fresh and clean as charity."

"It's my positive outlook." Heidi sat down beside Doreen. "Or maybe it's love." She folded herself over her legs to stretch her hamstrings.

"What, what? Love? Are you in love, Heidi Whelan? I didn't think it possible!"

"Why not? I'm a person, after all." After they'd said good night to Coburn and Doreen the previous evening, Peter led Heidi by the hand to the master bedroom. The house was cutting-edge contemporary and thoughtfully furnished with sharp-edged woods and metals and modern molded plastic. The concrete floors in the master bedroom were uncovered and cool underfoot. Windows lined one entire wall of the room. They made love while looking out at the expanse of ocean.

"Bully for you, my dear. He is very charming—and rich! Did you see the maid's quarters? And the meat fridge! A girl could do a lot worse than love a man with his resources. I can't say I feel the same about his little dimwitted chum, but he has a pleasing energy, don't you think?" Doreen yawned. "Do we really have to go back to dreary New Hampshire? Isn't it winter there? That is unacceptable to me."

"True, winter sucks. But without it there would be no après-ski. And what kind of life would that be?"

"Mmm. But to go back to Chandler? And do what? Learn about cosines? What an absurd idea."

"Speaking of Chandler." Heidi stood up and, balancing on one leg, pulled the opposite foot toward the back of her head. "I got a call from your cousin just this morning."

"Ugh. Sorry. It's just, she's a bit of a bore, isn't she?" Lately Doreen had no patience for Biz. Everything the girl said seemed to grate on Doreen's nerves, so she was often short-tempered, even rude. Of course, Biz was not the world's most glamorous companion, but Doreen's contempt seemed excessive, especially considering how much Biz worshipped her. Which was undoubtedly the problem. Poor Biz. Heidi was content to be the preferred roommate, but she hoped that Doreen's recent impatience was only temporary. Biz was one of the good guys.

"I can't speak to that, my pet, but she did have some juicy news to report. She's been on campus since Christmas."

"Of course she has."

"Preparing for her exhibit. It's coming up in March. Anyway, about a week ago she went into town. Some contraption of hers had run out of batteries."

"Please tell me it was a vibrator," said Doreen, grinning wickedly. "Wouldn't that be wonderful? For all of us?"

"Whatever it was, since the union is closed for break, she went into the hardware store in Hamilton. And who do you suppose she saw working there behind the counter?" Heidi released her foot and stood looking down at Doreen.

Doreen sighed and folded her hands behind her head. "I don't know, Heidi, and honestly, do I care? The hardware store in Hamilton, New Hampshire, seems a rather banal topic in this breathtaking—wait." Doreen sat up. She tipped her sunglasses onto her head and looked up at Heidi.

"Simon Vale," said Heidi with a nod. "He was there working. He didn't know who she was, of course, but she said she spotted him immediately. Apparently he's become doughy and marble-mouthed from medication."

"Doughy? Like, fat?"

"Yep. Those crazy pills will do that. Plus candy bars in the vending machines, no exercise, meals that go heavy on white bread. Anyway, she said he was a total zombie, shuffling around, fetching metal widgets for the local DIY-ers. Pathetic."

"I'm having the hardest time imagining it." Doreen gazed out onto the sea.

"She even asked if he went to Hamilton High. Our little Biz, getting the scoop! Aren't you proud? He said he didn't go to school anymore."

"He dropped out of school?"

"That's what Biz said. She said he probably couldn't have handled class in that state."

"Can I be honest with you, Heidi?"

"Of course!"

"I should feel something about this, right? I know I should feel something. But here? In this setting—I guess I'm just a little detached from all that now. I'm sitting here trying to picture Simon Vale fat and spaced out, and all I can think of is the scrumptious strawberries and pineapple we are going to have for breakfast."

"It's easy to feel disconnected."

"But seriously. What am I supposed to feel? Loss? Regret? Guilt? How life diminishing! I loved him once, and he blew it. I don't see what any of that has to do with me now. Brooding over lost causes seems a terrible waste of time. Anyway, I have to get wet now, it's sweltering."

Doreen untied her sarong and ran into the water. Heidi watched her friend's head bob up and down in the waves. How easy it was for her to let go and move on. But wasn't she right? What good would it do anyone for Doreen to get wrinkles fretting over something she could not do anything about? All she did was break up with the guy.

Probably he had always been unstable. If it wasn't Doreen, it would have been somebody else. Still, something about it left Heidi cold.

Like father, like daughter, she thought, then scolded herself. Doreen was much better than Roland could ever be, she was completely sure of that. Or, mostly sure. Somewhat sure?

The sun beamed down. "How's the water?" Heidi called out to Doreen. She shimmied out of her shorts.

"It's perfect!" Doreen yelled back. "It's just perfect!"

And it was.

21

Deep in the Bolivian countryside, an ancient *camioneta* zoomed around curves on the bad mountain road that led to La Paz. In the back of the truck, perched on a great bag of seed, Jane Vale braced herself for the bumps, staring straight ahead to avoid looking over the cliffs at her pending demise.

She tried not to be afraid. Could it have been only that morning that Jane woke up in her host family's shack, enjoyed a breakfast of boiled eggs and plantains, and prepared for a regular day of work in the village? Had only a few hours passed since she heard the words *emergencia* and *hermano*? Since she dropped everything to go, get out, get to Simon? But it seemed a lifetime ago, like she'd been a different, more carefree version of herself.

The *camioneta* took a particularly harrowing turn and Jane closed her eyes.

This, too, was ending. In a few hours she would be on a plane to Miami and from there on to Boston. The beautiful campo—broad and dry with squat trees and majestic blue mountains—would she ever see it again? When she volunteered for the Peace Corps, Jane had assumed it would change her, and that it would be the people she helped that would have the most lasting effect. And though she'd found the work rewarding, what moved Jane most of all was the landscape. After a childhood in a cramped house on a cramped block in a small-minded town, it had done her soul good to live in such vastness.

If she could have brought Simon with her, if he, too, could have left Leaving Place, seen how large and far the world stretched . . . but it was no use thinking about it. She opened her eyes. Take it in, miss nothing. A great sadness filled her heart, as if she was saying good-bye forever to an intimate friend.

Houses began to crop up as they approached the out-skirts of La Paz. Back, backward. How much like a failure it seemed.

———•◦•———

Simon's doctor suggested that school might be too much for him right away, and that football was out of the question. But it was good to have a routine, he said, so Jane and her mother decided that installing Simon at the hardware store would be a reasonable solution. One benefit of the store having so few customers was that the job would demand little of him.

And at first, the plan seemed to be working. Not that Si-mon returned instantly to his old, jovial self, but the light re-sponsibilities of the job appeared to do him good. Jane saw little improvements—an occasional smile, a flash of whimsy. One evening near Christmas, when she came to pick him up at the store, he said, "How you living, Janey-Jane?" in a voice that sounded so much like the brother she'd known and loved that Jane had to bury a sob of relief.

But the glimmers of hope were painfully infrequent. Most of the time he moved around silently, heavy of body and spirit. He almost never laughed or kidded her, and he accepted hugs the way he seemed to accept everything now—as a passive, unmoved recipient. Jane found herself spending much of her day unconsciously praying. *Let him smile today,* she would beg. *Let him laugh.* Once, while they were sitting on the couch after dinner, she took his once-chiseled chin in her hands and stared deep into his eyes.

"I know you're in there, little brother," she said. He blinked at her stoically, through a fog of meds. She moved her face even closer to his. "I know my Simon is in there, and he's going to come out when he's ready, better than ever." When she released him and settled back into the couch, he patted her lightly on the knee and changed the channel.

Doreen Gray. Jane knew who was responsible for what had happened to her brother, and she resolved that as soon as Simon was a little better she would plot her revenge. She'd already googled the girl, of course, but no pictures came up at all. What kind of person had zero Internet presence? She apparently belonged to no clubs. She wasn't listed in any local article and she had no profiles on social media. And as the mystery around Doreen Gray grew, so did Jane's anger and hate. Who was this phantom girl who had done this to her brother? Was she even real? Had Simon seen a ghost?

Then, one cold January day, Jane dropped Simon off at the store on her way to the public library, where she fulfilled requirements for the online college classes she was taking. At noon she came back to the store, as usual, to have lunch with her brother and check on the daily sales. She saw that Simon was helping a customer, and at first she didn't think much about it, just went into the back room and retrieved the turkey sandwiches she'd packed that morning. When she came back to the counter, the customer was still there, holding one of the paper sacks they used for small items like screws and bolts. It was a teenage girl, someone from Chandler, Jane assumed from the fancy clothes and headband.

"This ought to do it," said the girl. "Thanks for your help, Simon." Jane unwrapped the cellophane around the sandwiches and opened the bag of chips. She heard the bell ring as the girl left the store.

"Do you want a soda?" Jane asked, but Simon didn't answer. "Hey. Simon?" She looked up at her brother and saw an expression on his face unlike anything she had ever seen before. He appeared to be experiencing excruciating pain and rapturous joy simultaneously.

"Simon?" she said. He clutched a dollar bill the girl must have given him for whatever item she had used as an excuse to gape at her troubled little brother. The bill shook in his hand as he stood frozen, staring ahead.

Jane sprinted from behind the counter and pushed herself outside, coatless in the bitter wind. Black wavy hair and a red coat. That's what she remembered of the girl. Oh, why didn't she pay closer attention? She ran down Main Street toward the Chandler campus, but the girl—that evil witch who had turned her exceptional brother into a blubbering half-wit—had disappeared. Jane thought of running all the way to campus so she could claw her eyes out, drown her in that stupid man-made lake.

But Jane had seen Doreen Gray. And if she saw her once she could find her again. She tucked her hands into the sleeves of her sweater. The sweater was made of rough-hewn alpaca, a typical Andean design that had been a gift from her Bolivian host family. Doreen Gray had cost her everything! Her brother, her future, everything she loved was damaged or gone. And the girl would pay for all she'd taken, of that Jane had no doubt. But she had to be patient. She had to plan.

———●●———

Jane got herself employed at the Chandler library, reshelving books. Her smallness made her ill-suited for the job, and she had to lug around a ladder to reach shelves that would have been accessible to someone of average or even slightly below-average height. Something else she missed about Bolivia was how low to the ground everyone was, making her feel less shrimpy in comparison. But though the physical demands of the work were less than ideal, Jane thought it a perfect location from which to spy on the student body to try to catch the scent of the mysterious Doreen Gray. As she wove through the stacks, she scanned the tables and comfy chairs for the raven-haired, pale-skinned girl she'd seen so briefly in the store.

But the girl never appeared.

Maybe if she'd gotten nothing, Jane might have given up after a few weeks, but the name Doreen Gray rang loud at Chandler Academy, even in the supposedly quiet library.

Her name was constantly invoked by the students—as if she was somehow behind everything that was happening on campus. *Doreen suggested I do X. Doreen said I shouldn't do X. Did you see what Doreen was wearing today? Did you see Doreen?* Jane knew it was only a matter of time before the girl was revealed in the flesh.

Then, one afternoon, Jane was on a ladder re-alphabetizing the English History section, when she overheard a cell phone conversation that was happening on the other side of the stacks. Such malfeasance was typical of the entitled Chandler students, and Jane didn't think too much of it at first.

"Heidi," the voice hissed in a harsh whisper, "You have to stop calling, okay? I'm at the library and . . ." Here the girl paused and listened. "What? . . . Really? You're kidding! Uncle Roland? Of course, you can help yourself to whatever's in my closet. Is Doreen there now? She must be thrilled."

Jane froze at the sound of the name. Could it be the same Doreen? It seemed unlikely that there would be more than one. She left her pile of books on the top rung and climbed down. She crept around the back end of the stacks and crouched to the lowest shelf, staring out the corner of her eye at the girl on the phone.

"Lunch in Boston. Wow. Okay. Okay, I'll come right back. Just let me . . . okay, okay. Tell Doreen I'm on my way."

Jane recognized the girl on the phone. She even knew her name: Elizabeth Gibbons-Brown, a constant fixture in the library's daily life. Jane had heard the staff talk about

how she was this rich girl from some spectacularly important old family who preferred books to the company of her
fellow debutantes. She read voraciously, sitting at the center
table with a cheek in each hand, scanning pages as if they
were fuel or food. She never spoke to any of the other students, though she must have known at least a few of them.
And she never tired.

The girl interested Jane. When she wasn't daydreaming
revenge schemes about Doreen Gray, Jane sometimes imagined making a friend of Elizabeth Gibbons-Brown, as if
someone with her pedigree could ever condescend to speak
to a poor townie girl like herself.

After she clicked off the phone, the girl rushed back to
the table, where she'd been installed since early that morning. Peeking from behind the stacks, Jane watched her pack
papers and notebooks into her backpack, shrug into an
oversize wool coat, and make for the door. Jane ran into the
office behind the checkout desk and grabbed the Andean
sweater and alpaca cap.

"Sorry, um, family emergency?" Jane said to Mrs.
Turner, her fat, cross-eyed boss who sat at the office desk
snarfing caramel popcorn and playing solitaire. "I'll be
back in twenty. Okay?"

Mrs. Turner grunted. Jane raced out of the library, terrified that she would lose track of Elizabeth as she'd lost
track of Doreen in town. But when she emerged onto the
quad, Jane spotted the girl immediately, and maintaining
a safe distance, she followed her across campus. The frozen

grass crunched under her hiking boots, and her breath came out in visible gusts from her mouth and nose. But she barely registered the cold. She kept her eyes focused on her target.

They arrived at one of the dormitory buildings and Elizabeth keyed in. Jane stopped behind a large oak. Of course, she didn't have key card access to that building, but it didn't matter.

She stood her ground, leaning against the tree as the feeble late-winter sun faded into the thick clouds. The lights came on in the quad. Jane Vale huddled into her sweater. She waited for Doreen Gray.

22

"It's just so unexpected! I never . . . I mean, how could I have . . . oh, Biz! There you are! Did Heidi tell you? Isn't it just too wonderful?" Standing in Biz and Heidi's bedroom half-dressed, Doreen flung her arms around her cousin with uncharacteristic affection.

"Yes, I heard," said Biz happily. "You're having lunch? With Uncle Roland?"

"I am, I am. Taking the nine-eighteen train to Boston tomorrow morning. Heidi, what about this?" Doreen twirled around in a high-waisted black skirt and silk blouse from Biz's closet. "Heidi, hello? You there?"

"Hmm? Oh." Heidi stared at Doreen. "I, uh . . . sure! I mean, it's a start. You need a belt. And shoes." She poked into Biz's closet. "Maybe the red Mary Janes?"

Heidi was trying to keep it cool while she went through the motions of helping Doreen find an outfit, though inside she was in full-on panic mode. The moment she'd been fantasizing about, Doreen showing Roland all that she'd become, was finally upon them. But to Heidi's dismay, Doreen was actually excited to see him. Thrilled! She'd apparently forgotten all about their conversation in the back of Gordon's town car. Everything her father had done to her, the million ways he'd turned his back on his own daughter, did not seem to matter the least bit to Doreen now. She was happy he wanted to see her. She sought not revenge, but approval! It was an unmitigated catastrophe.

Doreen frowned at her reflection in the mirror. "Red?

Isn't that a little . . . I don't know. I want to seem young. You know, virtuous."

"Of course! But everyone loves a schoolgirl with a sense of fun," said Heidi, forcing a smile.

They'd made a plan, hadn't they?

But that was over. Heidi only had to look at Doreen glowing with happiness to realize that there would be no place at this luncheon for revenge. Doreen understood that Roland would treat her differently now that she looked and acted like one of his own. And she couldn't wait to bask in the light of his attention. Could Heidi blame her? It was wonderful there.

Heidi cinched a gold belt around Doreen's tiny waist. She waited while she stepped into the T-strap heels, fighting back tears. It would all be hers, Doreen's. She would have everything he promised Heidi—and what was more, she would have him. But so what? What did Heidi want with a bored, sadistic, superior jerk?

And the answer, of course, was everything. Heidi covered her mouth with her hand. She tried to find calm.

"So Dean Crotchett called you in?" Biz asked from her spot on her bed.

"Exactly," said Doreen, her attention fixed on her reflection. "It was crazy. When I got the notice that he wanted to see me, I thought I was toast. Don't look at me like that. I've been trying to buckle down, Bizzy, really. But it's so hard to focus here! Of everything going on in my life, my studies are the least interesting thing by a mile. So

I thought, okay, he's not going to kick me out. He'll just put me on academic probation. No big deal. I can handle it, I just have to concentrate more on schoolwork. But that wasn't it at all!"

The scheme was doomed from the beginning. No matter how angry Doreen might have been at Roland, he was her father. His cruelty only made Doreen *more* desperate to win him over. Heidi had imagined Doreen showing herself to him in her new glory and then *rejecting his attention.* Ludicrous! Short-sighted!

Oh well, oh well, oh well. The fixation on Roland Gibbons was just a crutch anyway. Doreen should go and have a beautiful reunion with dear old dad, and Heidi could cheer her on, hope for the best, let it all go.

But that presented more problems for Heidi. Doreen and Roland as separate entities were manageable to her. The minute they developed their own thing, away from Heidi, she lost control of the story. Roland could spill. He could tell Doreen that Heidi used blackmail and manipulation to secure a spot at Chandler. And that the person she'd blackmailed and manipulated had been Doreen's own father.

Heidi felt sweat beads forming on her usually pore-free forehead. Roland once again had all the power. He could take Doreen from Heidi with two words. And Doreen? With her new position at Chandler, she could easily take the rest. She certainly would not let Heidi go unpunished for turning her father into a chump. Heidi squeezed her eyes shut. She told herself to relax. Turning away from the girls, she tried to find space to breathe.

She'd been an idiot. Blind, stupid, negligent of her own security. Distracted by her dumb happiness, she'd dropped an army of henchmen into Doreen's lap. All she would have to do was give them a nod, and Heidi would be an outcast, friendless and alone.

"No!" Heidi cried.

"Huh?" asked Doreen. "What is it? The belt?"

"What?"

"You said no," said Biz. She gave her roommate an odd look. "No, what?"

"No! Uh, I mean, no way! Crazy. What you were saying about the dean—"

"Go on, Dorie," said Biz. "What did he say?"

"Only that he'd received a call from my father. He was giving me an overnight pass, he said. My dad was his buddy back when they were at Chandler, like a hundred million years ago."

Heidi needed to stop this from happening. She just had to talk Doreen out of seeing her father. And she could do it, too. She may have taken a little break from social engineering, but she was still the original Heidi Whelan. Doreen learned it all from her.

"So he was making an exception for me to be able to spend the night in Boston on Saturday. 'Your father really wants to see you.' That's what he said, can you believe it?" Doreen beamed. Heidi took a deep breath. Here was her chance.

"And you think that's true?" Heidi asked. "You think he really *wants* to see you?"

"Of course he does! I'm so happy for you, Doreen," said Biz.

But Doreen looked nervous. "Why?" she asked Heidi. "You think he doesn't?"

"No. It seems like an abrupt change, that's all."

"What's gotten into you, Heidi?" asked Biz.

"Nothing! But why should he . . . I mean, shouldn't Doreen . . . like, as long as he says jump, she says how high? Isn't that a little, ahem, *pathetic*?"

"He's her father. I think you should be supportive."

"I am, but why would he suddenly want to see her? I mean, out of the blue? I just don't want to see you get hurt again, Do-do. He hasn't exactly been a force for good in your life. We discussed this, if you remember, on our way back from New York. In Gordon Lichter's limo?"

"But why would the dean say he wanted to see me if he didn't?" Doreen's brow creased, her hands fluttered around as if unsure of where they could safely be placed on her person. "This is a mistake. Oh, he's going to mock me, humiliate me." She kicked off the heels and began to unbutton the blouse. "I'm not going. Screw Dean Crotchett and his stupid overnight pass! Screw Boston!" Tears streamed down Doreen's face. Heidi smiled.

"It's okay, Doreen. You're right, screw him. Hey! I have a great idea. Why don't I text John Elliott's townie friend to buy us some beer? We can have our own party right here. We can invite Claire and the Mi-Mi's and Lord Volde-mort—I mean Chastity." The bleach job had made the girl completely bald. "I can't imagine she has anything else on her social calendar."

"Now hold on a second," said Biz. She put a steady hand on her cousin's shoulder. "Just relax." She turned Doreen to face her and began to do up the tiny mother-of-pearl buttons on her own shirt. She brushed Doreen's hair out of her eyes and retrieved the red shoes, setting them down in front of Doreen so she could step into them. Then she squatted down at her feet and buckled the red straps. "Uncle Roland may not be winning any father-of-the-year awards, I'll give you that, but why would he go to such elaborate lengths—calling in a favor to Crotchett, setting up a place to meet in Boston—if he just wants to humiliate you? What is he going to do? Stand you up and watch, crouched beneath a window somewhere as you sit alone waiting for him? Doesn't it seem a bit far-fetched? Isn't it more likely that he simply wants to check in on you, his daughter? And his investment, I might add."

"That's true. He probably wants to make sure I'm not wasting his money. But I can show him how much I've changed, can't I? Oh, he's in for a real surprise."

"I don't think you've changed that much," Biz said warmly. "You're still that same little girl I remember from Amagansett all those years ago. The one who loved to dance."

"Oh, Bizzy," said Doreen. "You're right. This is all going to be great."

"The misguided triumph of hope over experience," said Heidi with a scowl. Biz shot her a look. "Just saying."

"Let it go, Heidi. No matter what they've been through, Doreen is Uncle Roland's daughter and he loves her. He is going to be so proud when he sees you, Doreen. Except I do think your outfit is missing something."

Doreen returned to her reflection. "What? What is it?"

Biz opened her underwear drawer and dug out a small black velvet box. "Grandmère Kiki's diamonds! They will be perfect."

Doreen's eyes brightened. "Oh, but I couldn't. Look at them! They're tremendous!"

"Just put them on, Dorie," said Biz. "I mean, she was your grandmother, too."

Doreen screwed the giant diamond earrings into her ears.

"Wait, but wasn't Grandmère Kiki your father's mother?" Heidi asked. Her head felt like it was about to burst a vessel. "So she wasn't related to Doreen at all."

"Yes, well." Biz leaned her head on Doreen's shoulder and looked into the mirror at their double-reflection. "No need to get technical about it. Anyway, they look really pretty on. I think Uncle Roland is going to be quite taken aback."

"Oh, thank you, Biz! They are too perfect!" Doreen flung her arms around her cousin again. "What do you think, Heidi?"

Heidi watched Doreen spin around joyfully. She saw how it would all go down. Doreen would show up at the restaurant with her gorgeous face and her longing for acceptance and suddenly Roland would have this perfect little daughter, an ideal expression of his worth. Humiliate him? Doreen's change was just another feather in his already overstuffed cap. He would love her and help her and Heidi would be where she always was, on her own. Helping her own damn self. Until Doreen said Heidi's name, that is. Then she'd be nowhere.

"You look stunning, Doreen," Heidi said. "It's the perfect outfit." What were her options? She could work on Doreen's insecurities, ensuring that she never saw Roland again. Or she could follow her to Boston and find a way to thwart the meeting altogether. But she just didn't want to do that anymore. She was out of practice, for one thing, and she was tired. She wanted to let go, to be optimistic for once. Maybe Doreen wouldn't mention her. They would have plenty of other things to discuss. And even if she did, would he really tell her the truth? It didn't exactly look great for Roland that he'd been outwitted by a high school girl. And if it came right down to it, she wasn't without resources.

Heidi could fight her way out of anything. But hopefully all she would need was a little faith. She swiped at her face, taking out the tear before it leaked.

"Just take care of yourself, okay? Not that I know him personally."

But Doreen didn't hear her. She was too invested in the way the diamonds caught the light as she turned her head from side to side.

———•◦———

Doreen said she was too nervous and excited to eat, which relieved Heidi somewhat, since she wasn't sure she could take much more of Doreen's enthusiasm. But as Biz and Heidi turned toward the dining hall, they were practically mowed down by a small girl in an Andean sweater.

"Ow! Watch where you're going, bitch!" Heidi yelled, pushing the girl with enough force to knock her onto the ground.

"Heidi!" said Biz.

"Sorry," said Jane Vale.

"You don't have to apologize." Biz helped Jane to her feet. "Hey, I know you. You work at the library, right? Do you go to school here? I'm Biz. I've been wanting to, I mean, I always thought you seemed, I don't know, kind of focused, I guess."

"Can we go please?" Heidi demanded.

"Hey, listen, what's your name? I'm Biz. Oh, but I said that, right?" Biz laughed again.

But the girl wasn't listening. With creepy intensity she looked at Heidi, then up at the dorm, her gaze searching.

"What the hell is your problem?" Heidi said. "Get the hell out of here. Now!"

"No!" said Biz. She shot Heidi a look. "I mean, you don't have to. Do you want to join us for dinner?" But before she could say more, the girl ran away across the quad.

"What the hell was that about?" asked Heidi. They fell into step toward the cafeteria.

"You were rude. There's no reason for that. No reason to be rude."

"What? Me? That little runt smacked right into me! And what was she wearing, a poncho? Is she late to play the pan flute or something?"

"That's not nice. Don't say stuff like that around me, okay? I don't like it."

"So quick to defend. All right, all right. Didn't realize you had such strong feelings for her. Let me know when the wedding is and I'll be sure to bring my llama." Heidi put her hands up. She didn't know why she was being so tough on the girl, or why she turned it on Biz, but it seemed to be happening without her.

"Look, maybe you should have dinner by yourself," said Biz as she stopped walking and looked hard at the ground. Even in the dark, Heidi could see she was hurt.

"What? Why?" What had Heidi said to embarrass Biz? She'd made fun of the girl, not her. But then, looking at her shamefaced friend, Heidi began to see. Of course, she was not the only one with an inner life. Biz had her own soul to contend with, and her own set of secrets. Which Heidi, too wrapped up in her own mess, had mocked and belittled.

"Oh, Bizzy, I'm sorry. I don't even know what I was saying, I'm a little confused right now. Please forgive me, I'm just . . . I'm really . . ." She was a horrible person. She'd tried to be good, but she couldn't help herself. She was mean to one of the few people in her life who gave her peace. It took everything she had not to burst into tears. "If you want to eat alone, I understand. You don't have to be with me now. I get it."

Biz's expression softened. "It's okay, Heidi."

"I shouldn't have said that. I don't care who you, I mean, I like you no matter what. Seriously. I'm just, I'm having a hard time."

"Look, you don't have to explain. It's about Doreen, isn't it? Doreen and Uncle Roland."

"Huh? What about them? No. No."

"It's okay, Heidi. I think I understand." They resumed their walk as Biz spoke. "I'm sure it must be a little complicated for you to have my uncle, the esteemed Roland Winthrop Gibbons IV, swoop in with his connections and his lineage. Part of what connected you to Doreen was this idea that she was an outsider like you, that you guys were infiltrating some prep school palace or something. Even though he hasn't been around—maybe because he hasn't been around—Doreen will obviously want her dad's approval. And now, due to her recent transformation, it seems likely that she will get it."

Heidi was impressed. Biz noticed more than she thought. Of course, it wasn't the whole story, not by a long shot. But it had elements of truth to it. In a flash Heidi saw Doreen's illustrious debut into high society: on Roland's arm at society functions, introductions to the most important people, photos of them together in the party pages. *Guest of Roland Gibbons.* A wave of nausea came over her.

"She will still need you, Heidi. I think you have more to offer than you think."

The tears were coming fast and free now. But she didn't have to indulge them. She told herself to buck up. *Buck up! Heidi Whelan does not cry in public.*

"Thanks, Biz. Of course, I want Doreen to have a better relationship with her father."

"You don't have to explain. You're a good friend, Heidi. And a good person—a better person than you think."

"You really think so? Even after how awful I was to you and that girl?"

"Yes. I do. I think you've got greatness inside you, Heidi Whelan."

"Maybe I could. Maybe I will. Thanks." They walked a few paces in silence. "I guess it feels a bit like the end of something. Like the end of some beautiful chapter." Heidi stopped and pulled on Biz's sleeve. They could see the dining hall ahead of them. "You mentioned Doreen's transformation. I think that's the first time either of us has said anything about it."

"Uncanny, wasn't it?"

"One minute she was this high school disaster."

"And then, poof! It was like a magic trick, wasn't it? So odd."

"I keep thinking of the picture. The one you took for the GryphPage profile. The one you photoshopped and then she got so upset."

"Me too! I asked Doreen for it. She said she destroyed it."

"It's the strangest thing . . ." Heidi was sure Biz would think her ridiculous for what she was about to say, and she wanted that, wanted to be told she had a crazy imagination, that it wasn't possible. "It's like she became that girl in the picture!"

"Right? That's what it seemed like to me." The girls looked at one another.

"But it happened so quickly, I sometimes wonder if I invented that other girl, the lumpy, frizzy-haired, pimple-faced, shy one. Did I just make up the whole thing?"

"I know just what you mean. If you weren't there with me, I'm sure I would think I'd hallucinated that other girl."

"But she was real, right? And this one, this current Doreen. She's real, too?"

"I think so. No, she is. She's real. Of course she's real." Even in the darkness of night, Heidi could see fear in Biz's eyes. "What other explanation is there?"

23

February 26. 9:14 a.m. I am writing these notes while sitting on a bench at the Hamilton Train Station. The subject, who I will henceforth refer to as the *Elephant,* is standing at the window, gazing onto the track. When I arrived ten minutes ago she was already here. She went into the bathroom once since then, but otherwise has just stood with her ticket in her hand.

11:20 a.m. Arrived in South Station. The train ride was without incident except the Elephant received attentions from a young man that she rejected outright. Not surprising. I changed in train bathroom into slacks and blazer, fake glasses, hair in bun. Want to seem businesswoman-ish. Want to avoid detection.

12:40 p.m. At uppity restaurant on Newbury St. Followed Elephant from South Station. Arrived thirty minutes ago but the Elephant walked around block four times before entering. She gave the maître d' her name, and they sat her at a back table near the kitchen. I am sitting alone at the bar, within earshot of Elephant's table. Prices outrageous. Ordered a cranberry and soda. Cost $3.

12:48 p.m. Sharp-dressed man (SDM) enters and sits with Elephant. (Father?) Seems surprised at her appearance. Happy. Yells at maître d' to move them away from "Siberia." Knows maître d' by name. Must be regular. Elephant and SDM move to table at front. I request a seat near window. Will have to order something. Soup $14. Outrageous.

Conversation btwn Elephant + SDM. (transcribed from recording on voice recorder in pocket of coat hanging on hook near table)

SDM: I'll admit it. When Crotchett said I'd be surprised to see how you've changed, I didn't think it would be for the better. But you look marvelous, Doreen, just marvelous. It's hard to believe it's even you.

E: Thanks. Yes, Chandler has been good to me.

SDM: I can see that! Let's get a drink. What would you like? A white wine maybe? Go on. It's an occasion, isn't it? Waiter! Waiter! Another Macallan for me, please, and be sharp about it. What would you like, dear?

E: Hm. Oh, a glass of champagne, I suppose. (Snobby French name) if you have it.

SDM: My, my. What a sophisticate you've become. And I love what you're wearing! You look like you're ready for high society. What happened to that embarrassment I picked up from the airport?

E: Oh. Well, Biz (Ref: E G-B) is very generous with her closet.

SDM: Biz? You mean you had to borrow these clothes from your cousin? (Ref: E G-B is E's cousin? Too bad.) Oh no, no. That won't do. Listen, let's order. She'll start with the pear and Roquefort salad and then—you like fish, don't you? The dover sole. I'll have the Caesar and a chopped steak. Medium well.

Yes. And after we're done here we'll go shopping, how's that? Neiman's is right down the street, and I don't want you borrowing clothes from Elizabeth, though I'm sure she has them to spare. My sister has spent a fortune trying to make that girl into something presentable. I can't tell you how many times I've told her to give up the ghost. I tell her, 'Gloria, what's wrong with having an intellectual in the family? We can't all be hostesses and charity mistresses.' But she embarrasses easily, my sister does. She doesn't love having an ugly duckling around, she doesn't like how it looks.

(Note: E appears very pleased and happy during this. Tries to act normal about it, but is beaming from ear to ear. Seems like she might cry. Snapped cell phone pic.)

SDM: Anyway, there's no reason why you can't have clothes of your own. Though it's good she's been so nice to you. Is it Biz I have to thank, then, for this utter transformation of yours?

E: In part, I suppose. And her roommate, maybe you met her before at Aunt Gloria's? Her name is Heidi Whelan.

(SDM coughing fit ensues.)

E: Dad, are you okay? Dad?

(SDM continues coughing. Waves to waiter for another round of drinks.)

E: Of course, it was mostly my own doing. I mean, I made a conscious decision to improve myself. To make a positive change.

(New drinks arrive.)

SDM: To youth!

(They drink.)

SDM: Your mother used to wear her hair just like this.

E: I know, I mean, only from pictures. Her hair is short now. And going gray. She dyes it. (E laughs)

SDM: Go ahead and laugh. The privilege of the young.

E: So, Aunt Gloria is embarrassed by Biz? I can totally see that. She is kind of, I don't know, hopeless? I mean, in some respects. Are you all right, Daddy? Daddy? Everything okay?

3:20 p.m. After Elephant + SDM finished lunch, they moved to the restaurant bar. Had to leave to avoid drawing suspicion. Moved to coffee shop across street. Changed in bathroom to disguise #3: jeans, Harvard sweatshirt, messy ponytail. College girl. What my life would have been before Elephant came in and ruined everything. Been sitting here for some time, transcribing recording above. No action at the restaurant. Not sure what I am doing here.

4:30 p.m. Still nothing. Third coffee. Feeling jittery.

5:15 p.m. Elephant emerges with SDM's arm around her neck. He is obviously intoxicated. They turn east. Will let them get ahead before following them. Really very drunk. How humiliating ☺ . Will take pictures.

6:25 p.m. Mandarin Oriental Hotel lobby. Followed E + SDM on meandering path with stop for SDM to lose his $80 lunch (priceless!). Caught all on camera. SDM wanted to have drink at hotel bar. E convinced him to rest. Went upstairs. That may be it, though am hoping she comes back down. Will stay on for a bit, see what happens.

7:38 p.m. E emerges! Settles into sofa to make phone call. Can't hear who she is calling. Clicks off. Appears to be waiting. Will get closer.

9:07 p.m. Pink-shirted boy (PSB) enters. E waves. We are going out, folks! Happy I changed to outfit #4: miniskirt, heels, see-through top. I will own you, ~~Doreen Gray~~ Elephant.

24

Now here is a man, Doreen thought. He slept on his stomach, his arms and legs stretched wide, a man accustomed to taking more than his share of everything, even space on the dorm room bed. The sun came through the window with that brightness reserved for mornings after a fresh snow, and the Charles River sparkled like a girl admired.

Doreen had a slightly stuffy head from the previous evening's indulgences, but otherwise she felt wonderful. She slid out of his bed, choosing one of a number of balled-up oxford shirts to button up over her naked body and, removing a pile of books from a chair near the window, she sat and looked out over the river. Everything glistened in the new snow. The world seemed full of possibilities.

". . . Hello?"

"Daddy!" The word tasted like ice cream on her tongue. She wanted it to remain there forever. "Good morning, Daddy!"

"Bianca? Why are you calling me now? I thought you were in Stockholm."

"No. No, it's not Bianca. It's your other daughter, Doreen."

"Oh, Dorie! I'm so sorry, sweetheart. Hello! Where are you calling from? Are you here at the hotel? What time is it?"

"It's about ten. I went to a friend's place." Her father had mentioned getting Doreen a room at the Mandarin but passed out before he could manage it. No matter. "Anyway, when should I come by the hotel? I can be there in about a half an hour I think."

"Come by? Here you mean?"

"Yes. We were supposed to have breakfast, remember?" After the bartender had cut him off at the restaurant, when it became clear that he was in no condition to take her to Neiman Marcus or any place, he had told her that they would get a fresh start in the morning. Breakfast, he had said, and then he would really take her shopping. He would buy her whatever she wanted, he said.

"Did I say that? Oh, yes. Of course, only . . . what time is it?"

"It's ten o'clock."

"Ten o'clock. No, well, I'm afraid this won't do. I have to get back to New York. Damn, I'm late already. You see, I'm trying to sell this painting, I won't bore you with the details, but really I should have left an hour ago. Please forgive me, my dear girl. Can we do it next time? And I didn't forget about the shopping, either, but we should do it in New York where the real clothes are. The only things worth buying in Boston are suspenders and snow boots. I can't imagine that would go over at the next dance."

Doreen giggled. "No, I suppose it wouldn't."

"So, until next time. And you keep up what you've been doing. I'm really very proud of you, my darling. What a miraculous surprise."

Tears of joy streamed down her cheeks. This was just the beginning.

"Peter! Peter!" she said.

"Mmm?"

"Peter, wake up. I feel an incredible need for pancakes.

Can you make that happen? Pancakes and bacon and raspberries."

The boy blinked up at Doreen's sunlit form. His face was marked with creases from the bedsheet.

"It's you," he said, like he was the luckiest man in the world. "Come here, come to bed."

"But, Peter. Pancakes!"

"Anything, anything, just please, I need to make sure I'm not dreaming."

Heidi was right. He was adorable.

———◦•◦———

It was winter; it was New England, but that didn't stop them from riding with the top down on Peter's black Jaguar road-ster. Doreen's belly felt warm from their hearty breakfast and she was almost sad to say good-bye. She loved the way she felt with Peter. There was none of the hair-pulling histrionics of the Simon Vale affair, but he was so much more interesting than the weaselly Gordon Lichter or the dull Coburn Ever-bock. She loved the thick flesh of his hands and the glint in his eye. But more than anything she loved his voice—rich and velvety, confident, full of insight and humor. Doreen thought she could talk to Peter Standish forever.

"Really, this is preposterous. We are already in the car! Why not let me drive you back to campus. We could stop on the way. I know a wonderful diner on Highway 1 that has the tiny jukeboxes on the table. We could go in separately, pretend to be strangers, and then make out in the bathroom. What do you say?"

"Tempting, tempting."

"Or how about this? We skip the whole thing and go back to mine, spend the rest of the day in bed. The rest of our lives in bed! We'll have a love-in. Surely there must be some worthy cause. Should I call my mother? She's very plugged in to all the latest charity fads. Child soldiers in Africa or somesuch. The underfed feline refugees of the Balkans."

"I hate cats."

"Do you? Well then, maybe we can support the other side? What about puppies? You can't possibly argue with puppies, can you?"

"I can't, no. But I think you might be able to. I have a feeling you could argue with anyone. There, isn't that South Station? Peter! I'm going to miss my train!"

He drove around the block, pretending to kidnap her, but they both knew he would have to give up and let her out. He couldn't risk driving her back to Chandler. She knew it and he knew it.

"I should have chosen you from the beginning," he said wistfully, almost to himself as she was leaving his car.

"Mmm?" she said, pretending not to hear. But she had heard. And didn't it feel grand?

———◦◦———

It's not like it had happened intentionally. Finding herself stranded at the Mandarin Oriental, she, of course, called Coburn first.

"Doreen! Quick, what, uh, are you wearing?"

"What? No. Coburn. I'm not calling for phone sex."

"No? Oh. That's okay. Be tough anyway since my mom is about to get in the car."

"Your mother? Where are you?"

"San Fran. Didn't I tell you? My mother made me come out for my grandfather's retirement soiree."

"San Francisco! Crap. What am I supposed to do now? I'm basically stuck here in Boston."

"Wait. What? You're in Boston? You're in Boston right now and I'm in San Francisco? What the—why didn't you tell me? Shit. Shit! How could this have happened? Oh man. This sucks. This sucks so hard!"

"Calm down, Coburn. Oh, never mind. I'll think of something."

"Wait. Doreen! Do-do, I miss you so much. Don't you miss me? Don't you miss little Cobey? We think about you all the—"

Doreen hung up. She looked around the hotel lobby and tried to think of what to do. She could simply stay there, on the upholstered bench. Who would try to move her? She certainly looked like she belonged. Or should she get a room and put it under her father's name? Would they let her do that? Even if they did, she couldn't risk it. Their reconnection was so new and tenuous, one little slipup could ruin everything.

And then she remembered Peter Standish. What gentleman would refuse to help his girlfriend's best friend? And was Heidi even his girlfriend? Of course, Heidi thought so, and Heidi was Doreen's friend. But Peter was in college. Surely he didn't think of Heidi as his one and only?

"I'll be there in thirty minutes," he told her.

"You're a good friend," said Doreen.

"I'm sure Coburn was shattered when you told him you were here while he was gone. But I can't say I'm upset about it."

"No?" They were walking, huddled together against the cold Boston night. Snow was just beginning to fall.

"Here we go. This is the place." They entered another hotel. Peter led her through the lobby, past the elevators and down some stairs to a dark lounge.

"Evening, Mr. Standish."

They settled into a small table. She picked up a drinks menu.

"Don't bother with that," Peter said. "She'll have a French 75. And I'll do a Macallan. Neat."

"Thank you very much."

"It's a good night to come," Peter told Doreen. He leaned back on the leather couch with his arms spread. "Not too busy. I despise crowds, don't you? It makes me feel like I'm spending my time unwisely, to be among loads of people at once."

"Mm," said Doreen. Heidi had chosen well. Coburn was prettier, but Peter had magic about him. He was so strong and confident. "You remind me of my father. Is that a strange thing to say?"

"That depends on your father," he said, a twinkle in his eye.

"It's a compliment, trust me. He's a dashing character. I just saw him tonight, in fact. Roland Gibbons? I thought you might know him. You know Addison, right? Addison Gibbons-Brown—Ad-rock—he's my cousin. I don't know if you knew that."

"Ah." Was he bored? He seemed to be looking around, distracted. "It's funny that you didn't call *him*."

Doreen flushed with embarrassment. Of course, that would seem odd, wouldn't it? But she hadn't seen Ad-rock in a decade or more! Would he even know her name?

"Though, he can be such a tool, no offense. I'm going to show you a much better time."

"That's exactly what I thought," said Doreen. "Cheers!"

"Cheers."

They had many, many drinks. Doreen could not be sure how many, but she seemed never to be without one. Along the way she moved from her seat across from him to the couch beside him, allowing her thigh to graze his, her fingers tracing the rim of her martini glass.

"Do you love Heidi?" Doreen asked at some point. "I mean, you don't have to answer that if you don't want to." Her tongue felt thick and uncooperative in her own mouth, but it was a delightful feeling, nonetheless, to be drinking like an adult at an adult's bar with a man.

"Love her? No. Well, I don't know. She's very beautiful and smart and everything." He leaned in secretively. "But she can be a bit calculating, don't you think? She comes from nowhere—as I expect you know—Irish Catholic Yonkers nowhere. And she's created this whole image for herself. Out of necessity, I suppose. I know that's what she believes. I just think it's hard, need I say it? When one comes from money, one attracts a certain amount of attention from people with ambition. Of course, I know I'm preaching to the choir here."

"Oh, yes. I know what you mean exactly. You have to be careful."

Peter nodded. He looked at her with hungry-wolf eyes. Doreen pressed her leg against his and leaned back on the couch, thrusting out her chest. She rolled her head toward him and breathed into his ear.

"Wouldn't you like to kiss me, Peter?" She played with a button on his pink shirt. "Come on, nobody's here."

The bar was more or less empty. Only a few people, the bartender, a girl sitting by herself typing into a tablet. Doreen took Peter's hand and put it on her hip. "Peter, don't you want me?"

And he did. He wanted her. Did he ever.

Well, they were young and nobody was married or anything. It was a pity they had to uphold these inane loyalties to people, people like Heidi Whelan. Heidi was only interested in Peter for what he could do for her. But Doreen didn't need Peter. She had her father now and everything that came with being Roland Gibbons's daughter.

Doreen gazed out the train window at the passing suburban landscape and considered whether she should change her name back. Gibbons was her rightful surname anyway. Gray. Blech! How much more dreary and lifeless could a name get?

Of course, changing her name to Doreen Gibbons would signal to her mother that she was taking her father's side against her. She would be heartbroken. People and their feelings—her mother, Heidi. How dull it all was! Peter wanted her, not Heidi. Her father wanted her, not her mother. Was any of that her fault? People will make their own choices in this life, she thought. If they choose her over somebody else, that was up to them.

She wouldn't say anything to Heidi about Peter. Let him break it off with her if he wanted to or not. What did any of that have to do with her? She stepped off the train at the Hamilton stop and began her journey back to campus. Everything felt so different now than it had when she'd left the previous day. Yesterday she'd been her father's burden, his obligation. Now she was his prize. Peter would be lucky to have her. They all would.

25

Jane Vale turned onto Main Street about a minute after Doreen did. The two girls walked, separated by a few feet, past Bread the News Café and the Vale family's hardware store. Doreen checked her own reflection in the plate glass window of a clothing store and Jane paused, backed into a shadow. She could be patient. It would all be over soon.

After Doreen left the hotel bar with the pink-shirted boy, Jane found a twenty-four-hour diner nearby where she could await the dawn. She went over her notes, her recordings, her pictures, and made her plan. She was proud of what she'd compiled. The girl was hers; she was sure of it. Jane could not remember the last time she'd felt like she won something.

The energy of victory, along with cup after cup of acid coffee, kept her awake through the night until it was time for the early train back to Hamilton. She didn't find Doreen on the train as she'd hoped, but it made no difference. She could wait. In Hamilton she sat on the bench in the station until she spotted the raven hair, the red coat.

They approached the Peabody Street Bridge. *If she looks over the edge*, thought Jane, *if she thinks of Simon even once, even in passing, I will delete everything. I will call it off.* Of course, Doreen didn't even pause, made no indication that the place meant anything to her. Was Jane relieved? Happy? Vindicated? She turned to her phone. She had all the pictures lined up. She was prepared. Her finger trembled as she pressed SEND.

The cell phone beep shook Doreen from her daydream. Probably it was Heidi checking in. She would have to come up with a story. She'd say her father got her a room at the Mandarin. Of course! They had a sweet little breakfast together, and he dropped her off at the train.

But the text came from an unrecognized number. And there was no message, just a picture of herself—with Peter. They were sitting beside one another at the hotel bar. "What the hell?" she said. She looked around. Was somebody following her? Her cell phone dinged again. Another picture. This one of Doreen and Peter kissing. And another—one of his hands up her shirt, the other with a firm grasp on the back of her hair, empty glasses crowding the little table in front of them.

Was this someone's idea of a joke? "Ha ha," Doreen wrote back. "Very funny." But the pictures didn't stop. The next one was of Doreen in the lobby of the Mandarin Ori ental, her father's arm around her neck. Then she was on the street, looking around as her father vomited behind a trash can. Then she was in the restaurant, her face lit up and happy as she sat across from her father. That was the most humiliating picture of all—even worse than the trashy ones from the bar. Her face was so open and willing, so vulnerable. Doreen's desperation for her father's affection was so obvious it made her sick. That smile! So revoltingly eager to please. "Delete!" she yelled. "Delete!" Finally, in the last picture, she saw herself in the Hamilton train station, perfectly coiffed, waiting for the train to Boston.

"Who are you?" she typed to her torturer. She felt violated, and queasy with fear. Someone had been following her, but who? And for how long? What were their intentions? The wind whipped the back of her neck.

Her phone rang. "Hello? Hello?! Who is this? What do you want?" But nobody answered. Instead she heard the sound of her own voice—some sort of crazy person's remix of things she said over the course of the previous day. "Do you love Heidi?" she heard herself asking. "Don't you want to kiss me, Peter? Daddy? Daddy? Don't you—don't you—don't you want to kiss me? What's wrong Daddy? I'm too tired to go shopping. Daddy? Daddy? Don't you want to kiss me? There's nobody here."

Doreen turned off the phone. She looked around. "Stop this! Stop what you're doing!" she yelled. She would kill whoever was behind this, she would strangle that person with her own two hands. "Reveal yourself, you coward!"

"Ha!"

Doreen spun around. A tiny hippie girl materialized near the bridge.

"Funny for you of all people to call someone a coward, Doreen Gray. Ha ha ha."

Doreen marched over to the girl. "Who are you? What do you want?"

"Personally, I think that a person who steps out with her best friend's boyfriend is pretty cowardly. But that's me. I have, you know, morals."

"Who the hell are you?!" Doreen demanded. She gripped the girl's arm, but she seemed unperturbed by

Doreen. She stood her ground in her alpaca sweater, her backpack. "What do you want from me?"

"I want to ruin your life," the girl said, grinning.

"But I don't even know you! Why would a perfect stranger want to . . ." And then a picture came into Doreen's mind. A family portrait of a graduation. Simon, his mother, and a girl in a cap and gown. This girl, the deranged socio-path who was out to get her now. Doreen had paused over the photograph on the mantel of the house on Leaving Place because something in the girl's face disturbed her. While Simon and his mother leaned in with their heads and flashed their teeth, his sister's lips were pursed closed. She stared directly out of the frame as if challenging Doreen to look harder and deeper. Doreen had brought the frame right up to her face. *You think you see me?* The girl's face taunted from under her graduation cap. *You don't see me, I see you!*

"Jane Vale," Doreen said.

"Marvelous to meet you," said Jane. "A real treat."

Doreen's mind raced. What did she have on this girl? How could she stop her from sending out those pictures? She had to play it cool. Bullies want to see you freak out, and she couldn't give Jane that power.

"And I'm so pleased to meet *you* finally," Doreen said in her most pleasant voice. She grasped Jane's rough little hand and shook it, looking deep into her eyes. She would have to think of something—fast.

Jane pulled her hand away. "Ha! You won't be so pleased when everyone you know sees these pictures!" She thumbed through the pictures on her phone. "Which one shall I send first? I have access to the whole school's e-mail, by the way. Let me see, the one with you and your best friend's boyfriend? Or maybe the one of your drunken buffoon of a father yacking all over Newbury Street."

"Give me that phone!"

"I have to say, you sounded *pathetic* in that restaurant. Like a little baby. Oh *Daddy*, do you weawy think I'm pwetty? Do you wuv me, Daddy?" Jane laughed. "Meanwhile, the guy was sucking down scotches like they were cherry soda. You could tell he didn't give a shit about you."

"Give me that phone! Now!"

"What, this phone? This one right here?"

"Yes!" Doreen seized the phone out of Jane's grip and hurled it over the Peabody Street Bridge. It shattered against the rocks.

"Well, that was dramatic. But worry not, your pictures are safe. I've got them all ready to send on my e-mail. Life with the Internet—glorious, isn't it?"

Doreen lunged at Jane. The girl was small, but she had a lot of fight in her. She elbowed and kicked, but Doreen got her arms behind her back. She pushed her up against the railing of the bridge.

"Delete those photos. Do it!"

"Or what? You'll kill me? Isn't that a little extreme? Even for you?" Jane squeaked. Doreen pushed her cheek against the railing. She had her fingers around her throat.

"Why shouldn't I? Who would miss you? You,

rodent! Anyway, haven't I already sent one Vale over the Peabody Street Bridge?" She laughed. "Why not the whole family?" She laughed harder. "Your mom, too! And that horrible couch!"

"Stop laughing! Shut up!" With a mighty heave, Jane Vale pushed Doreen off her, into the dirt. She gasped for air. "You don't get to laugh at my family. Do you hear me? You don't have the right."

"Don't I? But it's so funny! Ha ha ha." Doreen stood up and wiped the dirt off the back of her red coat.

"Shut up! Shut up, I said! I'll send the pictures right now. I have my tablet, you know. I can do it right here. I'll destroy you. I'll end you, Doreen Gray!"

Watching the red-faced girl stumble toward her backpack, Doreen realized she knew how to stop her. Of course! Why hadn't she thought of it before?

Jane dug around in her backpack. "Wait until everybody sees what you've been up to. Then you won't think it's so funny!"

"And who is going to show them, you?" Doreen asked coolly.

Jane held her tablet in the air. "You're damned right I am. And you haven't even seen the half of it. I have the goods on you, Doreen Gray. You're going to rue the day you ever heard the name Simon Vale."

"You're not stupid, Jane. And I don't think you are a liar. So why don't you give up this whole charade? Give me the tablet—or don't. Actually, it makes no difference.

You and I both know you are never going to publish those pictures."

"That's where you're wrong, you dumb tramp. Don't even think for a second that you can stop me."

"Stop you?" Doreen shook her head and clucked her tongue. "I have no intention of stopping you. I won't have to. You see, on the day those pictures go public, I will walk over to Hamilton Hardware. I know the clerk there, you know. He hasn't been himself lately, but I am sure he would enjoy hearing from me—about how much I love him. I need him. How I can't live without him."

"Leave Simon out of it!"

"Oh, Simon, I'll say. Every day without you has been torture."

"I'll keep him from the store! I'll hide him from you, don't think I won't!"

"And I'll keep at it. Day after day. I'm patient, you know. Soon we'll be taking walks together. I'll let him tell me how he feels and I'll let him think I feel the same way. Won't he just love that? Won't it just fill him with joy?"

Jane covered her ears. "Leave him alone! Haven't you done enough?"

"And then one day—" Doreen gazed meaningfully over the railing of the Peabody Street Bridge. Her hair whipped her face in the wind. "One day I'll turn to him and I'll tell him how I despise him." A dark disgust crossed her face. "'Love you?' I'll say, 'I could never love you! You're an insect. You're less than nothing!'"

"That would kill him!" Jane said. "That's what you're saying, you know. You're saying you would kill my brother, a boy you claimed to love! He's already—" Jane looked down. Her hands were shaking. "Haven't you done enough?"

"I don't know, have I? It's up to you. This could end right here. You destroy those images and disappear from my life. And I will disappear from yours . . . and Simon's."

Jane nodded. She hunched into herself. "Okay. Okay. You win." Doreen almost felt sorry for her. But the girl had brought it on herself. Nobody messes with me, Doreen thought, not anymore.

"Give it to me." Jane handed over her tablet. Doreen threw it over the railing into the ravine. The girl said she had already uploaded the pictures, but Doreen felt safe. Jane would never put her brother in danger.

"If I see anything," Doreen warned.

"You won't."

"I'd say it was nice to meet you, but I think we both know that's not true."

"I hate you, Doreen Gray. You—I despise you."

"That's your right, I suppose." Doreen left Jane peering out over the bridge railing—at her broken electronics? Her broken future? Whatever it was no longer concerned Doreen. It had been, all things considered, a remarkably easy and satisfying encounter. But there was one thing she still didn't understand. She turned back to the girl.

"Why did you show me this? I mean, if you had the

addresses, why didn't you simply send the pictures out? That's what I would have done."

"I don't know. I guess I wanted, I thought, I mean if Simon loved you . . . and Simon is so good. I wanted to give you a chance to . . . to . . ."

"Apologize? Redeem myself?"

Jane shrugged miserably.

"Oh, *honey*," said Doreen with a laugh and skipped on toward home.

What was the lesson? All she did was identify Jane's chief weakness and exploit it for her own benefit. Love, that was Jane's problem. What Jane had done to avenge Simon's broken heart required patience and selflessness. Doreen could not think of a soul for whom she would go to such trouble—or who would do anything of the kind for her. Except, of course, Simon Vale. Was that irony? "Oh well," Doreen thought. "Probably it's all a bit overrated. Love."

She was proud of herself. She'd grown accustomed to a certain kind of life and Jane Vale threatened to annihilate it. Without consulting Heidi, Doreen had quashed the problem. That success, along with her triumphant reunion with her father, seemed reason enough for Doreen to feel happy.

But she didn't feel happy, not at all. She was aware of an aching dread in the depth of her chest as she approached her dorm. What she had done to Jane was efficient and thorough—but it was basically blackmail. She may have saved her reputation, but what was she doing to her soul?

Ugh! She wouldn't even care if it weren't for that damned picture! The picture was always watching. And she couldn't help but think of what it would look like now that she'd slept with Peter, destroyed Jane Vale, and more! There was Graham's virginity (captured), Chastity's hair (burned off). The time she made Brian Whitaker break up with Cynthia Stern because Cynthia supposedly told Whitney Owens that she thought Doreen was a snob. Or how she talked Alex Cummings into asking Madison Morrison to sit with him at dinner, knowing that she would reject him and it would make his stutter go bananas. Or how she'd gotten Mr. Bugiali to give her an A in choir even though she never attended a single class, rehearsal, or recital. It was her stage fright, she said, her eyes big, her eyelashes aflutter.

She climbed up the stairs to her floor, her head throbbing. The picture knew all about what she'd done. It frightened her to think of how it would look now, after every misdeed, every connivance, every time she used someone to get what she wanted. It was supposed to free her to do as she liked, and it had, but at what cost? Why did victory feel so foul? Back in her room, she collapsed on her bed, hugging Mopey tight. Was she lost? Doomed? Why couldn't she just be happy to have won?

If only she could tell someone. Confess her secret, bare her soul! Certainly she knew someone worthy of her confidence, someone to whom she might bring her story, to seek comfort in candor and companionship. Heidi? Biz? They were her friends, weren't they? They could offer her understanding. But then they would know. Everything she did would be subject to their judgment. They would think of her soul decaying into putrescence and so would she. No. It would diminish the gift. The only way for her to live this beautiful life was to endure the loneliness that accompanied it. It was the price she had to pay. Mopey would have to remain her soul confessor.

She threw her stuffed elephant off the bed and sobbed into her pillows. Small, grubby, pathetic Jane Vale had more than she did, more than she could ever have. She had love! And Doreen, despite how thoroughly she had trounced her enemy, felt jealous of her. Jealousy was the constant companion of her old life, and feeling it now put her right back in it.

Doreen turned to her reflection in the mirror. Even with tears in her eyes she looked flawless. No matter what was happening to her on the inside, everything she'd gone through had only made her more beautiful. She gazed at herself and allowed the sight of her own face to calm her aching heart. So she was lonely, so what? Anyone who possessed greatness had to feel a little solitary. It was the burden of excellence. And if she allowed herself to give in to despair, then there was no purpose to any of it.

Doreen straightened her back and wiped the tears from her cheeks with the corner of her old duvet. She felt herself returning. The whole miracle of the picture was that it could absorb any and all ugliness in Doreen's life. The least she could do was enjoy it. And to prove it to herself, she spent the rest of the afternoon devising a scheme to turn Misha and Miyuki against one another, just to see if she could.

It worked like magic.

———•◦———

When Jane finally left the bridge and walked back to Leaving Place it was with a heavy heart. Doreen's victory over her had demolished her momentum and emptied her life of purpose. For as long as she could remember, she'd seen her mother bear the weight of what their father had done to her like wet clothes, and Jane swore she would never give anyone the means to defeat her so utterly.

So she was guarded; she had few friends. She let her ambition for herself be her only concern other than the welfare of her brother. And that had been enough. Let him have the social life—the athletic glory, the dates to prom. Let him live enough for both of them while she focused on her future. But now? When he jumped off that bridge he sacrificed more than his body and his potential. He had sacrificed Jane, too. Who was she now? The Peace Corps was done. She could apply to college, but with Simon sick, she would have to go somewhere local and the prospects were dismal.

It pained her to admit that being the quarterback's sister had meant something to her. As much as she used to rib him about it, she was proud of his talent, the way he took charge of the field, how invulnerable he seemed. But no one was invulnerable, that's what this whole thing had taught her. Everyone could be taken down—everyone, that is, except Doreen Gray.

Jane saw her house and stopped. She wasn't ready to go in yet, to face her brother's neutral gape in the light of the old TV. Through the kitchen window, she could see her mother heating up dinner with the same disappointed expression she carried around day after day. Jane felt her body stiffen as if she was afraid to take one step closer, afraid of what it meant to belong here.

"I'm still young," Jane said aloud. The wind dried the tears on her cheeks. "Anything could happen. I'm young. I'm still so young!" But she didn't feel young. She felt very, very old.

26

Black leggings. Black miniskirt. Black turtleneck sweater. Black boots. Hair tied into a low, messy bun. Clear lip gloss. Killer diamond earrings.

"Well, well, Elizabeth, look at you," said Mr. Cameron. In the evening light the pictures looked different than they looked during the day. Biz wondered if anyone would even notice them—or if they did, what they would think. The opening was less than an hour away, and Biz was so anxious she felt as if she was moving in gauze. She was happy to see Mr. Cameron. One more minute alone with her work and things might have gotten ugly.

"Doreen did it," said Biz. "I don't know. She said I had to make an effort."

Mr. Cameron nodded approvingly. "You look serious, my dear, like an artist."

Biz looked down. She liked the boots. They made her feel strong. "Really? Well, I guess that's good."

"Of course it is!" Mr. Cameron pulled off his knit cap, tucked it into a pocket of his coat, and looked around at the installation. A large guy, despite his light mannerisms, with a full gray mustache, gray ponytail, and bald pate, Mr. Cameron was goofy the way that boarding school teachers are often goofy—a combination of overenthusiasm and limited time with the outside world. His arm on Biz's shoulder communicated a mother's pride and hope and fear. She breathed in his contact and tried to calm down.

"I'm not sure I should have allowed you to talk me into this," said Biz. Everyone was coming—her mother, her uncle, Doreen and Heidi, the entire school and their connected parents. Seth Greenbaum told her he was bringing his mother, Eloise Peek, the famous gallery owner. Biz even went to the library to invite the girl in the funny sweater, but the librarian said she had quit. Maybe it was better that way. Already Biz was so nervous, she was afraid she might puke.

"Oh, you'll be fine. Just try to relax. And have fun! These things go by faster than you think."

———⊶⊷———

Heidi padded down the hall to the showers in a towel and flip-flops, weighing the pros and cons of attending Biz's opening. The problem, of course, was Roland Gibbons, the man himself. To Doreen's delight (and Heidi's disbelief) he'd showed up for Parents' Weekend, which meant he would be there, at the gallery. Roland Gibbons in the flesh.

The last time Heidi saw him he made it perfectly clear that she was never to make contact with him again, or else. Could it have been three years ago? It felt like a lifetime had passed, but also like she could click her heels together and be back there in a flash. In the shower, she leaned back and closed her eyes.

You'll get your education, my dear. You'll get your chance. Don't blow it. Oh, and don't contact me. If I hear from you again it's all over. Understand? Marvelous. I expect you can let yourself out.

Heidi watched herself in the mirror as she blow-dried her hair. She wished she knew if he had told his daughter about their arrangement. She had watched Doreen closely ever since she'd returned from Boston, and though she seemed more or less the same, Heidi was sure there was something different about her, a new distance, as if the girl was keeping a secret. Heidi piled the hair on her head as she paced around in her towel. Could Doreen know? Did her father spill? Heidi looked for signs obsessively, but she really could never be certain one way or the other. And then Doreen would be so sweet and attentive that Heidi would tell herself that nothing had changed between them, it was all in her head.

But even if Doreen was still in the dark, being in the presence of her and Roland simultaneously seemed like pushing it. Would he tell their secret there, in front of his family? And what if Doreen did know? Would she be able to contain herself when she saw Heidi and Roland in the same place? The whole school would be there. She could lose everything she worked for. Heidi knew the wise thing would be to skip the event altogether, lay low, hope it all blew over. She fell back on her bed and stared at the ceiling. Yes, she decided. The thing to do was play sick, stay in bed. Skip it.

But then she turned and saw Biz's empty bed. How would she react when Heidi blew off her big opening? Biz practically lived at the photo lab for the entire semester. It would break her heart if Heidi ditched her now. And the moment at the Hamilton Inn when she was honest with Peter about herself marked the beginning of a momentous change inside Heidi. She craved honesty now. Biz had risen in her estimation for that reason. This was a girl who lived with integrity. Heidi wouldn't allow the sins of her past to get in the way of Biz's night.

Heidi pushed aside the covers and attacked her closet. Well, she'd say this, the evening would certainly be interesting. That was guaranteed. And Heidi could never stay away from interesting. Plus, she'd called in reinforcements. Peter was on his way and he would make it all better. Though, when they spoke on the phone earlier she thought Peter sounded irritated—and not for the first time. He was overwhelmed, she told herself. He was juggling a lot. And Heidi had been annoying about this event. It wasn't his fault he didn't know what was riding on it for her.

He mentioned something he wanted to talk about. In person. What was so important that he couldn't say what it was on the phone? It was probably about their future. Of course! He was going to tell her that he loved her! Finally! Heidi had heard the declaration many times from a variety of unworthy boys. But now at last she would get to say those magical words of reciprocation: *I love you, too.*

That's why he'd been so moody lately. It was all a buildup to the big declaration. Giddy with anticipation, Heidi finished dressing in no time. She looked at the clock. The gallery would be opening soon. She wanted to go, get on with it, get it all started, but she knew she had to wait. The power move was to be the last one to arrive. She sat on her bed and opened a magazine. When she looked at the clock again, one minute had passed.

———•◦•———

Desperate for an activity, students and their parents arrived in droves to see Biz's art. They milled around the large lobby turned gallery at Douglas Hall, clutching plastic cups of sparkling water and apple juice, happy to have something to distract them from one another. By the time Biz's family arrived, the place was packed.

"Isn't there anything stronger?" Mumzy asked, frowning at the soft drink handed to her by an underclassman.

"Oh, calm down," said Roland. "You can get through one event without alcohol."

"I can. But can you? Oh, hello, Elizabeth. Well done." Mumzy kissed her daughter on both cheeks.

"Yes, very nice. Though I thought there would be a picture or two of my girl." Roland put an arm around Doreen.

"Oh, Daddy," said Doreen. She looked prim in a blue ruffled shirtdress and flats. She held tight to her father's elbow. "Great job, Bizzy. They are so good."

"Pictures of Doreen are never in focus for some reason," said Biz. "Except for one, but—"

"Hey!" said Addison, his mouth full of pretzels. "Hey, that's Peter Standish. What is he doing here?"

"What?"

"Pete! Pedro! Over here!" Addison waved madly over the crowd and Peter acknowledged him with a nod of his chin. He turned sideways and slithered through the swarms of people.

"I didn't realize he'd be here." Doreen smoothed the front of her dress.

"Mother, you remember Peter Standish, don't you? A Harvard chum," said Addison.

"Hello again, Ms. Gibbons-Brown."

"Gloria, please. Lovely to see you again, Peter."

"And uh . . ."

"Doreen Gray." Doreen shook Peter's hand.

"You guys met at the dance," said Biz. "You're bad with names, huh?"

"Of course. Doreen Gray. Doreen, yes. Uh, hello. Hello again."

"Hello, Peter," said Doreen softly. She introduced her father.

"What the hell are you doing at Chandler?" said Adrock with a playful punch in the arm.

"Hm? Oh. Well, this may be awkward." Peter's grin was charmingly sheepish. "We seem to have a, well, a buddy in common."

"Is Heidi coming?" said Biz. "I haven't seen her yet."

"She told me to meet her here. I thought she'd have arrived by now."

"Wait. You're with Heidi Whelan?" said Addison. "You old goat. Good luck with that. She's a piece of work, that girl."

"Who now?" asked Gloria. She shook her head at a tray of sushi on offer. Addison grabbed a handful of California rolls. He popped them into his mouth one at a time.

"Heidi, mother. Heidi Whelan. My roommate," said Biz with a roll of her eyes. "Heidi Whelan! You've met her like a thousand times."

Roland began to cough uncontrollably.

"You don't have to take that tone with me, young lady. I don't know why you expect me to keep all of your little friends straight. Roland, are you quite all right?"

"Fine. Fine. I think I will get another drink," he croaked. "Want anything, anyone?"

"Poor Daddy," said Doreen. "Have you got a cold?"

"I'm just a bit parched is all. We should have brought some little bottles from the hotel."

"You act like I have a hundred friends," Biz mumbled.

"Ha! Now who can't get through an event without alcohol?" said Gloria.

"Will this help?" Peter fished his flask out from the inside pocket of his coat.

"Oh, my dear boy." Roland reached his plastic cup out and let Peter fill it.

"Elizabeth, there you are!" Mr. Cameron approached the group. "There's someone I want you to meet. Hang on, is this your proud father?"

"No, my indifferent uncle. Roland Gibbons. And this is my mother, Gloria Gibbons-Brown. Mother, this is—Mom! Where are you going?"

"I need some sparkling, my darling. I will return shortly."

"I'm coming with you," said Roland. "What have you got in there, kid? Gasoline?"

"Dewar's. If I'd known . . ."

"No need to apologize," said Roland.

"I wasn't."

"Should I come with you, Daddy?"

"I'm Elizabeth's photography teacher," Mr. Cameron explained to Addison, since he seemed to be the only one paying attention.

"I know, Mr. C. I was in your class, like, three years ago. Addison Gibbons-Brown. I made the series called *Animal Buttholes.*"

"Oh, oh yes. My apologies. How could I forget?"

"Animal what?" It was Heidi. She slipped up to Peter's side wearing a snug, emerald-green suit with a deeply plunging neckline and high heels. "Hello, babe," she said to Peter and kissed him lightly on the lips. "Sorry I'm late."

"Buttholes. Animal Buttholes."

"You look nice," said Peter.

"Hello, hello." Heidi kissed greetings all around.

"Ad-rock was telling us about his own artistic explorations," said Peter. "I don't understand. What were the pictures of, exactly?"

"Bizzy." Heidi grasped Biz's wrist and looked straight into her eyes. "The installation is just gorgeous. I'm so proud of you."

"Isn't it, though?" said Mr. Cameron. "Now, Elizabeth, if I might steal you away for a moment."

"Buttholes. It was a lot of different animals' buttholes. Like a dog butthole. And a cat. And a horse."

"Ah. That explains it."

"You really like it, Heidi?" Biz asked.

"It's—it's just astonishing, Biz. Really. I didn't know that you were paying attention. The self-portraits are a revelation."

"Congratulations," said Peter.

"Thanks. Thanks, you guys. That means a lot. Okay, okay. I guess I have to go meet someone now."

"The belle of the ball," said Doreen.

"Where's, uh, your father?" Heidi asked. "I'm, obviously, you know, keen to meet him."

"Oh, he just stepped away for a minute with Aunt Gloria. He'll be back in a sec."

"Uh."

A caterer walked by and bumped Doreen. She used Peter's arm to stop her fall.

"Sorry," said Doreen. "I mean, excuse me."

"That's okay," said Peter with a smile.

Addison picked a spring roll off a tray. "Wait a minute! Now I remember cousin Doreen. Hold on, but weren't you kind of fat before? Yeah. Fat and super dorky. Sure. Doreen. With the crazy mother. I remember you."

"Ad-rock, isn't there something else you could be eating?" said Heidi.

"There they are!" said Doreen. "That's my father, there—with Gloria."

"Sorry we tarried. Needless to say, Roland knows everyone here. Gloria Gibbons-Brown," she said.

"Yes. Heidi Whelan. We've met."

"And this is my father," Doreen said proudly. "Roland Gibbons. Daddy, this is my dear friend, Heidi."

He turned his body so that they stood facing one another. It was a moment or two before one of them thought to extend a hand, to shake. *Here goes nothing*, Heidi thought.

"Heidi Wello," he said.

"Whelan," she said, clearing her throat. So they were going to act like strangers. She could do that. She caught Doreen out of the corner of her eye to see if she was in on the ruse, but she was saying something to Peter, totally unaware. That was a good sign. "Heidi Whelan." Okay, she thought. Okay. Doreen doesn't know. And she's not going to find out.

"Have we met before?" Roland asked, still grasping her hand. He cocked his head to one side and looked deeper. It was unsettling.

"N-no. No, I don't think so."

"No? You sure we never met?"

Heidi shook her head. She pulled her hand away and grabbed Peter's hand. Roland was taking the strangers thing a little far. Why wouldn't he just let it go?

"People often think I look familiar." And Heidi heard it then, the old Yonkers accent. *People awfen tink I look familiah.* What the hell! "Ahem. I mean, famili*ar*." She would not let him turn her into her old self.

"Do they really?" he said. He shook his head slowly. "I find that hard to believe." He took a sip from his drink.

"You cold, babe?" asked Peter.

Roland took a small step closer to Heidi. She smelled scotch and cigars. "But I could swear we met before. You're absolutely positive? Do I not look familiar to you?"

". . . Because you're shivering."

"No. No, I'm sure we never did. Anyway, it's nice to meet you now, but I gotta . . . I mean, I'm afraid I must, you know, uh, pardon, I mean, excuse me."

"Well, never mind," said Roland. He stepped back to let Heidi pass.

"Where are you going?" Peter said.

"I just have to ask Franklin something. It's for school. Sorry, I, uh, I'll be right back."

The blast of night air on Heidi's face felt like salvation. She took it into her lungs in greedy gulps, leaning against the side of Alfred Douglas Hall as the comers and goers clustered near the gallery entrance. He was trying to get in her head, to mess with her. And it was working, goddamn it. And the accent coming back! What the hell was that about? She felt wobbly, unsure of herself. The conversation repeated itself over and over again in her mind—like that scene in the action picture when the one guy turns to the other guy and says: *But if you're out here, who's flying the plane?*

"Smoke?"

"Ahh! Shit, Gordon, you scared me!" Heidi put her hand on her heart.

"Sorry." Gordon Lichter stepped out from the shadows. He had the hood of his duffle coat up over his head and a cigarette in his mouth. The way his hair fell in his face as he squinted in the smoke gave him the look of a classic teenage brooder. "I thought you might want a smoke."

"No, no, thanks. I would take a handful of pistachios if you had them."

"Huh?"

"Nothing." Gordon leaned on the wall next to Heidi and took a long drag off his cigarette. "How are you doing, Gordon?"

"Me? I'm doing shitty. Thanks for asking. Doreen in there?"

"Yes."

Gordon nodded. "She with someone? That Harvard guy? What's his name? Dickface?"

"Do you mean Peter? He's inside, but he's with me. I mean, not right this second, but generally." Though, had she just imagined it? Or had he seemed a bit cold to her in there?

Gordon shook his head. "No, the other one. Everbastard."

"Oh, you mean Coburn. I didn't know you knew about him. No. He's not here."

"I know about all of them." He sounded almost boastful.

"Gordon, look, I know you feel a bit raw."

"Ha!"

"But don't you think you should move on? I mean, you're seventeen years old!"

"Could you not, please? I think we're beyond the 'other fish in the sea' speech, all right? I don't want to hear it."

"Fair enough." Heidi reached out a hand and Gordon gave her his cigarette. She took a drag and handed it back.

"Can I ask you something? You don't have to answer if you don't want to."

He shrugged. "Shoot."

"What is it about Doreen? I know that she's beautiful and everything, but the effect she has on boys. You know, not to brag, I have been told that I'm not bad-looking myself, but no one has ever—"

"Jumped off a bridge for you?"

Heidi nodded. The conversation rang with mild disloyalty, like she was breaking some kind of girl code, but she had to know.

"Beautiful doesn't cover it. Yeah, she's beautiful, but I've been with beautiful girls before, okay? And Doreen was different. Being with her, I felt like I was a part of something big, something important. I would have done anything for her—lie, cheat, get kicked out of school, I didn't care!"

"So then maybe it's best for you that it didn't work out."

"Maybe." Gordon scraped his cigarette against the wall and threw it into the bushes. "But it sure as hell doesn't feel like it's better. You know what I think about? That kid, the one from the dance."

"Simon."

"Yeah, Simon. I think of how I watched that poor jerk like, get your hands off, she's mine, you know? Because I thought she was." He shook his head. "I thought she was mine, you get it? It's funny, maybe. I don't know." Gordon shoved his hands in his pockets, his body looking even smaller than normal, like a kid in his father's coat.

Heidi put an arm on his back. "It'll be okay, Gordon. Just give it time."

"Anyway," he said.

And he was gone.

Heidi took a deep breath. Time to rejoin the party. It would look suspicious if she just left like that, plus she was supposed to be supporting Biz. Peter would help her. With him at her side she could muster up charming and witty and marvelous. Then, before she knew it, it would all be over.

"Go back in there or he wins," she mumbled to herself. She would not be a victim like Gordon. She would maintain control.

"There you are."

Heidi spun around. Stepping out of the shadows, looking perfectly dapper in his gray wool suit and tangerine-colored bowtie, was Roland Gibbons.

"I've been looking for you, *Heidi Whelan*."

Okay, she thought, gloves off.

"What do you want, Roland?" She hoped she sounded stronger than she felt.

"Oh, nothing much. I just wanted to thank you."

"Thank me?"

"Yes. I understand that you are responsible, at least partially, for the positive change that has come over my daughter since the fall. She has blossomed under your, how shall we call it? Your guidance."

He lay a hand on her shoulder. It wasn't a particularly big hand, but it was powerful.

"I learned from the best," said Heidi. She squirmed out of his grip.

"Isn't it just a small, small world? I take it you and Doreen have become intimate friends. I think that's so nice! For both of you."

"Why don't you cut the crap? What exactly are you trying to pull here, jerkoff?" Heidi hissed.

"Pull? Nothing."

"I think you're pressing your luck, okay? You've got Doreen. You don't deserve her, but you got her. Our friendship has nothing to do with that."

"Ah. Well. That's what I came to talk to you about. You see, I don't believe Doreen would feel so chummy about you if she knew certain facts about your, ahem, circumstances."

"Oh yeah? Well, what would she think of you if she knew you were a perverted statutory rapist? Huh?"

"That old line? My dear, you really need some new material."

"Don't you my dear me, pedophile."

"That's enough!" Roland grabbed her by the arm. Hard. "Listen to me, you little shrew. I want you to stay away from her. Do you hear me? She is my daughter and I don't want her socializing with the likes of you. I appreciate all you've done for her, I meant that seriously, but it's over. I will keep your secret and you can graduate and be on your way in just a few months. All you have to do is keep your grubby Yonkers mitts off my kid." He let her go and she rubbed her arm with a smile. She could not back down. She could not show fear.

"You're disgusting. You know that? Maybe you *should* tell her, so she can see what kind of creep her father is."

"What kind of creep is that? The kind who offers his wisdom to a lost little girl only to be paid back with lies and blackmail? I'm sorry, my dear, but it's hard for me to see how you come out ahead in her estimation."

"Stop calling me 'my dear'!"

Roland pinched the bridge of his nose. "I'm so tired of you. I don't know why I ever bothered, why I thought to lend some of my knowledge to the daughter of a sanitation worker." He ran his thumbs across the fingers of both hands, a look of disgust on his face, as if conversing with Heidi was equivalent to direct contact with garbage. "I would expect you to be grateful."

"Grateful? For what? For getting me fired?"

"You know that was not me, that was my wife."

"Ex-wife."

"Yes, how adorably astute of you. My ex-wife." The fury that had overtaken Roland a minute before vanished and he resumed the smug expression that Heidi remembered from their Hamptons days. "The poor imbecile misconstrued our friendship as a threat and she wanted you gone. I did not see the point of arguing. Happy wife, happy life. That sort of thing. You were beginning to bore me, anyway. So doting. So obedient. I thought you had more fire. More zip! You were so young, then. And quite pretty. Do you remember that little party I took you to? Oh, my sister was scandalized. It was marvelous." He chuckled to himself. Heidi let her face flush. That party was the single most important event of her life. To him it was nothing more than a practical joke.

"So happy I could entertain you."

"Yes," he said with a wave of his hand. "But by the time Constantina arrived I felt rather done with you. Our little lessons had become tedious, and it seemed that everywhere I looked, there you were. With your eager little face and your ponytail. Have you got a light?" Roland plucked a cigar out of his coat. He snipped off the end with a small contraption. He felt around in his pockets. "Never mind, here it is." He struck a match and turned his back to the wind to light his cigar.

"You make me sick, do you know that?"

"Oh please." He waved the lit match and dropped it into the grass. "You think you can play holier-than-thou with me? Even if I could have stopped Constantina from having you fired, which is doubtful, what are we talking about here? A summer job? Nine dollars an hour? You've taken me for much more than that now. Haven't you?" He stepped closer to Heidi, the light of the cigar reflected in the dark parts of his eyes. "You dare to pass judgment on me. When I find you standing in my own apartment, having connived my simple doorman with some lie about being my art dealer's assistant. But still I am polite. I offer you a drink. I invite you to sit down. And then what do you do? You sit there in your little outfit and threaten me!"

The stink of the cigar got stronger as he approached. Heidi closed her eyes. She saw herself there, inside the glowing white penthouse on lower Fifth Avenue with the wraparound deck and the famous art collection, just as it was described in the real estate section of the *New York Times*. It only took three days of waiting on a bench outside his building, eating sandwiches her mother made for the new job she thought she had in a Midtown hotel. Three days of reading books from the list he had given her, watching the well-heeled tenants enter and exit his building, until she saw him, heard him give orders to his doorman, made her move.

Roland's face was very close now. She could see the stubble on his cheek, the sprout of his eyebrow. "Statutory rape, you said. Second degree. Oh, you had it all figured out, didn't you? I, who never laid a hand on you! Never did a thing that wasn't decorous! I respected you, for some reason. I imagined remembering our time together with fondness. But not you. You had to turn it into something tawdry. Didn't you?"

He thrust the cigar toward her and she jumped back with a gasp. He laughed. All he ever did was laugh at her. He did it then, in his apartment. After she got everything she wanted, got him to agree to pay her way through his alma mater, the illustrious Chandler Academy. Before she had a chance to feel satisfied at her victory, he laughed. Aloud. He laughed and laughed and laughed, the kind of convulsive hysterics that cannot be faked or stopped. He wiped the tears from his face and laughed more. Then he changed the rules. He said he would pull the strings, pay her way, but only because he admired her pluck.

"I did it all, didn't I? I got you enrolled here, made sure your tuition was covered. I had but one requirement: that I never hear from you again. How hard could that have been? A small price to pay, I should think, for entrée into our closed world. But you could not do even that. The next thing I hear, you are dating my nephew, living with my niece. I let it go. She is nothing but a schoolgirl, I thought, let her have her little games. I didn't care enough, you see, to stop you. But this, with Doreen, no, I'm afraid this all ends now. Tonight. Whatever story you've concocted in that backwoods brain of yours, this little drama with me is over. Right now. Otherwise—"

"What?"

With his elbow dug into his side and his cigar floating lazily between two fingers, he looked at Heidi—really looked at her, scanning her from the top down. She saw his opinion of her reflected in his face. He did not care. Three years of wondering, longing for his approval, making decisions based on what she thought he would want her to do, and at last Heidi understood that to Roland Winthrop Gibbons IV, she was beneath consideration. The way he disregarded painters and composers who did not matter to him. "I don't rate him," he would say, and he may as well have been talking about her. She was a nuisance, that was all. A stain on his handkerchief would move him more than she did.

How could a single person have so much power? To Roland Gibbons she would always be an irrelevant Irish girl from Yonkers. Heidi wished she could be anywhere else than here, with this man who did not think enough of her, after everything she'd done, to hate her. She should take her cue from him and stop caring. But she couldn't! Why? Why?

Roland took a bored drag off his cigar. "I want you out of my life—and my daughter's. I can make things very uncomfortable for you."

"Daddy?" Doreen stood a few feet away in Biz's red coat. "What are you guys doing out here?"

Roland leaned into Heidi's ear. "Don't test me, little girl," he whispered before turning to his daughter. "Doreen! There you are, darling. I was just thanking your friend here for showing you the ropes here at the old Academy."

"Oh." Doreen looked from her father to her friend and back again. "Okay, cool, well, we are going. Do you want to say good-bye to Biz?"

"Of course, the young artiste!" said Roland.

"You coming, Heidi?"

"I uh, I'm—"

"Heidi's not feeling well," said Roland. "You should go home, Heidi. Take care of yourself." With that, he escorted Doreen back into the gallery.

"Piece of shit!" Head in her hands, Heidi paced back and forth, working herself into a froth. "No, no, no!" This was not how it was going to go down. Roland did not get a say in the company Heidi kept. She could—and would!—be friends with whomever she wanted to be friends with. She wasn't going to let him control her. If he thought she would just keep her mouth closed and do what she was told then he didn't know who he was talking to.

But then, graduation was *so* close. Heidi could almost touch the freedom awaiting her at the end of the year. It was like that moment when Dorothy finally approaches Emerald City. Heidi could see the city wall. And her diploma from Chandler Academy was all she needed to get to the other side. Roland could take it away from her with a snap of his perfectly manicured fingers. He knew it and she knew it.

What had he said? *She is my daughter and I don't want her socializing with the likes of you.* Had anyone ever made her feel so small and disgusting? But she could show him. She was no Yonkers nothing anymore. He would see she'd come into her own, that she'd become a person who mattered.

"Stop it!" she berated herself. "That's enough!" For her own survival she had to drop it, to forget him and move on, to end the cycle of striving and disappointment that had dominated her life. She had to get out, be free. He was never going to approve of her. So stop caring, she told herself, for real this time. What did she need them for? Any of them? All of this was keeping her tied down. The key was to think about her future. If she let Roland win this tiny battle, she could still turn it into a grand life for herself—for her and Peter. Wasn't that all that mattered? All she had to do was sever ties with Doreen. Cut it off and sail away. Never look back.

But how would Doreen react? Heidi had always assumed she was safe from Doreen's wrath, that she held a special position in Doreen's esteem that protected her. But now she wasn't so sure. In fact, the more she thought about cutting Doreen out of her life, the more frightened she became of the repercussions. Doreen would not take kindly to any sort of rejection. And while Heidi had been busily falling in love and dreaming of college, Doreen had been mastering the art of ruthless retribution.

And there was more. Since Doreen came into her life, everything had changed for the better. When she thought about who she'd been before—how lonely and cynical she'd been! Everything was an angle, a way to get a leg up. It was exhausting. And all that changed when Doreen arrived. Was it really a coincidence that the Fall Dance, where Doreen had treated Simon so heartlessly and jump-started her rise through the ranks at Chandler, also represented a transformative moment for Heidi?

Since then, she had opened herself up to Peter, been a better friend to Biz. It was as if by enacting the worst part of Heidi's own nature, Doreen left Heidi to thrive. What would happen if things changed back to how they were before? No. She wouldn't have it. Doreen Gray was Heidi's ticket to a better soul.

There would have to be a third option, a way to have it all.

Peter found Heidi standing there shivering, her brow furrowed in concentration. He carried her coat over his arm.

"There you are, at last. Everyone is leaving. They've invited us to dinner. Shall we join?"

She needed more time. She was on the verge of something—a solution. But she couldn't quite get it. "I don't think so. Is that okay? I don't feel up to it."

"Hm. You look a little pale. You're probably just cold. Come here." He buttoned her into her coat and rubbed her arms. He hugged her close to him, and in his embrace Heidi began to find strength. He wanted her. This wonderful person wanted her, after everything he knew. But of course! How had she not thought of it before?

"Hang on. Peter, all that stuff I told you before, about where I come from and everything, it never bothered you, did it?"

"Heidi, how many times have I told you? If anything it only made me like you more."

"Like me? Or love me?"

But he didn't hear her. He was looking behind his shoulder to where the Gibbons-Browns were huddled together near the entrance of the gallery. "I told Gloria we would be right back. Doreen—I mean, everyone is waiting." He turned back to Heidi. "Sorry, did you ask me something?"

"I want to talk to you, Peter," Heidi said, her eyes shining. "I have something, something else. It's the last thing, but it's important. I need to come clean about something. To you and to Doreen." If she told them everything, Roland would have nothing on her. She could live truthfully, as herself. It was the perfect solution. She flushed with the elegance of it.

"Can we do it later? It's just, you know, they're leaving. Can it wait? If you're not feeling well, maybe you should rest. I'll let them know."

"Wait. What? You're still going to go to dinner?"

"Do you mind?" Peter was already backing away toward the gallery. "I'm just really hungry. And I told them I would, so. Feel better, okay?" He blew her a kiss.

"What did you want to talk to me about?" she yelled after him. All at once she found herself alone.

It could wait. She would tell him tomorrow. She was very tired, after all. A night in by herself might do her a world of good, clear her head, give her time to figure out how she would tell the story. The important thing was that she had a plan. She would have her Oz. And she would expose Roland for the wizard that he was—just a sad, weak, old man behind a curtain.

27

Biz was not prone to skipping or leaping or sashaying, but that's just what she did. She danced and twirled and ran across the quad. It was late—almost curfew. The gallery had closed and all the parents had gone to their hotels. She should really head back to her own dorm, but she couldn't go, not yet. She wanted to see Doreen. Somehow, it wouldn't feel real until she told Doreen all about it.

Eloise Peek had red hair, but red like a stop sign, a reflection of conscious choice rather than arbitrary genetic disposition. She had thick arty jewelry and small green glasses.

"My dear," she said, "I want you to know that the last thing I ever expected when I came here was to find true talent, but I must say I am impressed. The way you use focus and color saturation, it's really quite brilliant. This one, for example." She waved her bracelets at a picture of Heidi sitting on the couch in their suite. "The way you blur the girl to nothing, just a flash of blondness, legs, lashes. She appears to be in the midst of saying something, some story or other, but since you've washed out everything but her eyes, all we see is this flash of burning blue in the center. It's beautiful but also somewhat sad."

"Lonely was what I was going for," said Biz.

"Yes. There is something haunting about it." The woman nodded. "And in the self-portraits." She stepped over to a series of pictures of Biz taken from the shoulders up. Biz faced the camera without glasses, without any visible clothing. She had blurred out the background, but her skin possessed exaggerated clarity. The pictures were almost identical, except for tiny changes in her expression and the location of her gaze.

Eloise Peek's face tightened as she viewed the series. Biz held her breath. The self-portraits were the result of her big moment of realization in the photo lab. They were a huge risk. She'd never exposed herself so honestly—especially not to total strangers. The gallerist stood silently in front of the pictures, her mouth twitching with concentration. Then, in a burst of sound, she spoke.

"Every pimple, freckle, birthmark, seems to rise off the surface of the body. It's about adolescence for me, that liminal zone between one's girlhood and womanhood. They are really extraordinary. And brave."

Biz exhaled. "Thank you, Ms. Peek. They were a big breakthrough for me. In a lot of ways. I'd never put myself in front of the camera before, but it felt necessary for me to do it. As an artist and, honestly, as a person."

"Do you know my son, Seth Greenbaum?" Eloise flipped her glasses onto her head. "He is a junior here. He asked me to attend this evening. He's a big fan of your work, as you may know. You see, I have a small gallery in Chelsea."

"Of course! The Peek Gallery. Not that, I mean, of course, you know the name of it." Biz felt her face flush.

"I do, yes. And so do you. Good! I'm glad you know us. Anyway, I'm very interested in you. You are young, of course, but that is hardly a detriment. Agnes Chase—"

"The photographer?"

"Yes, of course the photographer. She is a client and a dear friend and she was just saying to me that she would like to find an assistant. I'm sure she's looking for something more long-term than just the summer."

"I'll do it!"

"Wonderful enthusiasm, dear girl, but we must proceed step by step. Send me your portfolio and I will speak to Agnes. Here is my card, I will look for your e-mail."

Biz felt for the card in the breast pocket of her coat. There it was. Eloise Peek, President. Oh, to have this thing, something for herself, something she made for herself not because of her name or her family—but in spite of them, their materialism, their anti-intellectualism. It was all too good to contemplate. Imagine spending the summer as Agnes Chase's assistant! And then off to Yale, the best photography school in the world. Of course, she hadn't heard from Yale yet, but she would. She was the valedictorian of one of the highest ranked prep schools in the country. If Yale wasn't accepting Biz, then who in the world were they accepting?

She was so lost in her own good fortune that she collided head-on with someone coming out of West Hall.

"Ow!"

"Oh my god, I'm so sorry, I–Peter?" She helped him to his feet. "What are you doing here? I thought you left hours ago."

"Oh. I, uh," Peter looked back at West Hall. "I stayed for a bit, taking care of Heidi. I fell asleep."

"But our dorm is across campus. Doreen lives here."

"Does she?" said Peter. "What a coincidence. Anyway, great seeing you and congratulations again on your success." Peter's cell phone beeped.

"Is that a text? Who is it from?"

"Hm? Oh. I don't know, uh." He pulled out his phone and held it very close to his face. "Your brother. 'Good to see you, man.' Nice of him to say so."

Biz swiped the phone from him. The message on the screen was from Doreen: *I miss you already, Pinkie.*

"I don't understand. You and Doreen? But you're with Heidi."

"Look, Biz, I know you're Heidi's pal. She's great, okay? But Doreen and I . . . what we have . . . it's different. It's special, I–I can't explain it."

"But Heidi really likes you. She loves you. She doesn't love anyone and she loves you."

"I guess that's her problem. Are you going to tell her? It would be a favor to me if you did, actually, save me the trouble."

"And what about your friend? Coburn? Doesn't he count, either?"

Peter shook his head. "Not for me. Not now. It's just her that matters now. Nothing like this has ever happened to me before, I'm different around her."

"You're disgusting. You're in college, an adult, practically."

But Peter wasn't listening. He was scanning the windows of West Hall, obviously trying to figure out which one belonged to Doreen. When he turned back, he seemed surprised that Biz was still there. "Good to see you," he said and walked away.

Of course, it was none of her business, but as Biz climbed the stairs to Doreen's room she could not help feeling lost and disillusioned. She'd always admired Doreen, overlooked the backstage calculations. But this was too far. Poor Heidi. Biz's heart broke for her.

"I knew you couldn't stay away!" said Doreen when she opened to the door to her room. She wore nothing but a white lace corset and frilly shorts. "Oh. It's you."

"Disappointed?" said Biz. "Expecting someone else?"

"Who knows? Anyway, have you come to share your news? Tell me everything. I'll even play at being surprised, though I already heard it from Addison." She plucked a lilac satin robe from a hook on her door and slipped it over herself.

"Why? Are you sleeping with him, too? He's your first cousin, you know."

"Huh? Of course not! I ran into him at the hotel after I said good-bye to my father. What's gotten into you?"

"That's a funny question, coming from you."

"Bizzy. Come sit." Doreen patted a spot on her bed.

"I'll stand, thank you. Where's the picture?"

"Sorry? What picture?"

"You know what picture. The one of you in the red dress."

"This again? I told you I don't have it. And what do you need it for, anyway? The pictures from the show are much better. The one of me is just a copy from *Vogue*. You had much better stuff in the show. I liked the one of your mother. The diamonds looked like they were about to eat her face!"

"Mm-hmm. Fine. You want to play it that way?" Biz flung open the top drawer of Doreen's desk. She yanked out the notebooks and searched the pages for a folded sheet. When she didn't find anything, she pulled out the other drawers and dumped them on the carpet.

"Biz! What do you think you're doing?"

"Where is it? Where is the picture, Doreen?"

"I told you." And if Doreen was nervous about Biz finding the picture, she made no indication. She stood near her bed with her hands on her hips as her cousin ransacked her desk, her dresser, her closet. "I hope you are going to clean all this up."

"You'll never guess who I ran into just now, outside of your dorm. Peter Standish. You know, Heidi's boyfriend?"

"Says who?" Doreen said under her breath.

"What? What did you say?"

"Nothing, but go ahead. Commence the dull moralizing lecture, I'm sure you've got one all cued up."

"Yes, yes. I'm so uncool. I know. But I would never . . . she would never."

"Of course! Our friend Heidi, the model of moral rectitude, who considers men to be loathsome, bottom-dwelling vermin to be used and discarded."

"This isn't about how she feels about men! This is about how she feels about friendship!" Biz lay on her stomach and pulled stuff from under the bed, empty duffel bags, old sweaters.

"Please, spare me. You act like she isn't using you for your name, your position, the clothes in your closet, the bags, the shoes. Why do you think she agreed to be your roommate? Because of your charming personality? I know all sorts of stuff about Heidi that would turn you cold. Did you know she's a year older than you? Yeah. Her school was so bad Crotchett made her do a year over again. She's been lying to us about her age all this time. How's that for the sanctity of friendship? She's on some sort of secret scholarship that nobody ever got before or since. It wouldn't surprise me if she slept with some high-ranking Chandler board member or something."

"You're just trying to justify what you've done." Biz emptied shoeboxes and added them to the pile. Where was that picture? "But it won't work. Not on me. I know Heidi—I know who she really is." She turned to the bookshelf.

"You see what you want to see, Elizabeth. Heidi Whelan manipulates, she steals. She uses people to get what she wants. She used you and she used me. Pardon me if I don't feel obliged to treat her like a saint. And what any of this has to do with that stupid picture, I'll never understand. But go ahead, if it makes you feel better. Just let me know when you're finished." Doreen lay back against the pillows on her bed. She yawned luxuriously. "I'm gutted. What a day. What time is brunch tomorrow?"

Biz stood in the pile she'd created: clothes, shoes, coats, books, papers. She breathed hard. "You changed, Doreen."

"Yes, Biz. I have." Doreen pumped some cream into her palm and began to rub it into one elbow, then the other. "I know you love to wax nostalgic about our time at the beach when we were babies, but that was a lifetime ago. I have changed, okay? I've grown up. You may consider doing the same before you go out and light the world on fire."

"That's not the change I'm talking about. I'm talking about the morning after we took the picture. I'm talking about a painfully awkward girl who left my dorm room one evening, only to return the next day looking like a fashion model."

Doreen stiffened. "Don't be ridiculous." She continued moisturizing, moving on to her legs, feigning indifference, but Biz could see tension in her cousin's jaw. Her head cocked to one side with attention.

"Am I? Well, then show me the picture. That's it. Show me the picture and we'll be done with all this. Because it does sound ridiculous. To think that a picture I took and fixed up could have turned you into someone who would sacrifice anyone who gets in your way. That seems crazy to me! And yet, I can't stop thinking that it happened. And I must know now, Doreen. I must know what responsibility I have for what you've become. A beautiful *monster*."

Doreen sat up, her eyes blazing, chest heaving. Time seemed to stop while the two cousins stared at one another. An intense smile spread across Doreen's face. "What a spectacular idea!" She hopped off the bed and clapped. "Yes!" Wading through the mess on the floor to her closet, Doreen pulled rubber boots over her bare legs and retrieved a heavy metal flashlight, flicking it on and off, on and off.

"What are you doing?" asked Biz.

"Making sure it works. Now let's go!"

"Where are we going?" Biz's guts churned.

"I'm giving you what you want, Biz! Ain't it grand?" Doreen put a hand on Biz's shoulder. "We should have done this ages ago!" She laughed.

"What's so funny? I don't get it."

"You will." Doreen tightened the belt on her robe and with a final laugh she headed out the door. She raced down the hall and Biz hurried after her.

"Oh, wait till you see what I have in store for you, my Bizzy little bee!" Doreen sang as she scuttled down the stairs two flights to the ground floor.

Were they going outside? Had she buried the thing somewhere? But Doreen didn't stop, she kept going down the stairs to the basement, almost hitting Biz in the face with the fire door. The stink of rotting garbage made Biz's eyes water, but Doreen sped past the overflowing bins at the base of the garbage shoot, the blue barrels of recycled refuse. Biz tried to stay close, but she couldn't keep pace. She saw a flash of purple satin as Doreen entered a small room at the back.

"Hello! Doreen, where are you?" A switch on the wall made a dim fluorescent tube flicker to life overhead, revealing a mess of electrical wiring, plastic tubing, rotting mattresses, and old, broken furniture. The smell was of organic decomposition and turpentine.

"Doreen! Doreen, are you here?"

Biz heard a creaking from the back of the room. Carefully trying not to touch anything or imagine what horrible creatures made the stinking room their home, she crept past the broken-down bed frames, the burst cushions, the stores of pink insulating foam. Finally, at the back of the room she found a rusted metal ladder that descended from the ceiling. It led to a small crawl space, lit from within by Doreen's flashlight. The drywall that had covered it had been pushed aside and Biz heard the scraping of things being moved around.

"Doreen! Come down from there. I don't understand."

Doreen stuck her head out of the opening. "Patience! All will be revealed shortly." Biz watched her gingerly climb down the ladder with a shapeless package tucked under her arm. "Where shall we do this? But it's so dark here. Come on. I know just the place."

Doreen hummed to herself as she scurried past the junk, out of the storage room. Biz followed her into another room. The janitor's office, Biz supposed from the tools, the desk, the small television. Doreen turned on the desk lamp.

"Have a seat," she said. Biz did as she was told. Doreen ripped apart the parcel to reveal a manila envelope, and inside that another envelope, and inside that a folder. Biz had a feeling that whatever was in there would change her life forever. But she couldn't stop it. She had to know.

"Ah, yes," said Doreen, adding the folder to the pile of discarded packaging. "Here it is." She smiled at the picture and placed it facedown on the desk before sliding it toward Biz. "Go ahead. See for yourself. Go on." Her voice was steady, but her eyes were wide.

Biz looked down at the page. "I don't know."

"Just do it!" Doreen yelled. She slammed a fist on the metal desk. "Look. Look! Look for yourself at your beautiful monster." Doreen flipped the page over. Biz peered down at the image. She gasped.

"What happened to it? Did you do this? Why?"

"Don't stop." Doreen shined the lamp onto the image. "Get a close look, Elizabeth. Take it all in."

"No, no. I don't under—"

The composition of the picture remained the same—there was the green grass, darkening sky, even the red, strapless dress. But instead of the lovely girl on a chair Biz saw a hideous beast—with the eyes of a devil and a gaping, bloody, salivating mouth. A horrible tongue reached out from the depths. The creature was all appetite, burning desire, horrifying in its need for more. The hands were oozing, boil-covered, and they reached out from the body, ready to grab, take in, devour. It was flesh that craved, that hunted, that would not be satisfied.

Biz felt woozy, but Doreen slammed her hand against the desk again. "Keep looking!" she demanded, her perfect, porcelain brow creased, her lovely mouth sneering. She smelled of orange peel and lavender. What could she, who looked so innocent, so immaculate, have to do with the seeping, lecherous beast in the image?

"How did this happen? Tell me. Please, I have to know."

Doreen turned the flashlight in her hand. "Do you remember that day last summer, Biz? The day you took this picture. After you used your computer to turn the fat, ugly pig that I was into an ethereal, graceful beauty? I became agitated when you showed me what you'd done to the picture. Ring a bell?"

"You thought we were making fun of you." Biz imagined Doreen the way she looked that day when she arrived at Chandler, how sweet and scared and broken she was.

"Yes. I often think that, of course. But you reassured me, didn't you? You were only doing what they do in the magazines, you said. And then Heidi admonished me. She offered to destroy the picture—but I wouldn't let her. I clung to it. I wanted to keep it forever. I made a wish. Do you remember what it was? It wasn't so long ago, wasn't it? Only a few months."

"You, you wished . . ." Biz had trouble forming words. "You wanted to be that girl, the one in the picture." She blinked the tears out of her eyes.

"And so I did. And guess what? My wish came true! Tra-la-la! Sound unbelievable? I didn't believe it myself when I awoke the next morning. You see, at first I didn't notice it. When you look as I used to, you don't spend a lot of time looking in mirrors. In fact, before I even saw myself that morning, I took a quick look at the picture. But the picture didn't look anything like I remembered it. The girl, the beautiful one, the one you created, Biz, she was nowhere to be seen. The subject of the photo was just regular, plain-old, ugly Doreen Gray—pimples, frizzy hair, and all. Was it a trick of my eyes or of my memory? I didn't know, but I was so sad to lose that lovely girl. But, of course, I saw her again only a few minutes later. She looked me in the face the moment I looked in the mirror.

"I thought I must be having some sort of psychological break. People don't transform overnight. But then, when I arrived at your suite and I saw your reaction, and later still, at the cafeteria, the way people treated me. I knew that what I saw in the mirror was how the world saw me as well. It had come true! My wish had come true and life would be too wonderful. Sad little Doreen Gray was a thing of the past, replaced by this!" And she spun around.

"You said that the girl in the picture looked like you—the way you used to look." Biz flipped the page over. "But this is the face of a devil!"

"Yes. That happened over time. I noticed it after I broke up with Simon, the day of the terrible football game. Something compelled me to look at the picture when I returned to my room and I saw a small change. Nothing too significant, a hardness around the mouth, a widening of the eyes."

Doreen paced in and out of the light as she recounted her story. Her robe had loosened, the tie belt dragging on the ground. Biz sat on the desk chair and hugged her knees toward herself.

"The morning after the Fall Dance—that's when I really started to see a change. The face was becoming diabolical. It scared me. Of course, I knew I had behaved unkindly to Simon, and I realized the picture was reflecting those actions. And my evening with Gordon . . ." Doreen smiled.

"I resolved to be better. I would study harder, I would beg Simon to take me back. I would be the very picture of purity and kindness and hard work. I would be you, Biz. But then Heidi came to me, she told me about what happened to Simon, how he'd been institutionalized. She showed me the article in the paper."

"Oh god." Biz wanted to cover her ears to block out the rest of Doreen's story, but she couldn't. She had to sit there and take it.

"And I realized that there was nothing to be done. More importantly, I realized that I didn't want to do anything. It was a gift, you see? A free pass. I could do what I wanted— enjoy the best things that life had to offer freely, without consequences. The picture would absorb the consequences for me. It was so liberating! Let the picture fester while I enjoyed life to the fullest!" Doreen's smile turned to a scowl. "But it was you, of course, nosy, tedious Elizabeth Gibbons-Brown who came sniffing around, asking after the picture. It had been just in my drawer then, but I knew it wasn't safe. So I wrapped the thing up and that's when I came down here and found the crawl space. The picture's been there ever since." Doreen lifted the page off the desk and examined the image. "It's developed an impressive gruesomeness in there, I must say. And boy, have I had fun out in the world in the meantime."

"Stop it!" Biz snapped the picture out of Doreen's hand and slammed it onto the desk. She took her cousin by the shoulders and looked into her eyes. Was the old Doreen in there somewhere? Surely she hadn't completely evaporated. "You have to stop this. Right now." She pulled Doreen over to an empty part of the room and pushed her down to her knees. She collapsed beside her on the concrete floor, and gripping both of Doreen's hands with her own, she bowed her head.

"What are you doing? Let go of me!"

"Uh, hello? Um, God? This is . . ." Biz had never prayed in her life. She was an intellectual, she believed in science and logic. But there was nothing logical or scientific about what had happened to Doreen. And they had to appeal to whoever was in charge. It was their only hope. "Elizabeth Gibbons-Brown. And this is my cousin, Doreen Gray. She's sorry. She's so, so sorry."

"Let go of me, I said!" Doreen pushed Biz away as hard as she could, knocking her to the ground, and stood up. She wiped the grit off her bare knees. "Ugh! I should never have told you. This was a mistake. How could I have been so stupid! Let go!" Biz had launched herself over to Doreen and held her by the ankles. Doreen kicked her away with her rubber boot.

"Dorie!" Biz hunched on the floor, sobbing. "Please! PLEASE! We have to save you! We have to put an end to this." Biz grasped her hands together and looked up. "She's a good person. She's had a hard life. Please, forgive her! Doreen, ask. Ask for forgiveness."

"No!"

"Ask! Ask and you shall receive, right?"

"Receive what? My old life back? No, thank you. I had nothing—NOTHING! Hardship. Vicious bullies, poverty. You don't know what I've endured. Indiana? That was a life for suckers! I want this life! I want this glorious, perfect, delectable life—the life reserved for beautiful people. I don't care what happens to that damned picture."

"But it's not the picture that's damned, Doreen. It's you!"

Biz prayed fast and hard, her hands gripped together, her eyes closed tightly, eyeliner streaming down her face.

"And now you're going to tell everyone. I should never have brought you down here. I should have just ignored you. Oh, what difference would it have made? Damn. Damn!"

"She didn't mean any of it, you see? She's not a monster. She's kind. She's sweet. She loves classical music and dancing and making gardens in the backyard."

"Oh, shut up, won't you? I'm trying to think!"

"She loves making mosaics out of pieces of broken china."

"Shut up! Shut up! Shut up!"

"She's a good person on the inside. She's just lost her way a little bit."

"Quiet!" Doreen picked up the heavy flashlight and hurled it at Biz. It hit her hard on the head and she collapsed. Silence.

"Biz?" Doreen breathed hard. The body on the floor did not move. "Bizzy?" She crept over to her cousin and turned her onto her back. She put her two fingers to her neck, feeling for a pulse. Calmly, she stood up. Her mind was whirring, working out an idea. Everything would be okay! It would all work out in the end.

Well, not for Biz.

"Serves you right!" Doreen left Biz on the floor of the janitor's office and ran toward the stairwell and then—thinking again—came back and snatched the photo from the desk. Then she ran and ran and ran until she got to her room. She kicked off the rubber boots. She picked through the mess on the floor, finding an ugly, old flowered nightgown, a gift from her grandmother. Discarding the satin robe, the sexy underwear, she pulled the nightgown over her head. Her phone was on her bedside table. She worked up some tears before dialing.

She watched her face in the mirror. Innocent, frightened Doreen Gray. A damsel in distress. She played the part perfectly.

"Daddy? Are you awake? Daddy? Something terrible's happened. Can you come? I need you to come to my room right away. You're going to have to call Dean Crotchett. Daddy, I'm scared!"

The photo was there, on her bed. She slipped it into a drawer in her nightstand. She waited for the men to come save her.

28

Heidi awoke with a jolt. Today was the day she would tell her secret! Doreen and Peter and Biz, too (why not?)—everyone would come find out the full story of her life and she could stop hiding behind lies and half-truths. She jumped out of bed. She heard birds. Birds! Could it be spring? When had spring happened? Racing over to the window, she saw a sky that twinkled with possibility.

"Bizzy! Look out at the quad! It's gorgeous out." But her roommate was not in her bed. It must be later than she thought, what time was it? Oh, what did it matter? All was new! Soon she would be free!

With Biz gone, Peter would have to be first. That was better, anyway. After all, Peter had gotten her started on her path toward truth. She had revealed her real self to him and he loved her for it. How beautiful life could be when one lived it honestly! Roland created her persona and made her worship it like an idol. Then Peter came along with a base-ball bat and shattered it into a million pieces. Peter would love her no matter what. The conversation with Doreen would be more complicated, but she would think of that later. She picked up her phone.

"Hello?"

"Peter! Hi! Did I wake you?"

"Oh . . . Look, Heidi, you're going to be fine, okay?"

"Of course I am! Never better." A robin hopped up the stairs to the library. "And I wanted to talk to you about something. I've, you know, there's some stuff in my past—ugly stuff that has been holding me back. Wow, this is harder than I thought. Hm. Can we talk in person? I know you were just here, but would you mind? It's really important. And I promise to make it worth your while."

"Wait. Hold on, just wait a second. So Biz didn't tell you?"

"Biz? Tell me what? I—she's not here. I haven't seen her." Something in his tone made her heart slow down and sink toward her middle.

"Shit, okay. Well, let's do this now. Heidi, it's over. We're done. There. Okay? The end."

"Wait. What?"

"You and me. We're finished. I'm with Doreen now."

"You're with . . . Doreen Gray? But that's not possible."

"Yes. It started a while ago, when she was here in Boston. I came to keep her company—as a favor to you, actually. But then, I don't know, we have a special kind of connection. I know you fancy yourself . . . well, anyway, it's over. And that's all there is to it."

"No. No, that's not, Doreen wouldn't—"

"Good-bye, Heidi. Lose this number, okay?"

"No! I . . . Hello? Hello? Peter?"

The silence in the room rang like a scream in Heidi's ears. So that was what she'd sensed before. She thought she was keeping a secret from Doreen, but it had been the other way around. And Heidi knew it, too. Hadn't she felt it ever since she got back from Boston? She was sure Roland had ratted her out, but it was Doreen's guilt about Peter that made her cagey. They had lied to her. Lied! Heidi thought they were her friends, that they would help her live a new, honest life.

But now she was alone. She had no Peter, no Doreen. She didn't even have her position at the top of the Chandler food chain. Doreen had taken that, too. She took Chandler and Roland and Peter and left her to rot. How could she let this happen? Why did she make herself so vulnerable? She thought she could have it all. So naïve! As if she was somebody instead of nobody with nothing nothing nothing nothing.

Heidi broke down into sobs. She cried for everything she'd lost. Never in her life had she felt so empty. There was only one person in the world she could trust, and that was Biz. She hoped she would get home soon. She would tell it all to Biz, who was so good and righteous and supportive.

Keys scraped in the door.

"Biz? Oh, thank god!" She threw the door wide, but it wasn't Biz. It was Mumzy, Gloria Gibbons-Brown. Perfectly coiffed and made up, she looked haggard nonetheless, like she'd been up all night.

"No. It's not, I'm afraid it's not Elizabeth, no. I–I've come for her things."

"Her things?"

Mumzy crossed the common room and entered the bedroom.

Wiping her face on the edge of her tank top, Heidi followed close behind. "What is going on?"

"Luggage? Under the bed, right?" In her heels and skirt Gloria got down on her knees and pulled out a duffel bag and a wheeled trunk. Using the bed to hoist herself up, she turned to the closet. "I suppose I'll start with the clothes." She passed her fingers along the dresses, blouses, skirts. "Lovely, aren't they?" Mumzy pulled out a bloodred, dip-dyed silk scarf. She wrapped it around her neck.

"We bought this in Paris. Roland bought it, I think." In the mirror, she looked at herself, then pulled the scarf off and rubbed the silk against her cheek. "Of course, Biz never gave a hoot about any of this. All she wanted was books and art stuff. Cameras and drawing pads. Well, never mind. Do you want this stuff? It's yours. Take it if you want it." She let the scarf drop to the floor.

"I don't understand. Where is Bi—Elizabeth? Is she all right? Did something happen?"

"She's in the hospital. With a concussion."

"Oh my god."

"Oh, she'll be fine. She is awake now, doing better. She thinks so, anyway. I haven't the heart to tell her." Mumzy sat on Biz's bed. She stroked one of Biz's pillows with her hand, then moved her hand to her lap, and for a second Heidi could see a resemblance to her daughter. "Anyway. She's been expelled. So that's that."

"Expelled?" Heidi followed Mumzy into the common room. "Sorry? No. There's been some kind of mistake. Expelled? That can't be right. Biz Gibbons-Brown is the valedictorian!"

"She is also a sexual predator, at least according to Doreen Gray. What can I do with this?" She stood in front of Biz's desk. "I'll have to send someone. Should I just leave it all? Do you have a box or something?"

"No, no! I'm afraid I'm going to be sick." Heidi bent over and grabbed her knees, trying to find her breath.

Mumzy went into the bedroom and came back with the wheeled trunk. She slowly filled it with books. "Last night my niece called her father. She was distraught. She said that Biz had come on to her, that she'd threatened her with violence. My daughter apparently forced Doreen into a dodgy basement, and Doreen hit her in the head with a flashlight. She said she'd been defending herself."

"But this is completely ridiculous! Doreen is Biz's cousin."

"Yes, well. That's what makes it so depraved. At least, in my brother's eyes. And the dean's."

"She's lying!"

Mumzy picked up Biz's camera. She turned it over and over in her hands. "Is there a case for this? Oh, here it is. It's useless to argue. My brother is Doreen's staunch defender. Apparently fourteen minutes of unestrangement make him an expert on his daughter's moral character. And Dean Crotchett is his old chum, you know, school days and all that. His response is to lecture me about Chandler's strict no-tolerance policy on sexual misconduct. They won't stand for victim-blaming, he told me. You know, I'm obviously a horrible mother to have raised such a demon."

"No. No. This isn't right. You have to do something! After all your family has done for the school."

Mumzy turned to Heidi. She looked careworn, over-whelmed, but also, for the first time since she'd met her, like someone's mother. "She was this close to getting everything she wanted. The poor thing, my daughter." Her voice caught. She hugged herself, her neck collapsed as if her head was suddenly too heavy to hold up.

"Isn't there something we can do?"

"No." Mumzy straightened up and swatted it all away with a jewel-heavy hand. She sucked in her breath and resumed packing. "She'll be fine. We have resources. Crotchett has agreed to keep the thing mum. Better for the school to do so. Better for the students. But for Elizabeth, who can say? Maybe she will end up a society maven after all." She picked up a Rubik's Cube from Biz's bookshelf. "I was really very proud of her. I know it may sound strange, we often locked horns. But I admired her commitment to making something for herself. She was fearless. Don't you think?" She dropped the toy into the suitcase and turned to Heidi. "I know who you are, you know."

"Yes. We've met many times." Heidi paced around the suite, trying to land on a way to save her friend.

"But the first time was out at the beach, no? I suppose you were my brother's date. To that party in Bridgehamp-ton. I lent you my gown."

So Gloria had known all along. "Nothing ever happened between us. I hope you know that."

"Unless you count blackmail. And exploitation. Right? I know he makes fun of me, but Roland tells me all about his little intrigues. You weaseled your way into my brother's bank account, then when that wasn't enough, into my son's pants and my daughter's dorm room. Ruining everything in the process. Yes. It seems to me that all was fine and dandy before you came into our lives. You and your obsession with our family." Gloria's face was twisted with contempt.

"But that's not what it was. I mean, I can understand why you would think that."

"What did you expect him to do, hm? Marry you? Adopt you?" Gloria faced Heidi, her jaw tight. "He paid a little attention to you for a couple of weeks and then he got bored. Boo-hoo. It seems to me that a first-class education more than made up for any kind of slight you must have felt. I told him he was a fool for doing it. Let her tell who she wants to tell, I said. But the money didn't matter to him, and I think he was curious about what would become of you. As if you would just politely disappear. But I knew better. And I was right, of course."

Gloria slammed her hand on the desk. The sound of it felt like a slap on the face.

"This is not my fault."

"No? Isn't it? Then why are you here? Why are you always here?"

"I don't know." Heidi sunk down onto the carpet and buried her head in her knees. Gloria was right. Roland didn't owe Heidi anything. Was it his fault that she couldn't bear to call home? Was he really to blame for how ashamed she'd become of her family, and how ashamed she was of herself because of it? It was easier to hate him than it was to hate herself, but the fact was that the only one responsible for what she'd become was Heidi Whelan.

"I don't know what happened," said Heidi. "I got in over my head."

"Yes, well, pardon me for not caring." Gloria turned back toward Biz's desk.

"Biz is different," Heidi said. "She matters to me."

"How wonderful for her."

"No. Listen, this was Doreen. Okay? She's the one who did this. And I'm not going to let her get away with it. I'm going to make this right. I'm going to fix it. I can be good, too. You just have to trust me, I'm different now." Heidi changed into running shorts and a sports bra. She tied on her sneakers.

"Where are you going? To exercise?"

"I've made a lot of mistakes, Gloria. But I'm going to make this better for Biz. She doesn't deserve this. I'll do anything. I'll make this all go away somehow."

"I feel sorry for you. Don't you know by now that Roland always wins?"

"Not this time," Heidi said. She ran out the door.

29

Heidi ran as fast as she could through the quiet campus. She sped past the library and the science building, tripped down the steps behind Sherman Theater, curved around the field house. The office of the dean was there near the pond. Heidi slammed through the door. She bolted up the stairs, down the hall, past Miss Jenkins. She pushed into the dean's office.

"She's lying!" Heidi panted. The blood rushed to her face.

"Why, Miss Whelan!" said the dean, "You're certainly looking, ahem, casual."

"Doreen Gray is lying. Biz never touched her, do you understand? I'm her roommate, okay? I know these things. Doreen is a manipulative liar. You have to believe me. I . . ." *I created her*, Heidi thought. "Doreen . . . she's not, she's . . ."

The dean remained perfectly calm with a patronizing smile plastered on his face.

"You're ruining Biz's life. Listen, you can't, this isn't . . ."

Why couldn't she make her point more clearly? There was so much evidence, it was so obvious. But the dean just sat placidly with his fat cheeks and squinty eyes. He sat in his affected double-breasted suit and tie and waited for Heidi to finish, as if she was having some sort of embarrassing paroxysm that needed to be waited out. "She's lying! Do you understand? Why aren't you saying anything?"

"What would you have me say, my dear? You've stated your case. It's your right, after all. Everyone should have their day in court, so to speak."

"Right, yeah. That's it exactly." The idea appealed to Heidi. She imagined a courtroom. She'd be there, power suit, briefcase. Doreen would arrive in her most proper headband, trying to eyelash-bat her way out. But Heidi would get her. She had the goods on Doreen Gray. "Great idea. A jury of Biz's peers. Yes. I'll show them, I'll tell them everything." Maybe she didn't need Peter to live honestly. Maybe she could do it all on her own. "A hearing. That's the thing." A thrill beat deep in Heidi's chest. She would tell them, for Biz. "A hearing."

"Ha ha, yesss." The dean chortled. "Oh, you're serious? My dear girl. It's a figure of speech, of course. This is a high school, not *Law and Order*. And as dean, I'm afraid my word is final. I am judge and jury. So, what is the expression? The bulk stops here."

"Buck."

"I'm sorry?"

"It's the buck stops . . . oh, never mind." How could she get through to this dough-faced dimwit? She had to change tactics. "This is a grave injustice. Grave. There's no limit to what Elizabeth Gibbons-Brown might have done—for the school. She would have made Chandler proud! But I don't see how she can recover from this." The dean's comfy little grin did not change. Heidi would enjoy wringing his fat neck. "You're sending her out to pasture—at seventeen years old! It's not fair!"

"It absolutely is not fair, Ms. Whelan, but not because of the expulsion. The accusations against Elizabeth are quite serious, and as an esteemed institution, we cannot let our reputation be sullied by oversexed lesbian predators."

"What you're saying is completely insane. Oversexed? Biz Gibbons-Brown? Now that's funny. Ha. Ha. Ha."

The dean held up his index finger. "I wasn't finished. What is unfair about the situation, Ms. Whelan, is that grave as it may seem to you—that is the word you used, isn't it? Grave. Yes, well, dire though it may seem to you, Heidi Whelan, scholarship student, whose father's greatest achievement was his acceptance into the Sanitation Workers Union of Yonkers—"

"Excuse me?"

"What is unfair about this, my child, is how little it will matter. Elizabeth's family is one of the oldest and most established on the eastern seaboard. There are horses on their estate worth more than your father will make in his lifetime. That's just a fact. They have friends, relatives, long-standing relationships with people in positions powerful enough to overlook a few schoolgirl shenanigans. It will be a blip, less than that, a speck on her illustrious life story. But others are not so lucky. Others do not have it as easy as Elizabeth, do they? That's why there are scholarships, internships, et cetera, et cetera."

"What are you saying? Are you threatening me?"

"I'm not telling you anything you don't know, my dear. Your very presence at this school speaks to your precocious understanding of how the world works." He looked at Heidi over the top of his horn rims.

Heidi watched the dean move things around his desk. Did he know? Of course, Roland had spoken to him about her admission to the school, about the creation of the "City Scholars Fund"—into which he deposited exactly enough to cover three years' tuition—but had he also mentioned that she had blackmailed him into doing it?

"I don't know what you're talking about," she said in her toughest voice.

"Of course you don't." The dean stood up and looked out at the pond through the window. "The hawks should be coming back soon. I keep checking. I love the return of the birds, don't you?" He lifted a pair of small binoculars to his eyes. "I find it invigorating. Virgil, that's my spaniel, is not as fond of the hawks as I am. Last summer . . ." He turned to Heidi as if he was about to launch into a story, about his dog, of all things, but seeing her countenance, he changed his mind. "Anyway, if there's nothing else . . ." He returned his stupid face to the window.

To live honestly. To live with integrity. She could do it. Starting right now. She could do it for Biz. She joined the dean by the window.

"May I?" She held out a hand for the binoculars.

"Certainly. You a birder?"

Heidi looked at the sad, man-made pond. No doubt about it, it was still winter. "You know, Dean Crotchett, uh, Timothy." She passed him the binoculars and sat on the edge of his desk, crossing her legs in her tiny running shorts. "I have my own life story. It certainly isn't as illustrious as

Biz's, but it has a certain, um, tawdriness, I think, that many people would find fascinating. No diamonds or wings of fine art museums, no yachts or dog show ribbons or fancy bloodline. Just power and money. You know, the usual stuff. Institutions in the back pocket of millionaire playboys, secrets hidden under the library rug. Administrators at the beck and call of moneyed school chums. It's a good story. One I am itching to tell."

"Are you?" The dean frowned. She had him! "Ms. Whelan, there's something you should know."

"Yes?"

"The desk upon which you have parked your bottom belonged to Franklin Pierce, the fourteenth president of the United States—and a Chandler alum. Please give it the respect it deserves and do not add your backside to the list of things it has survived. If you would like to sit, I encourage you to use a chair."

"I'll take it under consideration." Heidi switched her legs.

"I thank you. Now, vis-à-vis your little performance, your play at threatening me—is that what it was? You did seem to be enjoying yourself, but I'm afraid playtime is over. We will now return to real life, the one in which you leave my office right now, grateful for the opportunity to finish out the rest of your time here at Chandler and then move on to what is sure to be an interesting, if unrefined, life."

"You think I won't do it? I will. I'll finish you, Crotchett."

"For what? For whom? For Elizabeth Gibbons-Brown? She doesn't need you, my dear. And expulsion, though inconsequential for her, would indeed be your undoing. Are you really going to fall on your sword for her? After everything you've done for yourself, all the hard work, the personal risk? Why, you are almost home free! These people, they are immune to you. You can't touch them. I can't touch them. They are invincible."

Heidi felt herself growing smaller and smaller as he spoke. "Expulsion? On what grounds? I haven't done anything wrong."

"It's a cruel world out there for people without resources. You're better off playing by the rules. Trust me. Alienate no one and you will be fine." The dean resumed his survey of the pond through the binoculars. "Now, please leave. I hope to see you one more time, at your graduation, and then it is my hope and expectation that I will never again have to suffer through your company. Good day, Ms. Whelan."

———●●———

Where to go? What to do? She couldn't go home. To face Gloria and her resentment, her painfully slow packing, to tell her that she was right, nothing could be done. Roland and Doreen would win this one. Heidi was worthless. And Biz, who worked so hard, broke no rules, Biz who wanted only to make something for her own self without having to rely on her family name, would have to do just that. But at least Biz had a name to rely upon.

It would be hard, Heidi conceded, but it would not be a tragedy. Returning to Yonkers, however, was a fate she could not endure. Yonkers would be a kind of death, and she would never risk it. Not for Biz, not for anyone.

They had her, those bastards. She hated them for it—and hated herself even more for being so easily had.

The only choice was to accept it, move on, graduate. Northwestern had offered her a full-ride—based on her merit and nothing else. And with only a few weeks left in the semester, she could keep her head down and get through it, and then she would be out from under Roland Gibbons and Chandler Academy and Dean Crotchett and all the rest of them. Then she could start a real, honest life. She would have a new story then: I am self-made, she would say. I am the product of loving parents and talent and brains and wit. She would never lie about who she was again. That, if nothing else, would be her consolation.

It was still Parents' Weekend. Kids and their folks wandered around with maps and program guides. She missed her own family. She imagined her mother here, in a terrible dress but beaming, careful about her pardon-mes and thank-you-kindlies, her father striking up conversation with everyone he passed. "As long as she stays a Yankees fan, I don't care who educates her." She should have invited them to one of the weekends at least. But now it was too late. They'd given her everything and she couldn't even give them that.

Well, there was graduation. They could all come! Her mother, her father, plus Katie and Donald, Aunt Rosemary, if her gout wasn't acting up. Then it would really be spring and Heidi could show her parents—this is where I've been, this is what I've been doing. Be proud of me. She could show everyone who she was and not give a damn what they thought about it. The air smelled clean and fresh. She made unhurried progress across the quad.

Chandler had always seemed to Heidi like a series of locked doors that required complex social maneuvering in order to gain entry. Expertly, using her body and her brains, Heidi had unlocked one after another after another. But they didn't lead anywhere, she saw that finally, only to more locked doors. Doors like the one that she stood before now, the front door to West Hall. But she had a key to that door. She let herself in.

She was Heidi effing Whelan. She didn't give up as easy as all that.

30

"Heidi?" Doreen flung open the door and hugged her friend. "Oh, thank god. I'm having the hardest time getting dressed. Come in. Are you coming from a run? I hope you're feeling better. I heard you weren't well." She sat down in front of her mirror.

"Who told you? Peter?"

"As a matter of fact." Doreen managed to pull her eyes off her own reflection for a nanosecond and find Heidi in the mirror, obviously trying to gauge her emotional state. She wore a purple strapless dress and a white cashmere sweater, neither of which Heidi had ever seen before. Gifts from her father, she supposed, or from Peter Standish. Returning her attention to herself, Doreen began to twist and pin up her hair.

"Look, I'm sorry he said anything to you about it, honestly. He just told me and I yelled at him. I think I may call the whole thing off. It was really just a dalliance."

"A dalliance? But I told you that I had feelings for him."

"So I did you a favor. Any man who can be so easily led astray is obviously not deserving of your, uh, feelings."

Heidi couldn't think of what to say. Had she indoctrinated this heartlessness in Doreen? The girl put in the last bobby pin and, pleased with the results, turned to her friend.

"You're upset. Of course you are. I don't mean to trivialize it, really. I'm sorry it didn't work out between you and Peter, but you seemed to have gotten something out of it while it lasted. Now you must tell me, what do you think of this?" She swished the skirt of the dress around her legs.

"Purple again? It's getting a bit overplayed, don't you think?"

"It's my signature! You don't like it?" Doreen ran back to the mirror.

"I don't know. It's fine. Kind of babyish."

"Babyish? I thought it was classy and feminine."

"Classy is not a word that classy people use, Doreen. My mother uses that word. She thinks that shrimp cocktail in a martini glass is the height of sophistication."

"Oh. You're mad at me. I get it. Okay." Doreen sprayed her updo with hairspray. "Can we get to the other side of this? It's, I don't know, a bit of a drag."

"Am I boring you? So sorry."

"Yes, you are. And anyway, I can't really get into it now. My father's on his way and we have a luncheon with the dean."

"Ah, yes. Old Crotchett. School buddies, aren't they? Your father and the dean."

"From Chandler and from *Harvard*."

"Uh-hunh. And will the Gibbons-Browns be joining you for luncheon? Will you be toasting Biz's successful opening last night? No?" In silence, her lips pursed, Doreen tweezed errant strands of eyebrow hair. "Why not? Your cousin must be delighted with the way everything went last night. I wouldn't know, I haven't seen her. Though I did see Gloria."

"Did you? How interesting."

"She came by the suite this morning. To pack up Elizabeth's things."

Heidi watched as Doreen trapped and pulled one tiny

hair after another. "I really don't want to talk about this now, Heidi. Maybe you should leave."

"For somebody who was just attacked by a crazed lesbian stalker, you are in remarkably good spirits."

"Thank you. I'm trying my best to put it all behind me."

"Cut the crap, Doreen." Heidi seized the tweezers from Doreen's hand and threw them on the floor. With mild irritation, Doreen picked up the tweezers and replaced them in the glass on her bookshelf. Never in her life had Heidi felt more inclined toward violence—and Doreen's stony face fueled her rage. "What did she have on you, huh? What could she have done to you that caused you to throw a flashlight at her head? You're lucky you didn't kill her. You should be in jail. Assault. Assault and false testimony."

"I don't know what you're talking about, Heidi. I did what I had to do to protect myself. You must admit that the intensity of Elizabeth's attachment to me was unnatural." Doreen stood before a collection of perfume bottles, opening and sniffing the tops before finally choosing one. "My cousin—my girl cousin—followed me around. She was in love with me. That much is clear now. And she's obviously very troubled. My only wish is that she gets the help she needs." She sprayed the air and walked through the spray, a trick Heidi taught her to avoid overscenting.

"Save it for the adoring masses, Do-do. It's Heidi here. I taught you everything you know."

"Did you? How kind of you. Though I must have picked some things up from elsewhere. For example, how to keep a man." Doreen snickered to herself. She picked up a sponge and began applying foundation to her face. She was her father's daughter, no question about it. Heidi could have ripped every hair from her scalp. But what good would that do? She would have to get her where she lived.

"You know what? You're right. It's boring to get all in a fizz over this kind of stuff. Here we are, fighting like a couple of middle school girls. I guess I was just upset to hear about Biz. I shouldn't be surprised—she was totally obsessed with you. But still, you should have told me."

"Really?" Doreen raised an eyebrow at Heidi. "Yes, I suppose I should have. I guess the whole thing with Peter stopped me."

"Oh, forget all that. Now let me help you. You always overdo it." Heidi snatched the sponge from Doreen and resumed the work, passing it over the bridge of her nose, her chin, her forehead. It was a perfect face, the face of an angel.

"Thank you, Heidi. Yes. That's more like it. I know, I have a heavy hand. What will I do when you go away next year?"

"I'm sure you'll manage. What are we doing this summer? Should we go to the Hamptons? Did I ever tell you about the summer I spent working as a desk girl at the Montauk Inn? Now this is a great story."

As she did Doreen's makeup, she told the story of a man in a perfect white linen suit who she checked into the Captain's Seaside Bungalow at the Montauk Inn. A lonely man, away from his family, he took an interest in

Heidi. He would talk to her—at the desk, at first, and then for longer stretches, at a table away from view, where he taught her how to infiltrate his very closed world. He gave away all the secrets of fitting in among the rich and powerful. She learned how to talk, how to walk, how to dress. He gave her books to read and films to see. He showed her everything.

Then one late afternoon he called down to the desk where Heidi was working. He wanted her to come up to his room, he said. Once there, she found a dress had been laid out for her. And a stylist was coming for hair and makeup. He wanted her to accompany him to a charity event.

"But before I could get dressed," said Heidi, "he said there was something he had to do first. And that's when he ravaged me. He tore me out of my work clothes and threw me onto the bed. Oh, but I loved it. He knew what he was doing, that's for sure. We pawed at each other, like we could never get enough. I screamed so loud, I was sure someone would call the police."

It was the truth, all but the sex part, which never happened. The truth plus sex, loads of it, in every conceivable position. Heidi told a Penthouse version of her own story. "I was so green then, Doreen. You wouldn't have recognized me!" Doreen submitted her face to Heidi's attention, and listened to her make up every dirty detail. She wanted Doreen to have a full-color image. She wanted to leave nothing out. Sex by the sea. At the party. In the supply closet. Under the concierge desk. Then the wife arrived and had her fired. Heidi took the train back to Yonkers, but she wasn't going to stop there.

So she tracked him to his Fifth Avenue apartment, gained entry. She threatened to expose him to his wife, the world. After one more mind-blowing tryst on the floor facing the view of the park, she got him to agree to pay for her education.

"'Who do you think you are?' he said to me. I had my clothes on by then." Heidi traced Doreen's mouth with a pencil and smudged it with her finger.

"'I'm just a beautiful girl with nothing to lose.' There," Heidi ran light pink lip gloss over her lips and turned Doreen toward the mirror. Doreen looked at herself from side to side.

"Perfect, thanks! So that's how you got to Chandler. You know I always wondered." Doreen screwed earrings into her ears—Grandmère Kiki's diamonds, Heidi saw. She must have swiped them off poor Biz. "Good for you. I better be—"

"Wait! Don't you want to know who he was? My lover, my benefactor, instructor in the ways of the flesh. Aren't you even curious about who this glamorous cad could be?"

"What?"

"Hold on." Heidi plucked Biz's pearl necklace from a hook on the wall and slowly strung it around Doreen's neck. She straightened the diamonds in each ear. They looked at each other in the mirror. The door buzzer sounded. Doreen jumped.

"Ah! Speak of the devil. Maybe he can tell you himself." Heidi handed Doreen her white clutch purse.

"What? What are you—"

"What did he drive here? Was it the turquoise Porsche? I did love that car. It was a bit small, difficult to satisfy your father's penchant for copulation *au naturel.*"

"You're lying."

"And how about that art dealer of his? Benedict, right? Is he still calling all the time? There's always some painting he's trying to sell. He got so upset when the auctions didn't go his way! I knew plenty of ways to soothe him, though. Mostly with my mouth."

"Shut up, Heidi!" The buzzer sounded again.

"You better get that. He hates to wait. For anything," Heidi said with a wink. Doreen's bottom lip trembled; she clenched both fists.

"Shut up! Shut up! You slut! You whore!" Doreen pushed her onto the bed and slapped her hard across the face. Heidi pulled out the bobby pins in Doreen's hair and mussed her head.

"Does he order for you? Fish and a salad. That's what he thought women should eat. Fish and a salad for the lady, I'll have a steak and a scotch."

"Shut up! Shut up! Shut your stupid mouth!" Doreen scratched Heidi's face, and Heidi pushed her off hard so she fell back onto the carpet.

"Careful of your hairdo, Doreen. He hates a hair out of place." Heidi sprinkled the bobby pins she'd pulled over Doreen.

"I could kill you. You make me sick!" Doreen furiously

tried recovering the bobby pins and fixing her hair, but it only made the situation worse.

"Yeah, right. In the meantime have fun with your lover. I mean, father!"

"GET THE HELL OUT OF HERE!" Doreen screamed. Her hair and makeup were ruined. The buzzer sounded again. Her phone started ringing.

"Whatever you say. Oh," Heidi said, her hand on the doorknob, "one more thing. You know, I heard all about Roland's kids. Oh sure. Bianca the beauty. Heinrich the soccer star. You want to know what I heard about you? Nothin'. Not one word. When I asked him how many kids he had, he said two. He didn't even acknowledge that you exist."

"Things are different now," said Doreen. She was cleaning the smudged mascara off her undereye with a fingernail.

"Are they? You better hope so. And you better hope you stay pretty. Otherwise it's over. Believe me. That guy would sooner spit on you than suffer anything less than perfect. Well, ta. Have a gorgeous luncheon. I'll tell him you'll be right down."

Heidi slammed the door closed behind her.

<hr/>

Doreen's hair and makeup were beyond repair. She would have to brush the whole thing out and start over, but there was no time and anyway, she couldn't make her hand move. Her whole body shook with rage. How dare she. How dare she come in and make up such vicious lies!

"She's just an ordinary liar!" Doreen told her reflection, but she couldn't be convinced. The phone and buzzer jangled over and over again, until they stopped altogether. Peace. He must have given up, left without her. She was all alone. Doreen allowed herself to be overcome with sobs.

She'd caught it immediately—dismissed it, of course, but the moment she introduced Heidi to her father, Doreen had the oddest feeling they knew one another already. And when she came upon them outside of the gallery it seemed like she'd interrupted a conversation, something heated. So she knew. Or she'd suspected and now it was confirmed. But so what? Heidi and her father had sex. Oh, it was too revolting!

"No!" Doreen swiped her hand across the shelf, sending brushes, bottles, and compacts flying. She paced in front of her bed. She had to think, think! But her mind replayed all the smutty details from Heidi's story, populating them with her own father. What about it was so troubling? Was it the sex? But she hardly knew her father. Why should his choice of lover be so hard for Doreen to take? Was it jealousy? Ugh! Gross! What kind of sicko was she? Doreen hit herself in the forehead, trying to erase the thought.

Anyway, if she asked him he would have his own side of the story. He would say that Heidi was the one who seduced him—she had it in her, after all. But back then Heidi was just a young girl. She was a lost, young girl far away from home. Doreen flung herself onto her bed and sobbed into her pillow. She sobbed for the girl that Heidi was—but mostly she cried for herself.

She, too, had been a lonely, innocent girl in a new place, far from home. She, too, had needed help navigating the unspoken rules and expectations of a society she knew nothing about. Heidi had taught her everything, like her father had taught Heidi. It was sickening! To think that she used that knowledge to get her father to love her. Maybe she hadn't used sex, but what difference did it make? Could she really claim a moral high ground? After Peter? And Biz? Doreen annihilated anyone who stood her way. She'd become what she hated most in the world, a bully. If she had never met Heidi Whelan! But that wasn't it. Heidi could only have done so much for the ugly, awkward girl she was the day she arrived on campus.

Doreen eyed the drawer where she'd hidden the picture. Since the last time she'd seen it, she had given her cousin a concussion and a one-way ticket out of Chandler, Yale, everything she wanted—everything she deserved. Biz had earned her achievements. And what about herself?

Everything Doreen had she'd gotten by lying, manipulating, making every relationship she had disposable. She'd destroyed her friendships with Biz and Heidi—the only friends she ever had. All she had now was a father who only loved her because she was beautiful. Heidi had said it, and she knew it was true. If Doreen still looked the way she used to, Roland would never have come for Parents' Weekend, he would never have bought the clothes and shoes and bags. His daughter? She was nothing but a pretty trinket to him, an accessory for his arm. Just as Heidi had been, and her poor aging mother, her poor, hard-working, loving, discarded mother, alone in Indiana. What a life she'd made for herself! What choices! If only she'd stayed ugly. At least then she would have a soul she could recognize as her own!

Doreen held the picture facedown in her hand. The fear in her heart was so deep and wild, it had a strangely calming effect on her body. Her breath was slow and even and sure, but the fire blazed from her insides. She had to see for herself what she'd done.

One day! It had only been one day! But it was so much worse than she could ever have imagined. Doreen dropped to her knees, her mouth agape at what she saw. Her soul had become a disgusting thing—a creature so wicked and corrupt, so twisted and ugly. It was wretched! Foul! Its eyes had bulged and yellowed, the body writhed in ecstasy, and the tongue, that horrible tongue, it dripped and oozed and thrust itself out of the frame, threatening to spread its scourge to whatever poor sap passed by. Her soul wasn't just sick, it was sickness itself, a disease of evil, a plague on anyone who should come in contact. And she was responsible. There was no one to blame—no one but her own awful self. She tried to breathe, she tried to talk herself out of her fear, but she could neither calm down nor look away. Her fate was printed out in full color. She was doomed to live in this beautiful body, to live with that hideous soul.

"No! No! I won't do it. I won't be this person. I'll be better. Please! I'll be so much better!" She railed her fists against the picture. "No! No! No!" She scraped her nails on the image. Then she began tearing. First into big shards, then into a thousand little pieces. She ripped and ripped, until the image of her soul fluttered all around her like parade confetti.

When pain becomes sound, it can zip through the atmosphere, penetrating eardrums for miles like a radio wave. When Dean Crotchett heard it from his post at his office window, he mistook the agonized scream for the call of a returning hawk. He searched the skies in vain. Roland heard it, too, as he walked toward the dean's office, and the sound was so piercing he momentarily forgot his irritation at being stood up by his own daughter. Jane Vale yelled at her brother to turn down the TV, the sound had disturbed her work on a short story tentatively called, "The Elephant Goes to Town." And just down the road, at Hamilton County Hospital, in a private room, the sound rattled Biz's aching head as she rested it against her mother's rib cage. Thinking it had emerged from her own insides, in the face of her wrecked life, she nudged even closer to her mother, clinging to her bony frame for comfort.

When Heidi Whelan heard that tortured shriek, she knew exactly what it was and from whom it had come. But she did not change course; she did not look back. She ran and ran and ran. She ran to forget, to start over, to begin again. Liberated from the past, charged by the possibilities of the future, she ran away from her very last lie.

In West Hall, the scream, and the loud crash that followed, alarmed several girls on the floor. They summoned the RA, who arrived with a key to Doreen's door.

There they found, on the floor, a photo of Doreen looking elegant and gorgeous in a red strapless dress. On the bed, hunched over in agony, was a pitted, frizzy-haired, bloated creature, a girl unlike any they had ever seen. Naked, in a pile of ripped purple fabric, she seemed to be suffering from some kind of disease, her skin covered in sores and her hair falling out in fistfuls, making her skull visible in scaly patches. She looked up at the small crowd at the door with terrified, violet eyes.

"Get out! Get out! Get out!" she yelled. "Get out of here! Leave me alone!"

Doreen Gray was never seen at Chandler again.

❧ *Epilogue* ❧

Biz got into Yale. The dean came, hat in hand, to the Gibbons-Brown family. The girl, he said, was not who they thought she was. She'd lied, cheated, been expelled. He begged for Elizabeth to take her rightful place on the podium as valedictorian. But Biz didn't bother. She got her internship with the photographer, moved to New York, and never looked back. Biza Brown. Maybe you've heard of her?

She blew up at Art Basel one year, and then everyone wanted her photographs. Celebrities begged to put her work on the walls of their mansions. The Standishes bought one for their glass house in Hawaii. Roland's dealer Benedict Ruehl called and called, but Biza refused to sell to him. Anyone but him, she told Eloise. She wouldn't have any more pictures in the hands of that family. She was afraid of what would happen.

———◦—

Heidi Whelan went to Northwestern. She made new friends there, nice people who'd never heard of her, who didn't know the difference between Yonkers and Yorkville. She studied art and literature and began writing little reviews for the paper that became longer reviews, more involved. The faculty advisor encouraged her and suggested journalism school. There was still a place in this world, he said, for people with refined taste and a sharp wit. Who had time for boys now, she wondered, when there were so many beautiful things to see? She went to black-and-white movies, to the ballet. She read sentences that made her believe.

———•◉———

Artist and critic. Their paths were destined to cross again. And so they did, years later. The occasion was Biza's latest solo exhibition at Peek Gallery. Having come from Venice, most of the work arrived at the gallery already sold, but that did not keep the mob away. The glitterati shoved past one another, their outfits appropriately flamboyant, their glasses of bubbly held high overhead as they moved through the space.

Heidi arrived in black. Biza recognized her immediately. They hadn't seen each other in such a long time; they'd gotten older. Heidi was impressed with her old friend's elegance (she wore Marni and tights, fabulous), her comfort in her own body. Biza found in Heidi a gravitas she didn't have as a girl. She was also more available, she gave more of herself away to the world, as if she'd opened her hand to let whatever she'd clung to flutter away. It made her more beautiful than ever.

Biza introduced a sinewy, tattooed woman as Agnes Chase, her fiancée. Of course, Heidi knew her work. She complimented her on her recent exhibition in Berlin, and Agnes accepted the praise but insisted it was Biza's night. They were sweet with one another.

Agnes was no beauty. She had big teeth and a long upper lip, and could have been twenty years older, an age that showed itself in the corners of her eyes, sunspots on her skin. But she was quick to laugh and beamed with pride for her future wife. Heidi could see what was sexy about Agnes, and she saw, too, that Biz was happy.

It was all very polite and cordial. The artist was congratulated for her work, her success, the critic for her sharp eye, her reliability. They asked after one another's family. Heidi's father had finally retired. Her mother was trying to convince him to move to Florida, but he wanted to travel, see the world.

"They seem happier and more in love than ever," said Heidi. "It's really remarkable. How's Ad-rock? Married with children?"

Biz nodded, three kids in Connecticut. The babies had crazy names. Biz laughed when she recited them, but she loved her nieces and nephew, doted upon them. Mumsy spent most of the year in Paris.

"Roland died," Biz said. "I don't know if you heard." Heidi nodded. She'd seen the write-up in the *Times*. Liver disease, it said. Booze, Heidi had assumed, surprised at how sad it made her to think of a man who once meant so much to her, drinking himself to death.

Neither woman mentioned the girl they'd known briefly all those years ago, the name neither had spoken aloud since. But her presence loomed larger and larger over the conversation, until neither could bear it anymore. With empty promises to call, to write, to get together, one roommate left to get back to her party while the other escaped to the street.

Heidi lived in a nondescript studio in a nondescript East Side neighborhood. She had work to do, but the night was so cool and nice, she thought she would walk home. It would give her a chance to think about Biz—Biza—about time and art, and about how she might write up the show. She was on assignment for a new job, and she had to make it great.

"Excuse me," someone said, brushing past Heidi en route to the gallery. The voice sent a chill through Heidi's body. She spun around to find the source—she saw a flash of a red coat. Could it be? What had she seen? She would know that voice anywhere; she had heard it for years in her dreams. Heidi shoved her way through the crowd, looking for a girl in a red coat, but she came up short. She ran back into the gallery, but she saw nobody.

"Heidi? Are you okay?" It was Agnes. "You look white. Biza. Biza!"

Biz heard her name and came over. Heidi looked pale.

"I thought you left. What happened? You look like you've seen a ghost!"

Heidi grasped Biz's hand. She looked deep into her eyes. "I saw . . . I could swear I saw . . ." But she didn't have to say anything more. Biz knew. "But then . . . when I came, she was gone!"

"It happens to me a lot." Biz patted Heidi's hand. "It happens all the time. But then, it's never her."

"So you haven't seen her? I thought maybe through family."

Biz shook her head. "Nobody knows where she is. Nobody's heard a word from her."

Heidi was beginning to calm down. Doreen wouldn't be a girl anymore, she'd be a grown woman. She gave a little laugh, trying to break up the tension. "Sorry, I—working too hard, I guess. Not sleeping enough."

"You're okay?"

"Yeah. Sorry. Enjoy the party, just . . . hey. Listen, Biz." Heidi could feel something rumble up from the depths of her body. An old shame, one of the many that she carried around with her. "I wanted to come see you," she said, her voice barely a whisper. "In the hospital and then later, too, but after everything, I thought you would be better off without me. I figured I'd caused enough damage, you know?"

"I didn't blame you. Really." Biz sighed. "We all needed a fresh start."

Heidi's smile was filled with warmth and gratitude. "Well, congratulations again. I'm proud of you." She pressed Biz's hand between her own and slipped out the door.

"What was that about?" said Agnes. She kissed her lightly on the lips.

"Mm? Oh, it's—it's a long story." Biz rested her head on the spot below Agnes's shoulder that always gave her comfort.

"Tell me about it someday?"

"What? Oh sure. I'll tell you all about it someday," said Biz. "I promise."

Forgive her, Agnes. Everybody lies sometimes.

Acknowledgments

Rebecca Sherman and I have been friends since we met at Jewish summer camp in Wisconsin in the mid-1990s. I don't know why she trusted me with her idea of writing a YA version of *The Picture of Dorian Gray*, providing me with her professional support, her keen editorial eye, and her unerring, baseless confidence in my abilities, but I am so grateful that she did. If you have arrived at this page and enjoyed yourself, please know that you too have Rebecca to thank, because this book would not exist without her.

Additional thanks go out to Andrea Morrison, Lisa Cheng, Marlo Scrimizzi, and Leslie Yazel. Robin Wasserman and Wistar Murray are always there to offer a bit of sleeve to cling to when I'm peering over my toes into the beckoning abyss. And to Gregory Edwards, who must live with all of this, thanks for hanging out with me all this time and for making every single hour I spent on this book possible.